MW00850417

WITHOUT PERMISSION

July 2024

To Mary —

I wrote this book for you —
for all of us. For these times.
Stay furious!

Charlotte

WITHOUT PERMISSION

Book One in the Jane Smith Trilogy

CHARLOTTE TAFT

Copyright © 2024 by Charlotte Taft
ISBN: 978-1-957176-26-0

All rights reserved. No part of this publication may be reproduced or transmitted in any form or by any means, mechanical or electronic, including photocopying and recording, or by any information storage and retrieval system, without permission in writing from the author/s and/or publisher.

Cover Art & Design by Avison Book Cover Design

EMPRESS
PUBLICATIONS
WWW.EMPRESSPUBLICATIONS.COM

My heart aches
And sings
With the hearts of other women
As if they were the children of my body
Attached by some
Umbilicus of memory.
~from the journal of Miss Jane Smith

Dedicated to Shelley, my love and best editor

Nancy McNary Smith, my ninth-grade Ethics teacher who opened my eyes to the world

Annie and Phyllis, who laughed and cried in all the right places, and saved Lucie.

CONTENTS

CHAPTER 1

THIS IS NOT A STORY
YOU HAVE HEARD BEFORE

Paris, Spring 1939

A scream came from the garden. I dropped the book I was reading to the girls and raced outside, black robes flying. I saw her red hair fanned out. No! Not Lucie! Crumpled under the Linden tree I had forbidden her to climb. So still. Yvette hovering over her, pinafore streaked with mud, tears, and grass.

"She won't wake up! Mam'selle, is she dead? I told her not to climb so high!"

My heart caved.

I made a quick visual scan. Everything seemed intact, except for the unnatural angle of her obviously broken left wrist. I knelt beside her and the cold wet of the morning rain soaked through my robes. Tenderly, I brushed golden madeleine crumbs off her blue sweater.

I tapped her cheek.

"Lucie. Lucie, wake up chérie."

Nothing.

Her face was so pale it made her freckles ghostly.

I leaned over to see if she was breathing.

Nothing.

I took her right wrist to check for a pulse.

Nothing. I moved my fingers to another spot. Nothing. I moved farther down her arm. Nothing.

Jane! Pull yourself together. You know how to do this.

I put my fingers just under her jaw, took a breath, and waited.

A pulse.

"She's alive!" I was crying out as much for myself as for the nine whimpering little girls in pinafores surrounding us. Behind me, the cook, Danielle, said, "Grâce à Dieu," and the housemaid, Brigitte, mumbled, "That troublemaker. She doesn't belong here. Madame Mathilde should send her back."

Since I didn't know whether she meant me or Lucie, I moved closer, as if I could protect either of us from Brigitte's foul intent. In the distance, the discordant bells of Notre Dame sounded. So different from the church bells at home. The practical Jane kicked in.

"Danielle, get me a badminton racket." She scurried off.

"Eveline, Paulette, I need your hair ribbons." They pulled them from their braids.

Danielle ran back, out of breath, holding the racket.

"I am going to use this to stabilize her wrist so I can carry her. Come over to this side and hold her." I tied Lucie's swelling arm to the racket and picked her up. Like lifting a shell. Such a tiny body to hold so much light.

"Brigitte, get smelling salts and inform Madame Mathilde." Brigitte trudged off. Danielle and I got Lucie inside and onto the sofa. By then my aunt, Madame Mathilde, had Dr. Levy on the phone. She proffered the heavy black receiver. I willed my voice not to quaver and told him everything.

Dr. Levy replied, "This child has had mishaps before. It is only a sprain. Smelling salts will wake her up. Keep the wrist cold, apply menthol, wrap it, give her aspirin, and she will be better in the morning."

"Doctor. Her wrist is broken. We need you. Come now. Please."

"She will be fine." He hung up the phone.

It was my fault. Lucie was my responsibility. I had only been there a few weeks, and already I had failed. Aunt Mathilde would say that twenty-five was too young to be responsible for ten seven-year-olds. She would send me home. I felt sick. My parents would be so disappointed. Lucie's fall was just another annotation in the ledger book of my imperfection. I tucked my hair under my cap and adjusted my belt. There was nothing to do about the mud and tears on my white collar. There was no way to avoid Mathilde's rebuke, but I could never stay mad at Lucie, no matter what befell me.

Brigitte grudgingly made an entrance and pulled the ammonia out of her pocket. She corralled the other girls back into the sunroom. I placed the tiny bottle of salts under Lucie's nose and she shook her head and opened her eyes.

Lucie gave me a wan smile. "I'm sorry I missed the Rumple story," she said so softly that I had to lean over. I had been reading Rumpelstiltskin.

"N'importe," I said, "I... I am just glad you are all right. Do you know where you are?"

"Madame Mathilde's school. It's Sunday."

"Exactement."

Thank God. Oriented as to place and time.

"And you are Mam'selle Jane, the best teacher in the whole world."

I never said she wasn't savvy.

I gave her aspirin and wrapped her swollen wrist the best I could, wrinkling my nose at the menthol. Once fully conscious, she writhed in pain. I attempted to comfort her, but aspirin every four hours wasn't enough. I dragged an old chintz chair into the girls' dormitory and sat by her bed all day, talking about everything and nothing. She dozed off and on and didn't want supper.

As the sun set in the nursery window, Danielle brought in a steaming bowl of vegetable soup. I was surprised she had thought about me. She set the tray on the dresser.

"Thank you."

"How is our petite?" She felt Lucie's forehead. "I hope she's not getting a fever."

"I'll keep checking."

Danielle nodded and returned to her kitchen.

My soup finished, I stood over Lucie and put my palm on her forehead. She was a bit warm.

She opened her eyes and looked at me pitifully. "It hurts, Mam'selle. I am trying to be very brave, but it really, really hurts."

"I'm sorry. I'll tell you a story and maybe you can go to sleep." She nestled back into her pillows, a pinched expression on her pale face.

"Once upon a time, there was a girl named Lucie. She was strong, and funny, and smart, and kind, and she liked to do things her own way. When she wanted to see the world and be free, she climbed to the very top of her favorite Linden tree...."

She rewarded me with the tiniest of smiles as she fell asleep.

I nodded off myself. In my dream, Brigitte shoved me. "It is your fault she died. We never should have trusted you." I looked behind me to see my girls in their two straight lines with a gap where Lucie should have been. "It is your fault the *salaud* doctor didn't come." The girls wore black pinafores for the funeral. Lucie's inert body lay on a table, her pale face haloed with red hair.

I woke to Lucie crying out. I was sweating as I jumped up from my chair and put my hand on her forehead. She was hot, so I pulled the bedclothes aside. Mathilde bounded into the room in her nightdress and robe, her long braid down her back, and cold cream on her face.

"Que'st-ce qui se passe? What is happening? Oh, petite!" She looked at me, eyes wide. "I will call the doctor." Mathilde was a substantial woman, in personality as well as girth. She turned around to see nine little girls out of their beds, chattering. "Silence. It is the middle of the night. Back to bed, enfants." She clapped her hands, and they ran back to their cots.

Lucie alternated between loud cries and whimpers as I gave her more aspirin and put a cold cloth on her forehead. "It hurts too much."

None of my ministrations seemed to help. The grandfather clock struck one and finally Dr. Levy came. He examined her with his ever-present cigarette clamped between his teeth.

"This is a fracture," he proclaimed, without a trace of irony. In the dark of night, the doctor took her to the hospital and confirmed it with an X-ray, then set the bone in plaster-of-Paris. Lucie recovered after a few weeks in a cast, decorated with many little-girl-painted flowers and butterflies.

The same Dr. Levy who dismissed me so thoroughly on that important occasion would later turn my life upside down.

Though my story begins with ten little girls in a school in Paris, don't be confused. This is not a story you have heard before. If you stay with me through my journey, you will learn that this is most decidedly not a children's book. Instead, it is the tale of women's lives, lived without permission, outside the lines of men's laws and customs.

Although I was not a typical 25-year-old woman in Paris in the spring-time, I did fall in love—with Clémentine, Eveline, Hélène, Lynnette, Nicole, Paulette, Socorro, Sofia, Yvette—and, of course, Lucie.

Since this story starts with the children, I must confess that I *did* make those little girls get into two straight lines on our daily walks. Well, have you ever tried to take care of ten seven-year-olds? The public saw ten well-be-haved little girls in blue striped pinafores accompanied by an extremely tall woman in a uniform of black robes and a white wimple. When I wore those robes, for the first time, I didn't feel too tall. I was architecture—like a flying buttress—there to protect those children. For the first time I can remember, I stood up straight. My mother would have been so proud. That uniform trans-formed me into someone I could never have imagined.

My aunt, Madame Mathilde Smith, was what the French call formidable. I guess it means the same in English. When we first met, she barely said hello to me before she turned and led the taxi driver who carried my trunk into the building. I'm not sure what I was expecting. More of a welcome? An em-brace? "How are your parents?" Her aloofness surprised me and put me on my guard. I had hoped she would be, if not a friend, at least kind. Instead, I avoided her stern face at all costs.

When the housemaid, Brigitte, showed me to my room, she handed me a long list of rules compiled by the former teacher.

"The girls who come to this school are the children of wealthy aristocrats. Madame Rochand was a proper teacher, not an imposter like you. American. Pfft. And I won't be cleaning up after you, Miss, even if you are related to Madame." Brigitte tossed her head as she left, as if expecting me to dump a load of dirt on the floor of my little room with the tiny bed and faded chintz chair.

I believed I had to follow the regulations to the letter, on pain of some punishment that I was too timid to discover. It is almost impossible that in those early days, I obeyed authority without a second thought. The most impossible rule was that I was forbidden to leave my room to comfort the girls when they wept in the night, as they invariably did. For the first few weeks, I cried myself to sleep in chorus with the weeping of my young charges, wondering what in the world I had gotten myself into.

I was in bed reading when the sobbing began. I am embarrassed to say that my homesickness gnawed at my heart, so hearing the cries of my little students was excruciating. In vain, I put a pillow over my head. What a fool I was to think I had to obey that stupid rule! I was about to turn on the radio to drown out the noise when a knock came at my door. I opened it to find Lucie.

She reached up and took my hand and said, "Mam'selle, we must do something."

I followed mutely as she led me into the dormitory. The girls were all awake and several were crying. I told them it was perfectly all right to cry when you feel sad. I couldn't think of anything else that would help—except a story. I wanted to begin with a tale they would be familiar with, so I asked if they knew of a girl named Joan who lived in Orléans. Of course, they all clamored to tell me about her.

"But her name is Jeanne, Mam'selle," Lucie insisted.

"Of course," I said. And Jeanne it was. "Once upon a time there lived a brave girl named Jeanne." I looked around—their faces were excited, even though some were streaked with tears. "Which one of you is most like Jeanne?" They all turned to Lucie. "All right, Lucie, will you portray Jeanne?" In a moment, Lucie stood by my side with a pillowcase around her neck in place of a cape. Her left arm was still in a cast, but she gesticulated wildly with her right, brandishing an imaginary sword.

"Now Jeanne, what did it take to be a warrior for your faith?"

Lucie thought for a moment. "I believed in things that no one else could see."

So perfect. "Yes, ma chérie!" I said, giving her a hug. "Were you aware that Jeanne had nine of the bravest and best girls in the country by her side?" I asked. They all fell silent. This was not a story they had heard before. I continued. "Now you won't believe the coincidence, but Jeanne's compatriots were named Clémentine, Eveline, Hélène, Lynnette, Yvette, Nicole, Paulette, Sofia, and Socorro!" The girls gasped. "Just imagine you were her helpers. What would you do for Jeanne?"

Paulette piped up, "I am strong. I can knock anyone down who tries to hurt her."

"Excellent. What else?" I looked around at the other girls. They all spoke at once. I put my hand up to quiet them. I turned to one of the shyest girls. "Lynnette?"

"I am very smart, and I can figure out any puzzle," she answered with a huge smile.

Hélène blurted, "I can talk louder than the soldiers," in a voice that made me shush her, lest my aunt be awakened on the other side of the building.

Nicole grabbed my arm and said, "I can brush her hair every night 100 times and make sure she feels very pretty." I would never have thought of that. The gifts continued until the only one who hadn't spoken was little Yvette, one of the girls sobbing when I first came into the room.

She looked at me with her sad, sweet face and said, "I can tell her it is perfectly all right to cry when you feel sad, and give her my hanky."

We all laughed, and she laughed too. Then we said goodnight with many hugs and kisses, and we slept peacefully until the morning when we woke to the chirping of the birds.

I did everything I knew to keep them safe, but a terrible storm was brewing.

CHAPTER 2

AMERICANS IN PARIS

Paris, Spring 1939

Returning from our walk to the park, I was brushing sweet-smelling lilac blossoms out of Lucie's hair when I saw the gendarmes. On the steps of the school, two officers flanked Madame Mathilde as if she might run off. I froze, and the girls in their two lines bumped into each other as they stopped behind me. I turned to shush them.

Well, really to shush Lucie, who asked loudly, "Why are they arresting Madame Mathilde?"

"Nothing to worry about, children," my aunt said, in her stentorian voice. Danielle, the cook, hovered behind her, looking worried, indeed.

Mathilde continued. "The police are interviewing the Americans in town. A bit of bureaucracy."

Thank goodness. Nothing was wrong.

"Come along, Jane dear."

I swung my head to see who she was talking to.

"Jane, look smart. I don't have all day. Danielle will look after the children."

My mouth open, I nearly tripped over my robes, catching up with her as she turned and marched to the small autobus. As soon as we got in, the gendarme pulled abruptly from the curb. I was relieved they didn't blare that horrible bahn-bah, bahn-bah alarm that I so hated. No sooner did I register the thought than the driver turned it on like a boy's plaything. The alarm made it too loud for any kind of conversation.

When we pulled into the police lot, Madame said, "You won't mention this to your father." She handed me my passport. "Best keep this with you these days." That was the most she had said to me in the entire month I had been in Paris.

A gendarme took me into a small concrete-block room painted in the dull green tint reserved for public offices and dormitories. I sat in one of the hard straight-backed chairs, still waiting to breathe out. No matter that I am exceedingly well-behaved and law-abiding, the police always make me feel guilty—as if I have done something terrible that I can't remember. A man in a gray suit came in, closed the door, and sat across from me. From the dark bags under his eyes, it looked as though he had been up all night. He hadn't shaved and needed a haircut. He had a clipboard and a pen.

"Bonjour, mademoiselle. I am Inspector Lavigne."

I was going to tell him that I didn't speak French fluently when he smiled broadly and said, "Don't worry about transmutation. My English is insatiable." He shuffled his papers and looked up at me.

"You are Miss Smith?"

"Yes."

"Miss Jane Smith?"

"Yes."

"This is your actual name?"

"Yes." I pushed my passport across the table. He looked at it, scrutinizing the picture.

In the mirror of my memory, he saw a plain girl with shoulder-length hair parted on the right that was eternally resistant to the multiple strategies for curling constantly imposed on it, with what my mother called a perfectly nice smile.

"You are very tall." He wrote something on his paper and pushed my passport back.

"So I have been told." Oh, my God.

"Harrumph," he said, as if I were trying to put something over on him. My heart beat so fast that I was panting to keep up with it.

Lavigne cocked his head to the side. "Miss Smith. Do not unstable yourself. This is routine. I simply need to ascertain your intentions."

"Excuse me? What do you mean?"

"For what reason are you in Paris?"

An easy question. "I am a teacher at my Aunt Mathilde's school."

"The American School?"

"That is not what it is called."

"That is what *we* call it."

"All right. Then, yes."

"And you are a religious? A brother?"

"A sister? No, I'm not. This is a uniform."

"A disguise, then? You wish to dismay the children?"

"Dismay them? No. It is just a uniform." If I hadn't been so scared, I would have laughed at his "insatiable" English.

"Ah." He made a note on his paper. "And your position on the war?"

"What war?"

"Miss Smith. There is only one war. The Grand War. Your country found it necessary to interview. To send soldiers to our shores. What is your position?"

"I don't have a position. I was only a child."

"Ah."

Why did his "'ahs" increase my nervousness?

"And your aunt? What was her role in the war? A spy, perhaps?"

"My aunt? A spy? Of course not."

"Ah." More notes on his form. He looked up at me. "It is my duty to inform you that every visitor to our country is required by law to report to this office any Communist, illegal ally, criminal or miscreant who comes to their attention. Failure to do so incurs a penalty of imprisoning. We are keeping our eyelids open on you. Do you understand?"

It was hard to imagine that any such person would come my way as a first-grade teacher. Little did I know.

"Yes, I understand."

"Bon. Good. That is all. Take my card." He dug underneath a pile of papers and pulled out a card with a stain and a bent corner. I stuffed it into my pocket.

He stood, opened the door, and pointed to a wooden bench with peeling green paint a shade darker than the walls. I sat there and waited for my aunt, every minute more certain that they had, in fact, arrested her. When I saw her coming down the hall, I stood. Her expression was dark. She trembled as she looked at her watch, yet her voice was strong.

"I shall be late for my meeting with the Archbishop."

That got their attention. In moments, we were back in the van.

"No alarm, please," Mathilde said. It was not a request.

"But…" the driver protested.

"No alarm."

We drove back to the school in silence.

I have no idea how my aunt went about her daily tasks after that unsettling interaction with the police, but I did what I always did. I put the business card in a drawer, tucked my feelings deep away, and pretended it had never happened.

CHAPTER 3

OUR FIRST GUEST

Paris, April 1940

My first year in Paris was like a fairy tale, and like all fairy tales, it had to end. I had gotten to know the children very well. Eveline, who had a story for everything and explained that chocolate got all over her skirt when a bush exploded; Paulette, who almost died because she wanted to be brave and didn't tell anyone when her appendix nearly burst; Lynette, so smart in math it scared me; Hélène, a bit bossy, but the one who managed to get everyone back in line; pretty Nicole, who loved to take care of the pumpkin seed plants we grew in an aquarium; tender Yvette, who guessed the answers to all my logic riddles; Clémentine, so earnest and in love with the rules, who always had the right answer about grammar; Socorro, fascinated by earth sciences and able to find any country on our globe in a jiffy; argumentative Sofia, who I swore would turn out to be a lawyer or politician one day; and Lucie.

How can I describe Lucie? She was a bit of all of those qualities, but it was her insistence on fairness that made us soul mates. If the cook made a cake for dessert, Lucie asked Lynette to measure it and divide it into ten exact pieces. When we walked by a kitten in the outdoor market, Lucie picked it up and told me we needed to stop by each booth until we found the owner. Which we did. She wanted to play every game until each girl had a chance to win. Clearly a Unitarian at heart, like my mother.

Over that year, we played, learned addition and subtraction, explored the nature of gravity, read about how plants make chlorophyll, memorized the major French holidays, practiced penmanship, and rehearsed sounding out big words. All the while, the world—our world—was going to Hell. The adults feared war, and yet put their hands over their eyes and pretended it would never happen. The year before, in March of 1939, the Nazis had "annexed" Czechoslovakia with a political sleight–of–hand that allowed most of the world to ignore it. But by that fall, they had ruthlessly invaded Poland. Finally, reacting to the Nazis' clear intent to ravage Europe, Great Britain and France declared war on Germany. We trembled to imagine what might happen to us. Millions of Parisians fled the city to their country homes. Those who were not able to leave were huddled indoors. The streets were deserted. The Paris I loved became a ghost.

I completed my daily tasks, seeing little of Aunt Mathilde, which was fine with me. The truth is, even after a year, she intimidated me. I scurried down the hall when she raised her voice in displeasure at the cost of chicken, or talked on the phone in French too fast for me to understand, or scolded the plumber for leaving a mess. Mathilde ate alone in the office next to her bedchamber. I took my meals in the enormous white-tiled kitchen with the cook, Danielle; the housekeeper, Brigitte; and the caretaker, Marcel. They had worked together for years, so I didn't expect them to welcome or trust me. And they didn't. I especially tried not to annoy Brigitte. As she reminded me frequently, she had been a friend of the dearly departed teacher, Madame Rochand.

One night, everyone was on edge.

"This dinner is not your best, Danielle," Brigitte said, frowning as she took a second helping.

"The butcher had very few good cuts of meat to choose from," Danielle answered in a grumpy voice. "War is coming, and people are already hoarding."

"Don't be ridiculous," Brigitte retorted. "This country has been going downhill for years. When the Germans come they will put things to right and eliminate the undesirable elements that have plagued us for generations." She took a large bite.

Danielle grimaced. Marcel snorted and said, "Quel bordel."

Danielle said, "Chut," to let us know she was uncomfortable with even the tamest curse. I had nothing to add. I was wary of voicing any opinion, even though the idea of Nazis horrified me.

Brigitte turned her scowl on me. "You are awfully dressy tonight. Strict Carmelite nuns raised my brother and me. They taught us never to lord it over others. Do you wear that ring to show us you are better than we are? That you come from a wealthy family?"

Mortified, I didn't just want to take the ring off, I wanted to remove my entire hand.

"My family is not wealthy. This was a gift from my parents. Wearing it makes me feel closer to them. I have never been so far away from home before."

Was the covetous look on her face meant to be a smile? "May I?" she asked, assuming that I would be too embarrassed to say I would not let her try on my ring.

Of course, she was right. I pulled the ring off and passed it to her. When she slid it onto her finger, Danielle gave me a look I interpreted as "Make sure you get that back."

"It's lovely. Topaz, isn't it? And are the diamonds real?"

"Uh, I think so." I felt like a fool. After an extremely long time, Brigitte took off the ring and placed it back in my open hand.

"Your parents have excellent taste. In jewelry." I was obviously dismissed, so I said goodnight and headed for the safety of my room.

After a nightmare, I couldn't get back to sleep, so I went to the kitchen for some warm milk. I had to go past my aunt's office. The door was slightly open and I could hear her on the telephone. Her voice rose, and as I tiptoed past, I distinctly heard my name! Of course I stopped.

"No. No. Jane? No. Being American is protection for the moment. They asked me to give a list of Communists. No, they didn't ask about Jews. This is not a joke. You think you are immune, but you are not, my friend. Just keep your head down." Then the other person said something I couldn't hear.

"Jane is my niece, Bernard. What would you have me do? It was a mistake to have her come here… No, they can count on me, but this is going to get worse. No, of course I can't tell her. I have put us all in a terrible position. D'accord. Bonsoir chéri."

Bernard. The infamous school doctor, Bernard Levy.

I held my breath and turned back to my room. No amount of warm milk was going to help me sleep after this. She was talking to the doctor who ignored me when Lucie fell. Did she think I was a bad teacher? Was it the stories?—that I was breaking the rule about going to the children when they cried? I got back in bed, my feet freezing cold, and wondered if I should just pack my bags. But I didn't want to go. I loved my girls. I loved Paris. In the wee hours of the morning, I decided to be the best teacher possible and let the chips fall where they might. And to stay out of my aunt's way.

A few days later, when the girls were napping, I overheard Danielle and Madame Mathilde talking in hushed tones in the kitchen.

Danielle said, "Her name is Esther. She is just a child. They arrested her father on suspicion of being a Communist. He is all she has. Madame, can't you help us? Just for a day or two until we can get her out of Paris?"

"Chérie, I would like to help, but what can I do? Hide her in the cupboard?" Mathilde gestured to the cabinets filled with Danielle's pots and pans. "I have enough to worry about. And I certainly can't involve Jane. Her father would never forgive me. No, Danielle. No, there is nothing I can do."

Yet two things happened the next day. What Madame Mathilde might have intended as a private conference became a shouting match. I herded the children outside, but we overheard the argument because Brigitte stood in the doorway to Aunt Mathilde's office.

"Madame Mathilde, I have been faithful to this school for ten years, long before you got here. You cannot sack me," she bellowed.

Mathilde answered in a steely voice. "Because of all the upheaval, many parents have not paid their school fees. I cannot afford to employ you any-more."

"Those rich parents cannot pay enough to keep their little brats in a clean place? Who will wash their nasty underwear and clean their snotty sheets?"

Mathilde didn't answer right away. She folded her arms across her chest. "Jane and Danielle, of course." Then she pulled Brigitte into her office and shut the door, muffling their conversation. Before the end of the day, Brigitte had cleared out her small room and loaded her belongings onto a wagon driven by her brother.

Supper was quieter than usual. Danielle served a filet of sole almandine that smelled of lemons and butter, but I just picked at it. After a while, she said, "It's good that Brigitte's brother came to get her right away. I think they live in the South of France."

Marcel scowled and hissed, "Zut."

Danielle followed with her usual "Chut!" She obviously disapproved of Marcel's coarse language. They were like a call and response at my father's church.

Marcel's expression scared me. We finished our dinner in tense silence.

The next night, just before bedtime, the girls were laughing and playing when Madame Mathilde abruptly entered their room. We weren't used to see-ing her in the dormitory, and my charges and I glanced at each other in dis-tress.

"Lines!" Mathilde said, clapping her hands sharply.

The girls stepped into formation so quickly they almost knocked me down.

Madame Mathilde cleared her throat. "Mes enfants, we have a special guest with us tonight who needs peace and isolation. She has an extremely contagious illness called pink eye. She will have a bed separated from all of you, and you are not to go near her, talk to her, or disturb her." At this Madame Mathilde produced from behind her long black robes a tiny girl with pale skin and long dark hair. "This is…" she hesitated. "This is Elinor." The little girl tried to melt back behind her.

Mathilde stayed to supervise as the girls brushed their teeth, combed their hair, said their prayers, and went to bed, making sure that the supposed little "Elinor" did everything last and at a distance. She tucked the silent child into a cot at the far end of the room and gave me a fierce look, as if to dare me to

interfere. Of course, I did not. I recognized the child didn't have conjunctivi-
tis, but I was certainly not going to rock the boat.

I woke in the middle of the night with the sense that something was not
right. I put on my pink flowered bathrobe and tiptoed into the dormitory. My
girls were clustered around our little guest, who was sobbing quietly.

"Elinor called out for her papa," Lucie said. "We didn't know what to
do."

"It's all right, enfants," I said. "Get back in bed."

I approached the girl slowly, not wanting to add to her fear. She was not
more than six years old. I reached out to her.

She flinched. "No touching. No talking. No crying for Papa."

I pulled my hand back and sat on the floor beside her cot, my face level
with hers. I wanted to cry myself. *Oh, little one, what have we done to you?* I
recognized that anything I did, or anything I didn't do, would put her at risk.
Would put all of us at risk. She curled up and burrowed under the covers until
I was sitting beside a small hump. I lay my hand on her back and sat, my hand
moving as she breathed. I listened to the murmur of ten little girls, safe in bed.
Our girls had so much—enough to eat, families who loved them. Futures. This
one had lost her parents, and been told she was dangerous in an effort to protect her—that she was contagious, and must not speak a word.

I realized I should get Madame Mathilde, but I couldn't bear the thought
of her anger—at my girls. At this one. At me.

A bony little back pressed against mine. There was no need to look. I
reached behind and Lucie clasped my hand. I wasn't thinking logically. How
could I take part in this little one thinking there was something wrong with
her? What life would she have then? I was ashamed that I had pretended not
to see the obvious. Under my hand, she sobbed. I was clear about what I was
not supposed to do. But I didn't know what was *right* to do.

I had to change position on the hard floor. I drew Lucie next to me as I
shifted. She looked at me as though I had the answers to everything. I touched
my forehead to hers and smiled. Maybe I did.

I patted the hump under the covers and said, "Come out, little one." A
tear-stained face emerged. She trusted me to be the grown-up that I looked
like. So I followed my heart and hoped beyond hope I could make it right.

I reached my hand out. She put her hand in mine and looked up at me
with eyes I shall never forget. I did the only thing I could think of to bring her
into a safe circle.

"A wonderful thing has happened. Our new guest has gotten well, so it is
safe for us all to be together." Lots of rustling as my troop left their beds. I
gathered the girls on the floor around the cot at the back of the room and
asked, "Who would like to hear a story?" Instead of the usual clamor and
excitement, the girls murmured a quiet, "Yes, please."

"This is the story of a brave woman named Queen Esther." The tiny girl exclaimed, "My name is Esther!" and then clapped her hand over her mouth.

"Don't worry, chérie. You are safe here. And since you are Esther, you must come and sit in my lap as I tell the story of a queen who shares your name." She climbed down from the bed and curled up onto my lap with the weight of a kitten. My mind was whirling with how to make the story of Esther simple enough for bedtime and tame enough for little girls.

"Once upon a time in a Kingdom called Persia there lived a beautiful young Jewish girl named Esther." My little kitten wriggled, excited at hearing her name spoken aloud. I told the Old Testament story, interrupted several times by Lucie when the story illustrated prejudice against Jewish people.

"Why?" Lucie asked.

"Because some people don't like Jews," I answered, knowing I was way out of my depth.

"Why?" Lucie demanded. "Why don't they like the Jews?"

"I don't know. I honestly can't explain it."

The girls were silent for the rest of the story. I thought about how much death and hate are in the narrative. I might not have told that story at a different time in a different world. But this was our reality—their reality. I ended with, "And you can see how Queen Esther's courage saved her people."

In a tiny voice, Esther said, "But that Esther Queen told the King that she was Jewish, and I'm not supposed to tell."

I looked down at her with tears in my eyes. "That's right, chérie. I'm afraid we don't have a Queen Esther who has the power to tell the Nazis not to hurt the Jews, so we must stay secret. That is how we use our courage—to love each other and protect each other the best we can."

I turned to the other girls and asked, "Do you know what a secret is?"

They all nodded their heads, but I wasn't convinced.

"If you are keeping a secret, who can you tell?" I asked.

Yvette scrunched up her brow. "Maman?" she asked.

"No!" Lucie insisted. "You can't tell anyone."

"That's right," I said. "This is a very special secret that we cannot tell anyone at all. I am sure you will be the best secret-keepers ever." I felt sick. I was not at all certain they could keep quiet. I tucked them in, gave each girl a kiss on her forehead and told them that angels were watching over them. As always, I hoped the angels were listening.

The grandfather clock in the hall struck two. I walked down the corridor and stood outside my aunt's door. My throat was dry, and I could smell my perspiration. It was much too late to wake her. *The time for being a good girl is over.* I knew I might only have the courage to knock once, so I made it a good one.

Mathilde surprised me by opening the door right away. She was in her dressing gown, her hair still pinned up and her light on. Next to the lamp was a cup of the tisane she drank that Danielle said would calm her nerves. I couldn't imagine any herbal tea that would be enough to make my heart stop pounding.

She frowned. "Yes, Jane. How may I help you?"

"Ithinkitisbestiflcomein," I said. Then I slowed down. "I don't think you want anyone else to hear this."

"Come in, then," she said, ushering me into her room, which was a riot of papers piled everywhere. "There is no place to sit, I am afraid. Use that chair," she motioned to a tall pile. "Just put the papers on the floor."

I did as I was told.

"What do you want?"

I took a deep breath. "I know about Esther," I said. "I know who she is and what she is, and I want to help."

"Nonsense. You know nothing." Her tone was so sharp that I winced. "I instructed you to stay away from that child."

I gulped down my fear. "She is Jewish, and you are helping her get out of Paris before the Nazis come."

"Don't even say that out loud," she hissed, holding her hand up in a stop motion. Then Mathilde seemed to sink into herself. "I knew I should have insisted that you go back to America. I knew it." She said this last part almost to herself. I lowered my voice.

"If you wanted the girls to keep this secret, telling them to keep away from her would never work. They trust me. If you are going to do this, you will need my help."

Suddenly, she looked exhausted. "My dear, of course you are right. I should never have let Danielle talk me into it. But what can I do?"

"Is that why you fired Brigitte? Because she sympathizes with the Germans?"

"Exactement. She would have put me in a terrible position. I never liked her very much. She only cares about herself. She worked at the school before I bought it, so I just kept her on. My mistake." She gave a wry smile.

"Is this why you thought you should have sent me back home?"

"Bien sûr. I don't want to put you in danger. Why else?" She put her hands in the air and shrugged her shoulders.

I didn't know whether to laugh or cry. I said, "I imagine Esther will not be our last guest?"

"I have already had two more requests for help. How can I say no?" Mathilde reached out and clasped my hand. "My dear, I am afraid you do not fully realize what you are risking. What they will do if we are found out."

After that night, I often stopped in before bedtime to talk with my aunt. We were a team.

CHAPTER 4

COLORING OUTSIDE THE LINES

Paris, May 1940

One afternoon, the girls wanted to color. I found crayons and coloring book pages in the cupboard and took them to my favorite place in the school, the sunroom. It had enormous windows and lots of light. I loved the freedom in that space. The girls each chose a picture to color, and I passed out boxes of crayons. Three girls sat on each side of the long monks' table to work, bent over, their shoulders moving furiously. Three of them sat at a round table with a mosaic surface. And then there was Lucie, flopped on her stomach on the floor, knees bent, feet in the air. Madame Mathilde would probably clap her hands and make her get up, but I didn't care. I walked around the room looking over shoulders, offering encouragement. The three at the round table colored exactly the same pictures in exactly the same colors—like a flock of birds that magically knows the same moment to take off. They had each chosen an image of a man and woman with a little girl in the park. I suggested they could use their imaginations and at least give the girl different colored dresses, but Clémentine was adamant.

"Mam'selle, we want to do it correctly. The daughter's dress is brown. The maman's dress is gray. The papa is wearing a black coat. No imagination is necessary."

"But you might each see it differently," I attempted.

"Non. This is how it is," she countered. "Madame Rochand told us."

Another encounter with the legacy of rules left by the now-deceased Madame Rochand. There did not appear to be room for discussion.

The girls at the long table at least chose different images. Eveline colored a brown kitten playing with a green spool of yarn. Lynette worked on a brown horse, drawing a brown wagon with a wagon driver wearing a brown coat and a black hat; Sophia colored a green frog sitting atop a green lily pad in the middle of a brown pond; Yvette created a mercifully yellow sunflower with green leaves in front of a brown gate; Nicole's was a magician with a black cape pulling a black rabbit out of his black top hat; and Socorro produced a black train with black smoke coming out of its engine with three men in black coats standing on a brown station platform. Madame Rochand obviously preferred the darker colors. I wondered why the inventors of crayons had even bothered to include blue, red, purple, orange, and yellow. Nicole was working assiduously to stay exactly within the lines—the tip of her tongue just sticking out of the side of her mouth. Eveline noticed the precision.

"Look, Mam'selle! Nicole has done it just right." All the other girls, except Lucie, stopped what they were doing and crowded around Nicole to appreciate the perfection of her magician. I had to admit that it was very neat. Hélène stepped back to glance over Lucie's shoulder at her drawing of a kitten playing with a spool of yarn.

"Mam'selle," she alerted me in a loud voice. "Lucie is coloring outside the lines. And she is not using the right colors. And she has made her own drawing without permission. Madame Rochand would never allow this."

Like that flock of birds, the girls and I moved over to look at Lucie's paper. She had colored the kitten purple with red zebra-like stripes that indeed extended outside the lines to give the impression of long red angora fur. The yarn was green, made fuzzy with an aura of yellow. The loose end of yarn that the kitten was theoretically batting about, connected to a green vine extending into the sky. The vine led to an enormous arc fashioned of red, green, purple, orange, yellow, and blue, in that order. While not scientifically accurate, it was quite clearly a rainbow. A small blue and yellow striped creature climbed up the vine. A figure in a blue gown with long red hair and golden wings sat atop the rainbow. When the other girls looked at the page and laughed, Lucie's expression grew dark, but she said nothing. I realized she had never been quiet for so long.

"What a wonderful drawing," I said gently. "Do you want to tell us about it?" I wasn't sure if that was the best thing to do, but the energy in the room was combustible.

"Papa told me that my mother is an angel who lives on a rainbow. This magic kitten can grant my wish to turn into a caterpillar and climb up to see her," she explained in a small voice.

"Chérie. What a wonderful way to visit your maman," I said.

Hélène was pulling on my sleeve. She leaned over and whispered in my ear, "Madame Rochand took away the paper when Lucie colored that way."

Oh, I didn't like that Madame Rochand.

I wanted to cry, but I remembered that I was supposed to be the grownup. I had to salvage the situation and comfort Lucie without casting aspersions on their departed teacher. As I looked at Lucie's vibrant page, I thought of Marc Chagall and the Fauves—artists I had studied in college. Then I recalled a footnote in my art history class and I had my story. I gathered the girls into a circle, putting Lucie next to me to give her time to get over her shame.

"In honor of all of your artwork, I am going to share the very special story of Émilie Charmy. Once upon a time, Émilie was born in Toulouse. She loved to paint and to make music. When she grew up, she had lots of friends who became famous. Their paintings hung in galleries. Émilie was a painter, too, but there was one problem."

"What was the one problem?" Good. Lucie was back.

I smiled at her. "The problem was that in those days, people didn't think that girls or women could be artists."

"The olden days?" Lucie asked, considerably perked up.

"Not so long ago," I said. "No matter how well Émilie painted, nobody would include her paintings in the big exhibits with the men. But about twenty years ago, someone took a chance and put on a show just for her. It was such a success they awarded her a knighthood in the Légion d'Honneur."

"A girl is a knight?" Clémentine asked, unconvinced.

"Yes. And she is still painting today right here in Paris."

"Girls can't wear armor," Sofia said.

"She doesn't have to wear armor. This kind of knighthood is more like getting a prize for being very good at what you do. But the reason I am telling you this story is that one of her paintings reminds me of Lucie's."

"It does?" Lucie's mouth hung open for a moment.

"Yes. It is a painting of a woman wearing green slippers, floating on an orange cloud."

"Is she really on a cloud?" Clémentine furrowed her brow.

"I think it's just the way Émilie imagined her. She made drawings and paintings that are magical, like Lucie's magic kitten." Thinking about all the risks Charmy took for her art made me wistful. I longed to care about something that much.

Clémentine remained skeptical. "But Madame Rochand would...."

"Madame Rochand was teaching you one very good way to draw—to see with your eyes. Today Lucie showed us another very good way—to see with your heart."

"Lucie, maybe they will put your picture in an exhibit someday," Socorro said.

I turned to Lucie and said, "If it is all right with you, I'd like to keep this one on the wall in my room." She beamed at me and nodded. "Just one thing," I added. "You need to sign it." And with that, Lucie picked up the red crayon and wrote her name with a flourish right under the kitten.

CHAPTER 5

TRASH ON THE STREET

Occupied Paris, June 1940

In the early morning of June 22, the screech of a loudspeaker rudely woke me from a fitful sleep.

"Citizens of Paris… There is no longer any efficacious resistance you can mount… It is useless to continue the struggle. The glorious army of the Third Reich has defeated France. Starting this evening, you are subject to an 8 p.m. curfew."

Our worst fears had been realized. It only took a month for the Nazis to overcome the storied French army. We dreaded what we feared would become of us.

After the girls had their breakfast, Danielle convinced me to walk into town with her. We had been told so many times about the barbarians threatening to overrun us, that we had to see this army. Mathilde dismissed the idea, but agreed to watch the children if we were "determined to be part of the rabble."

It looked like every man, woman, and child still in Paris was lining the Champs Elysees. Packed together as if waiting for a parade, we stood as silent as a funeral.

"Can you see anything?" Since I was the tallest, Danielle assumed I had a bird's eye view.

I felt it in my stomach before I saw them. The stomp of thousands of boots created a relentless bass drum. The heartbeat of our loss. The crowd exhaled and my knees buckled, as soldiers appeared four abreast. Carrying rifles, their uniforms sharp, and black boots shining, they marched into our lives and nothing was ever the same.

It was hard to believe, but some Parisians welcomed the Nazis. I was surprised at the nonchalant expressions of prejudice I heard against immigrants, Jews, and Communists. In the New England world of my upbringing, there may have been hatred, but people had the manners to keep it to themselves.

"There are so many! And they are tall, like you, Jane," Danielle said. Indeed, it was a good-looking army straight out of Hollywood.

"Of course they are, what did you expect? They are magnificent," a woman standing next to us crowed. People around us reacted in different ways. Some clapping. Some weeping. Most, in shock. Some Parisians killed themselves that day. The army's music was angry and defiant. Thousands and thousands of soldiers marched in coordination, like a machine that would grind us up. This was their celebration of victory and our ignominious defeat. I cried.

We stayed long enough to watch the rows of soldiers replaced by tank after tank, and motorcycle after motorcycle, and horse-drawn wagon after wagon. They came as if there were no end to them.

Although they sent their most handsome, fit soldiers to daunt us, they were the opposite of Parisians in every way—coarse to our elegant; guttural to our musical; militaristic to our laissez-faire. The Nazis succeeded in displaying their might that morning. We covered our windows with bedsheets, somehow feeling safer from the invaders if we could not be seen. We learned that Hitler himself planned to come to Paris. I couldn't bear to see our Tour Eiffel desecrated by his presence. The day Hitler came, I stayed home.

Mathilde decreed we should keep the girls in for a week, until she realized the Nazis weren't going anywhere, and we would have to figure out a semblance of life.

France tore in two, like a piece of tissue paper. They divided the country into the Occupied Zone, which included Paris, and the so-called Free Zone in the south. Marshall Pétain, the Great War hero that so many people revered, stepped up to "save France" by creating a collaborationist government in the South. His Vichy Government did the Nazis' dirty work. French officials and French police turned against their own people. Pétain said collaboration would spare France from the devastation wreaked on other countries, but he was as fascist as the Nazis. I saw the slogan of the Vichy Government pasted on billboards all over the city. "Work, Family, Fatherland." Difficult to distinguish one from the other.

It was harder and harder to take the children for walks, with soldiers everywhere—eating in our cafés, patrolling our parks in their brown uniforms with their guns, even claiming the best seats at the cinéma, where movies gave us a brief reprieve from reality. Paris became a tourist spot for German soldiers and the nurses, secretaries, and administrators who followed them. They came by bus, and they crowded the Metro. They had their pictures taken in front of the Eiffel Tower. They even changed the clocks to match German time. We disobeyed in a tiny way by keeping our personal pocket watches and the old grandfather clock at the school on French time.

It was a year before anyone mounted a real resistance.

We were afraid and disgusted, and we learned to keep both emotions a secret. My parents sent letters and telegrams begging me to come home, but by then I was devoted to the children. If they had realized the dangers I would encounter, they would have sent the Canadian Mounties to collect me.

You may have read charming stories set in wartime about little girls in Paris and their escapades in the park and at the zoo. But there are other stories too dark to tell in a book for children. One is the story of a gentle old man who parked his cart near the Notre Dame Cathedral. He sold antique books and pastel drawings of Paris landmarks. He loved the girls, especially Lucie, and they loved him. Whenever we walked past him, our two straight lines dissolved into a gaggle of girls. He always stopped and entertained them by creating drawings of animals and birds. He would never accept payment, though he wore layers of ratty black coats even in the summer. His tattered shoes, held together by tape, were quite a contrast to the clean pinafores and shiny patent leather Mary Janes sported by my girls.

One warm summer afternoon, the year after I arrived in Paris, we were visiting with our bookseller friend. When he leaned down to give a painting to Lucie, she noticed his yarmulke. She asked, "Why are you wearing that funny hat?"

I tried to shush her, but the man looked at her kindly, and in a heavy accent said, "I wear this to honor the holy one. Ha-Elohim. I am a Jew." Just then, a burly man in a brown uniform pushed past us.

"You do not have a permit to sell in public. That is now required for all you trash on the street. Pack up this mess and report to the city hall to pay your fine." Lucie stood up tall in front of the soldier and said, "Don't yell at my friend. This is his corner!" In terror, I dragged her and the other girls away as the old man was being pushed and prodded to hurry.

In a voice much louder than necessary, the soldier barked, "I would tell these *kinder* to be careful, Sister. There is no tolerance for insolence from the French, young or old."

From across the street, we watched in silence as the bookseller wheeled his cart down the street, hounded by the man in the brown uniform. Our friend turned to us and gave a little wave, and that was the last we ever saw of him.

I say we watched in silence because I had my hand clamped over Lucie's mouth as she squirmed and protested. The angry voice of the soldier stunned the rest of the girls. Whatever my own feelings were, the safety of those children was my only priority. I reeled at the responsibility, then squared my shoulders. With a snap of my fingers, I got them back into their two straight lines. A stern look finally subdued Lucie, and we made our way to a park. My mind was racing. Because of Aunt Mathilde's influential friends, our little school had been protected from the harsh realities of the Nazi occupation. I had a hard time accepting what had befallen the country I had come to love. I didn't know how to explain any of it to these innocents.

By the time we got back to the ivy-covered house that had always felt safe, I was afraid I had succeeded in confusing and terrorizing the children. I told them that some men were not kind, and that it was very dangerous for any of us to talk back to the soldiers in the brown uniforms. I lamely explained that there were some bad things happening that the grownups were going to sort out. Looking back, I wonder if I was counting on FDR to get into the war—or if I thought that Marshal Pétain had something up his sleeve besides collaboration.

The girls seemed to calm down and had a nap. That evening at bedtime when they were crowded into the bathroom brushing their teeth, Lucie began to cry.

I wiped a spot of minty toothpaste off her chin and asked what was wrong. She said, "Mam'selle—my papa and me are Jewish. I'm not supposed to tell anyone, but I don't understand why it is a secret. Is that the bad thing? Is Jewish the bad thing?"

I could hardly hide my dismay. I pulled her to me and drew all the girls into a tight circle. By then, they were all crying, and I cursed the men who were turning the world upside down.

"No, my darling. Being Jewish is not a bad thing. It is like being in a big family that loves the world and loves each other. But these men in the brown shirts don't like Jewish people, and they are very mean and powerful and they can hurt us." I looked around at all of them. "That is why you need to keep it a secret that Lucie is Jewish."

I asked the girls to share their religions. All of them were Catholic. Then I did my best to explain what, in Heaven's name, a Unitarian was. I wasn't quite brave enough to stun them with the heresy that I didn't believe in God.

After the girls were all tucked into bed, I knocked on Mathilde's door.

"Come in, Jane dear," she said.

I went into the sitting room that opened onto her office. Even though it was still early, she was in her dressing gown with her long hair released from its habitual chignon. A glass of sherry was on the table next to her, and stacks of paper surrounded her on the couch.

"Ah, chérie. I am so glad to see you. Please excuse this terrible mess. The government is driving me insane with paperwork. I can't wait for these monsters to leave." She moved a pile onto the floor and patted the sofa to invite me to sit. In the warm light of the lamp, her face looked drawn.

"Aunt Mathilde," I began, and then I started to cry as if I were no more grown up than Lucie. "I am terrified." I told her what had happened to the bookseller and about Lucie's confession.

She embraced me. "Ah, yes. These are dangerous times. I am surprised that Lucie told you she was Jewish. She must trust you. I had hoped that the other girls would not find out. I didn't want to add this on to asking them not to tell anyone about our guests." She took a sip of sherry. "It is terrible to ask children to keep so many secrets. Lucie's mother is dead. Her father is a scientist, working somewhere in Russia. You can see how important it is that no one else knows. I will depend on you to find a way to keep the other girls silent on this matter."

I knew I would have to be very stern so that they'd understand that this was a very important secret. And I realized that there would be many more secrets to keep.

One night I finished telling a lovely story about Marie Curie, the brilliant Polish-born Nobel-prize-winning scientist who studied radioactivity with her husband at the Sorbonne in Paris. Lucie looked at me seriously and said, "Mam'selle, your stories begin the way they should, 'Once upon a time.' But they don't end the right way." The other little girls agreed.

"How are stories supposed to end?" I asked.

"You know, 'they lived happily ever after,'" Yvette said.

"Hmm. That's not very honest, is it?" I asked.

The girls looked surprised and then shook their heads.

"People try to be happy—they want to be—but sometimes they cannot," Paulette said.

Socorro added, "There are good times and bad times in life. Everyone has problems, but they try their best."

"How do you think stories should end?" I asked.

Lucie looked thoughtful. "You should say 'They had their good days and their bad days, and they took care of their problems the best they knew how.'"

From that moment, all our stories ended that way, and the little girls said it with me as if it were a mantra with magical powers. Little did we know how much magic we would need.

When it seemed inevitable that war would come, the parents of our original girls began to contact us in a frenzy. The most troublesome question remained where to send them. The United States was pretending not to know the extent of the danger. We learned the sad story of the Ocean Liner St. Louis, which sailed from Hamburg to Havana in May 1939, around the same time I sailed to Paris. The ship carried nearly a thousand passengers seeking asylum from Nazi Germany. The travelers applied for U.S. visas and planned to disembark in Cuba before going to America. The Cuban government turned most of them away. Then the ship sailed to Florida, and the United States government turned them away as well. Grâce à Dieu, most of them were taken in by other countries. I burned with shame that my beloved president FDR didn't open the arms of my country.

Money always seems to be power, and our girls had wealthy parents. They whisked our students away, one by one, to Switzerland, to South America, to Sweden. All but three—Paulette, Socorro, and Lucie. Paulette and Socorro's fathers held government appointments in Italy and Peru. It took them forever to send for their daughters. As for Lucie? We had no idea about her father. For months Lucie, Socorro, and Paulette played host to our guests, some who stayed as briefly as a couple of days, others as long as a couple of weeks.

At first, Lucie took it in stride that her friends were being sent away. So many girls came and went that the chaos distracted her. Then, in June, Paulette and Socorro were scheduled to leave. The three girls realized they might never see each other again, and they had a heartbreaking goodbye. As I look back, I can see why those three girls forged a bond that lasted their entire lives.

Only Lucie remained. Mathilde had her birth certificate, but it clearly documented her religion. As Shakespeare said, we were in a pickle.

CHAPTER 6

KEEPING SECRETS

Occupied Paris, Summer 1940

In Paris in the 1940s, secrets meant survival. Overnight, an entire nation learned to keep secrets. Children learned not to mention a stray baguette that might have a folded code baked into it; or hitherto unknown "cousins" who appeared and disappeared; or a strange door at the back of the cupboard; or a friend, like Lucie, who turned out to be Jewish.

One afternoon as I sat reading in the conservatory, I could hear the girls in the garden batting shuttlecocks back and forth. Lucie appeared at my side, a look of consternation on her face.

"Mam'selle?"

"Yes, petite?"

"What is the difference between a secret and a lie?"

I didn't answer right away. I didn't know how to answer.

I took her hands in mine. "A secret is something you keep to yourself. A lie is something you tell someone else."

"But if someone asks me about a secret—like if I am Jewish—don't I have to lie to keep the secret?"

I looked down at my little friend whose mind was always going a mile a minute.

"That is true. I want to tell you that a lie is bad, but sometimes it is necessary to protect yourself or someone you love."

She nodded. Then smiled and skipped outside to join the others. I looked at my hands, as if there would be some deeper wisdom in the whorls of my palms. But none was there.

Lies and secrets were necessary in those terrible times. We pretended things were normal when they were not. People in the Resistance took enormous risks as a matter of their daily routines. The people *I* knew resisted in small ways. They moved street signs so the Nazis would get lost; saved up old batteries and mixed them with new shipments to sabotage the Nazis' machinery; put bleach in the Nazis' gas tanks to wreck the motors—and when no more bleach could be had, they used sand. The waiters spat in their food. And we all pretended we didn't understand their angry guttural French. As I look back now, I can hardly imagine how I, who never even returned a library book late, found the courage to do these minor acts of rebellion.

Extra beds appeared in our dormitory. The two straight lines of five girls that we walked in, ate in and slept in sometimes became two lines of seven or even ten. It was a challenge to accommodate twenty children, but we did whatever we had to. The visitors ranged from toddlers to teenagers. We stretched and pinned extra uniforms to meet the need. Many girls came into and out of the school in just a few days. Our eight-year-olds didn't ask questions and treated our guests with great kindness.

Life changed in other ways. You couldn't trust anyone. Nice people informed on their neighbors and even their family members to get dispensation from the Nazis. French women slept with German officers to get food for their children.

With Brigitte gone, Mathilde and I did the shopping and cleaning. Thank goodness our loyal cook Danielle stayed with us, so we ate well. Danielle had a cousin with a large farm in the country, so we had access to fresh food. Marcel cared for the school grounds and planted a small vegetable garden. He brought in new cots and moved everything around, in spite of the limp he sustained in the Great War. He brought sweets for the girls. He didn't say much, but his constant cursing taught me all the bad words I know in French. I suspected Marcel was part of the Resistance, but no one ever said.

Mathilde had taught half of the daughters of Paris to read, which protected us. She also cultivated friends in the Church. They kept us stocked with petrol for our bus long after it was unavailable to others. Our field trips to Danielle's cousins in the country became a routine part of our lives. Mathilde obtained rudimentary papers for every girl, though she said the documents wouldn't be authentic enough for scrutiny by border guards. But even with credentials, we worried. We worried about having enough to eat when the rationing began. We worried about our neighbors noticing our "new" students. We worried about the men in brown uniforms with headquarters altogether too near the school. We worried about everything.

Our trips to the country accomplished more than a bit of fresh air and some food. They allowed us to hand off our "extra" girls to the brave souls who would take them on harrowing trips across borders. I drove Mathilde's rickety blue bus always certain it was going to break down. I was never a confident driver, so we went gingerly over the country roads, more appropriate for horse and cart than for the behemoth I steered. When we returned, we had eggs, onions, milk, butter, an occasional chicken, and a satchel stuffed with the no-longer-needed uniforms that distinguished Madame Mathilde's School.

I marveled at the courage of our guests. War separated them from their families and left them at the mercy of strangers, yet I seldom heard a whimper. I didn't have any idea what happened to those children when they left us, so I pictured them traveling safely, and finding their own stories in their own worlds.

There were moments of sheer terror, like the time I took fourteen girls to the zoo and Lucie threw a stone at a young soldier, who turned and raised his gun. When he recognized he had been attacked by a child, he swore and turned away. I nearly fainted.

There were also moments of such sorrow. The French word *désolé* says it eloquently—desolation. Ever since I arrived in Paris, we had been trying to reach Lucie's father, but we had not heard from Professor Fastion. Our attempts to reach him at his university failed. He left a bank account with Mathilde for Lucie's care, but like so many other people, he had disappeared. Even before the Nazis invaded Russia in the spring of 1941, things were terrible for Jews there, especially in the countryside. People were detained, imprisoned, and even murdered for no reason other than that they were Jewish or immigrants.

Like most of the children at our school, Lucie was accustomed to not hearing from her father. No one found it unusual that he didn't come when she was injured. It appeared that many wealthy people thought of their children in the same way they thought of the fancy cars they stored in their fancy garages. They thought of them not at all.

One day Lucie asked, "When is my papa going to send for me?"

I told her we hadn't heard from him in quite a while—that he may have been detained—a euphemism everyone employed when they could not bear to imagine what might have happened. In those innocent days, the death camps were still rumors, impossible to believe. Within a few months, Germany embarked on its ghastly final solution and, as Yeats wrote in his poem "The Second Coming": "The ceremony of innocence is drowned; The best lack all conviction, while the worst are full of passionate intensity."

CHAPTER 7

DR. LEVY CALLS

Occupied Paris, Summer 1940

You'll recall Dr. Levy's dismissal of my concerns about Lucie. I would assure you that he had barely noticed my existence. Despite the fact that I cared for the girls, he spoke only to Madame Mathilde when he made his occasional visits. Even though I was the person who recognized Lucie's fracture, he didn't offer a word of apology or thanks. He never offered me a word of any kind. So I was surprised when Mathilde knocked on my bedroom door one evening to say that Dr. Levy was on the phone for me. I followed her to her office. She held out the receiver and left the room with a mysterious expression. The doctor announced himself in his formal English and thanked me for speaking with him. I feared there was something wrong with Lucie, or my aunt. When I asked, he answered in that lovely voice that he seemed to reserve for his most vulnerable patients.

"Non, non. Don't worry. They are fine."

"Then why, may I ask, are you calling me?" I admit I harbored a bit of resentment for what I considered his impolite treatment.

"I need some help, and I am hoping you have an understanding heart."

That softened me a bit, and I was intrigued.

"I like to think I do. But I can't imagine how I could help you."

"I recall your aunt telling me that you have some nursing training. If I had listened to your concern about Lucie, I would have known you were correct about her broken wrist."

"Thank you for saying that. My training is very basic—what they call practical nursing—rudimentary and, well, as the name says, practical."

"And you," he said. "Are you practical? You see what needs to be done, and then do it?" he asked.

"I... I think I am," I answered, fearing that I was stepping into some sort of trap.

"Mathilde tells me your parents are not Catholic?"

"That's right. My mother is Unitarian, and my father is Episcopalian."

"Ah, the American person's Catholicism."

"Not exactly…."

"And you? Do you have, as they say, an open mind?"

"I like to think of myself as having an open mind. I'm not religious at all. Where you are going with this…?"

"And about the woman question? Where do you stand? This problem I have involves the secrets of women."

"Secrets? Now I really don't know what you are getting at. Can't you just say what you need?"

"Mademoiselle Smith, I presume you are not foolhardy. Nor am I. In these times, it is not always wise to be direct."

By then I felt like a dunce. "No, Doctor, of course not. Please forgive me. Yes, I support rights for women. And yes, I am open-minded. And of course I am willing to help you if I can."

The doctor was quiet.

"Are you willing to take a risk for something you believe in?"

"Well… yes."

"Bon. In that case, I need your open-minded assistance. I don't like to talk about these things on the telephone. Will you come to my home? Will you come right away? Mathilde can give you directions. Wear your uniform. Bring a change of clothes. And please, if you are stopped, don't tell them you are coming here."

I had already put the girls to bed. There was still time to go before the curfew, but I could hardly imagine my aunt allowing me to leave the school alone at night. She surprised me by coming back into the room and proffering a piece of paper that had directions written in her elegant Spencerian cursive. She gave me a steady look and said, "I trust Dr. Levy. I hope you will too." I nodded uncertainly and packed a bag with my passport and papers. I was still wearing my black robes—what he had referred to as my "uniform"—so I kissed Mathilde on the cheek and hurried out into the night. As I was going out the door, she said, "Be careful."

I was glad I had directions. It wasn't smart to ask for information from the French police who worked for the Nazis. It was already impossible to know whom to trust, unless your Aunt Mathilde told you. Dr. Levy seemed to trust *me*, but with what, I had no idea.

If I had known what he was going to ask of me, I would never have gone.

CHAPTER 8

FRANÇOISE

Occupied Paris, 1940

It was just a short walk to the large, brightly lit apartment house. The concierge was sweeping the sidewalk. She said, "Sister, Dr. Levy is expecting you. Third floor."

The elevator had an intricate wrought-iron gate. I slid it open, pushed the button, and up I went. In those days, Dr. and Madame Levy occupied the entire third floor of the building. I stood in front of the door with a trepidation I hadn't expected, despite all the mystery. I almost turned around, but I found my courage and knocked resolutely. The doctor opened the door so quickly that I had no time to process my thoughts as he bustled me into the foyer.

Doctor Bernard Levy was not a tall man. But he was so authoritative that it always seemed as though he towered above me. He had black hair and piercing dark eyes, and a tendency toward five o'clock shadow. As always, he was impeccably dressed. He wore a red silk scarf around his neck, adding a bit of color to his dark gray suit, and he had a cigarette hanging from his mouth. In my eyes, he was Hollywood's idea of the perfect French man.

"Bonsoir, mademoiselle. Thank you for coming. Desolé for not being able to be frank with you."

The apartment was enormous and elegant, with high ceilings. It smelled like lemons. The wallpaper was a beautiful pale green watered silk. Light bounced off crystal chandeliers, and under my feet were thick Oriental carpets. The walls were lined with bookcases, and there were small ceramic figurines on every table.

Dr. Levy showed me into a study with dark red leather chairs and couches. He gestured to a huge armchair, and I sank into it.

"Mademoiselle Smith…" he began.

"Please, Dr. Levy. Call me Jane, or I shall be looking everywhere for my aunt."

He laughed gently.

"Jane then. Good. Can I offer you some tea?"

I nodded, and he poured a cup. I shook my head to lemon and nodded for cream and sugar. The doctor was already drinking something else, scotch, perhaps? My knowledge of alcohol was limited to the gin and tonics my parents drank in the summer.

He gave me a serious look. "I have asked you here to help me with a sensitive matter. I'm sure I can count on your discretion." As he exhaled, the smoke was like an underscore.

"Of course," I replied, shifting in my chair.

"I have been caring for a Catholic family for years. The oldest daughter is nineteen. I met her when she was just a child."

I nodded, although I'm not sure why.

"She is engaged to be married. This is not a love match. It is a union that will be advantageous to the family and protect them in these uncertain times. While Françoise isn't happy about it, she is reconciled." He looked directly at me. "She has been promised in marriage to a high-ranking German official."

I stopped nodding and just looked at him.

"Do you judge them?" he said, with a gaze I could only describe as intense.

"Wouldn't you call that collaboration?" I asked.

"Yes. That is exactly what I would call it. And I would also call it survival. This family is part of my community. And...."

"And...?" I asked, a bit indignantly.

"And this girl is in a terrible—what do you Americans call it? A predicament."

"It sounds to me as though they have everything quite figured out for themselves," I said. I *was* judging them. "What could possibly be wrong?"

"Françoise has made a dreadful mistake. She is in love with a boy named Claude. They were going to run away together, but she realized the Nazis would punish her family for humiliating the commandant. She told her lover they couldn't be together and broke it off. He went into the army and was captured."

I couldn't get used to the casual French way of using that word "lover."

"That's terrible! She broke it off, and now he is in a prison camp? She must blame herself."

"Yes, but you see, there is another problem. They were together. She told me she couldn't imagine going on with her life without ever experiencing love with Claude. And...."

"Oh, my." The fog was lifting. "Is she going to have a baby?" Though I was twenty-five, my experience with men was not just limited, it was nonexistent. My cousins referred to me as the Old Maid. I didn't have any first-hand knowledge of sex and love, but I had a technical understanding of the birds and the bees. If I hadn't been talking with a doctor, I would have been embarrassed. But the science of it all fascinated me.

"Ah, yes. She is with child. So now you understand it—the predicament," Dr. Levy said. "The family has come to me for their salvation. If the Nazis find out she has lain with another man, they will call off the wedding and harm will come to the family. So you see... they have come to me for a... termination... for an abortion."

The word hung in the air. I had heard it before, but only as a sordid and dangerous secret. Then I remembered that Dr. Levy had said, "one of the secrets of women." Was that what he meant? Abortion was part of some netherworld that frightened me. I thought women died from it. I had never associated it with an actual doctor, and the connection made me wonder for a moment if he was some kind of charlatan. And how could he, a Jew, add doing illegal abortions to the risks he was already taking with the underground?

"I don't... I don't know anything about that, Dr. Levy. I can't help you." I started to get up.

He motioned me to sit back down. I can't describe the expression of pleading on his face. "I have seen the way you care for the girls," he said. "You are magnificent. You understand how to calm them. That is all I need from you. Françoise is like a terrified child. I just need you to hold her hand and help her keep still. I will do the rest. It is a simple and quick procedure. It will take ten or fifteen minutes. I will give her a dose of Laudanum to take the edge off any discomfort."

"Laudanum? Isn't that dangerous?"

"Non, mademoiselle. A few drops in a glass of sherry—very safe. Please think about helping her, won't you?"

I realized that, all of a sudden, I was helping *her*. I recognized it would be unwise to underestimate Dr. Levy.

"Dr. Levy, you are involved in something I cannot be part of. You'll need to find someone else to help you."

He jumped up and walked to a door hidden in the wood paneling. He opened it and said, "Françoise, won't you come in?" Looking back, I recognize how unfair it was to bring her into the room before I had agreed to help. But perhaps he sensed that seeing her would make my decision.

The girl named Françoise came tentatively into the room. My first impression was that he had summoned an angel. I am a tall woman by any reckoning, so it was startling to see how tiny she was, like a doll. She was pale, with golden blonde hair and dark brown eyes rimmed with red. She was wearing a pinafore, like my girls wore. It was pale blue with little yellow flowers. The short white gloves edged in lace seemed out of place. I thought of Alice in Wonderland. She was holding a small white leather-bound book and what

I thought might be rosary beads. I felt very conspicuous in my long black robe.

She looked nothing like the damaged women I had imagined when I read newspaper stories about abortion—women found dead in motel rooms or arrested for prostitution, which was always associated with abortion in my mind. She glanced down and her face was flushed. Of course, I realized how embarrassed she must be that a stranger was privy to her intimate secrets. I wanted to leave, but I also had compassion for this girl and wondered if it would be possible for me to bring a bit of grace to her sad story.

Françoise looked up at me and said in a tiny voice, "Oh, Sister—I am so grateful you are here. Will you pray for me?"

"I'm not..." I began, but stopped when I saw Dr. Levy's glare. "Of course I will," I answered. I bowed my head in what I hoped would look like reverence. I was not accustomed to lying about something as important as being a nun, but the heightened energy of this encounter seemed to be changing all the rules.

Dr. Levy gave me an approving look. He gestured to Françoise to sit on the couch and dragged a smaller chair over so that he was sitting in front of us.

"Françoise, allow me to introduce you to Sister Jane."

We nodded at each other.

"Now that we are acquainted with one another," he began, "I want to share with both of you what we will be doing this evening."

"*This* evening?" I yelped.

"Yes, of course. In matters like this, time is of the essence. And don't worry. I have informed your convent that you will stay with us overnight."

So my aunt knew. Of course, she had to have known or she would never have let me go out this late with no explanation. But could she approve of this?

He turned to face Françoise and looked at her tenderly.

"Françoise, it is important that you tell me it is your intention and desire not to have a baby. Is that correct?"

Françoise looked like she was in shock. She nodded her head slowly.

Then Dr. Levy began what seemed to be a university lecture.

"Before we proceed, I want you to understand your body and how it works. It is a crime that women are never taught about this, so they are helpless to regulate their fertility."

Françoise and I both blushed. Françoise spoke hesitantly. "But Docteur, doesn't that violate the dictates of the Church?"

"Not at all," he answered. "When the Church accepted the reality that the earth orbits the sun, it also accepted science. All I am sharing with you is science." He smiled. Françoise looked doubtful. I nearly choked on his dubious interpretation of Catholic doctrine, but kept my nunly peace. Levy pulled out a pad and pen and drew a picture I had seen once before in a text-book about childbirth.

"This is a picture of a woman's reproductive organs as one would see it from the front. In the middle here," he tapped with his pen, "is the uterus. This is the muscle that provides a nine-month home for a baby and then opens to release it when it is ready."

Françoise hung her head. I didn't think he was being at all sensitive with his "science." I put my hand on her arm to comfort her.

"I can't have this baby," she said.

"My dear, what is inside you now is not a baby. It has the size and shape of... of a shrimp. You don't need to be ashamed of removing this shrimp to save your family."

"Really?" she said. "Really? It is not a baby now?"

"Absolutely not," said Dr. Levy. "It starts as something so small you can't even see it, and then develops the way a tadpole develops into a frog."

I struggled to recall the diagrams I had seen of how a pregnancy develops. I remembered learning that "ontogeny recapitulates phylogeny" but didn't re-call what that meant. So I nodded, hoping that this would make her feel better. In the back of my mind were the summer smells of catching tadpoles in the pond in the woods behind our house in Connecticut.

"It is like that. But allow me to go back to the beginning, if you will." Dr. Levy proceeded to explain fertility and ovulation in a practical way that I'm sure Françoise wished she had known before.

He continued. "While men's bodies continually manufacture their seed, women are born with all the eggs they will have already in their ovaries."

Françoise and I glanced at each other, wondering if he saw that as some kind of accomplishment.

"Every month, one or the other of the ovaries releases a tiny egg. It travels down these conduits called the Fallopian tubes, named for an Italian, Dr. Fal-lopius. If you ever study this, you will find that many parts of a woman's body are named for men."

Given what I had already learned about the world, I didn't find that sur-prising. I had to break the tension, so I said, "My aunt's friends run a farm. They hold the eggs up to a candle to see if they are fertilized." I don't think I have ever in my life said anything so inane. Apparently, the doctor agreed, and he glared at me.

"That's right, *Sister*." Did I imagine the emphasis on the word? "Not all eggs are fertilized. When a woman's egg has been fertilized and implants it-self in the uterus, there are chemical changes in her body that signal preg-nancy. The uterus has a lining, like the lining of your coat. It thickens in order to provide the nutrients needed by the early pregnancy. If the tiny egg isn't fertilized, it passes out unknown, released from the woman's body with her menstrual flow."

"My mother told me that my monthly flow is my body weeping because it does not have a child," Françoise offered, emboldened, I think, by my chicken observations.

"Yes, well, that is a very sentimental way to explain it." Dr. Levy sounded a bit grumpy. "The body does not weep except from the eyes, and the woman does not always want a child," he said, pointedly.

Françoise looked chastened. This time I glared at Levy, who continued. When he finally completed his interminable lecture, he asked if Françoise had any questions. I had about a hundred, but I wasn't the designated student.

She looked lost and overwhelmed and shook her head no.

"All right then. Now, I'll give you a brief explanation of what we are about to do. As you know, it is called abortion."

Françoise blanched and swayed. I sat forward and caught her.

"Dr. Levy," I asked, "Could we have a moment? I think Françoise needs a sip of water."

He looked at me, surprised, and then pleased. "Yes, yes, of course."

I had noticed a pitcher on a side table and I poured some water for her into one of the porcelain coffee cups on the tray. She grabbed my arm and whispered, "Thank you," and took a sip.

I had to say something. "Dr. Levy, is it necessary to know all of this? I think Françoise is ready to proceed, are you not?" I looked at her and she nodded energetically. It was the most life I had seen from her.

Dr. Levy stood and drew himself up to his full five feet eight inches.

"Sister," he said in a serious tone, "Abortion is a very grave matter. I do this because I know it is a life-saving procedure. But it also ends life. It cannot be taken lightly, and I must ask that you respect my process."

"Of course, Doctor. I apologize." So much for piping up.

He nodded toward Françoise. "I will give a very gentle medication that will help you relax and be comfortable. The sister will hold your hand and keep me apprised of your well-being." I raised my eyebrows to show that I did not know what that comprised. Levy made a dismissive "don't worry about it" gesture.

"I will use an instrument like a slender spoon to remove that little shrimp. It will take about 10 to 15 minutes. When I am done, you will have bleeding similar to your monthly flow for a week or two. Your body chemistry will soon go back to normal, as if this had never happened."

Françoise was weeping softly.

"Why are you crying, my dear?" Dr. Levy asked in his kind voice.

"I will lose the only thing I have of Claude. The only thing that is mine," she said.

Neither the doctor nor I said anything. There was nothing to say.

The grandfather clock in the hall struck ten. Françoise looked up at Dr. Levy with more strength than I had seen in her before, and said, "I am ready." She stood up, and the two of us obediently followed the doctor back into the foyer and down a long corridor. He opened a door at the end of the hall to a small room with an adjoining bathroom. It was bright white and smelled like antiseptic. There was an examining table and a counter with shelves and drawers above and below it. The doctor showed her the cotton gown folded on the examining table.

"After you use the toilet, undress and put on this gown with the opening in the back. You can fold your clothes and put them here," he gestured to the wooden chair. "Then, sit at the end of the table. Sister and I will be back shortly."

"Do I have to remove everything?" Françoise asked, her eyes wide.

"Only your dress, your slip, stockings, and panties."

That was pretty much everything, I thought. He didn't mention the white gloves, so perhaps he considered them optional.

I followed Dr. Levy out another door into a small office.

"Mademoiselle Smith—" he began sternly.

I stopped him, holding my hand up.

"Dr. Levy, I am here and I will help you in any way I can. But you must not be cross with me. I am frightened. I feel like a big phony every time you call me sister, and I don't have any idea how to help you. Is this even legal?"

"Well, well. Your aunt said you had some spunk. I am glad to see it. As for all that, I am scared as well. I am scared of what would happen to this girl if I don't help her. I am scared of what would happen to her family. I am scared of what could happen to you and to me because, of course, abortion is not legal in France. The Nazis oppose it for the people they consider Aryans because they are determined to take over the world. I'm afraid of putting such a burden on you—a young woman I hardly know. If it weren't for my complete confidence in your aunt, I would never have dared ask you. But I cannot do this alone. I have never had to ask for help before. My wife has always assisted me, but she is away with her family, perhaps for some while. As for being a nun, as you can see, I am going to give this young woman what she needs, and I hope you will do the same."

"I don't know what to say. I have never broken the law."

"Really?" he sputtered. "Just what do you think you are doing when you help those girls escape?"

CHAPTER 9

INEXTRICABLY BRAIDED

Occupied Paris, 1940

The conversation continued.

"But that's breaking an unjust law—it's not the same."

"Isn't it? Think of what would happen to Françoise. To her family. Is that justice?"

I, the girl who insisted that I cared about justice but didn't want to be disobedient, had to face the fact that I had indeed been breaking a great many laws. I couldn't argue with him, so I turned my attention to our patient.

"We can't leave her sitting in there alone. Tell me what I must do to help you."

"Bon. First, keep her distracted. The laudanum will relax her. I'll give her enough to make the pain manageable, but not enough to knock her out. The procedure will be much easier if you can keep her mind off what we are doing. Talk with her, sing to her, Mon Dieu, pray with her if you can. Alert me if she becomes extremely pale, if her breathing becomes rapid, or if she faints."

"She could faint?"

"Yes, on occasion, the vagal nerve is stimulated. But don't worry. If that should happen while I am operating, you will come to the end of the table and put her legs over your shoulders. That sends the blood back to her head and, voilà, she will be back with us."

"Like Trendelenburg?" I asked, wanting to show off my familiarity with the medical term for elevating a patient's feet.

"Exactement! Very good. So, can you do these things?"

"I will do my best," I answered, trying to keep my voice from shaking.

I tapped on the examining room door and found Françoise sitting on the side of the bed, shivering. The room was warm, so I guessed that her trembling, like mine, came from fear. Dr. Levy helped her move back to the head of the table. He addressed both of us.

"Sister, since Françoise hasn't had a woman's examination before, I'll explain it. I'm going to put her knees over these rests." I, also apparently not having had what he called a "woman's examination," did not understand what he was doing. He placed her knees over stirrups, which kept her legs open and her feet dangling in the air. Francoise and I were both horrified at the exposed position.

He saw the look on our faces.

"I assure you, mesdemoiselles, that if there were another way I could do what is necessary, I would be more than happy."

Levy gave Françoise the laudanum.

Then there was nothing to do but begin.

I made myself busy, looking anywhere but at Françoise. She had folded her clothes, which smelled like lavender, neatly on the chair. The toe of a silk stocking peeked out from underneath the lace of her slip. Stockings of any kind were rare in Paris by then, and I could only imagine the conversation Françoise must have had with her mother about the appropriate apparel for this particular rendezvous.

The doctor gave me a small pillow to put under her head—a gesture I appreciated. Françoise looked at me with pleading eyes and pointed to the rosary beads on top of her clothes.

"Sister, pray for me. Please."

I picked them up and took her hand in both of mine in a gesture that I hoped looked holy. She had bitten her fingernails down to the nub.

I didn't have any idea what to say. I thought I remembered a part of the rosary:

> Hail Mary, full of grace
> Among all women blessed art, thou
> And blessed the fruit of thy womb, Jesus.

Drat! That would not work. Then I thought of a Gregorian chant I had learned once:

> Hail holy Queen
> Mother of mercy,
> Show unto us
> The blessed fruit
> Of thy womb, Jesus.

Oh no! Did everything have that inopportune fruit of the womb? Françoise whimpered. I tried to invent something that sounded like what she needed, and that might also be construed as Catholic. I held the beads in our entwined hands, trying not to cry out when she gripped me with such ferocity. I hoped she was too distracted to know or care about the authenticity of the prayer.

I intoned the same verses over and over.

> Hail, holy Queen
> Mother of Mercy—
> Our Lady of Perpetual Grace—
> Honor our love and courage—
> Remember our goodness.
> Show unto us
> Thy forgiveness
> And thy mercy.

My first, but not my last, encounter with Our Lady of Perpetual Grace.

True to his word, the doctor finished in about ten minutes. Françoise hardly made a sound, but she squeezed my hand so hard I believe I can still see the imprint of her rosary beads all these years after.

By the time he had finished, it was late in the evening. Dr. Levy put a pad between Françoise's legs and I helped her don a simple cotton nightgown. We led her to a room with three small cots. She lay down and closed her eyes right away. I kissed her forehead and told her that the angels were watching over her. As I turned to go, she grabbed my arm and whispered, "You—you are my angel."

Back in the study, Dr. Levy lit a cigarette, and poured us each a small glass of sherry as we sat across from each other. It wasn't my first drink. Well, maybe it *was* my first. I didn't like the taste very much, but it seemed like the thing to do after such a night.

"You were extraordinary!" he beamed. "I knew you would be." Too tired to speak, I smiled. As silly as I had felt repeating that same made-up prayer over and over, I was certain I had helped Françoise. I was to find helping women addictive.

Dr. Levy showed me to an elegant guest room with a pale pink silk coverlet. I removed the garments that comprised my uniform. As I folded my robes, I remembered Françoise's hand in mine. I have never cared a whit for the idea of God, and I wasn't ashamed for being his stand-in, or rather, the stand-in for the Virgin Mother. Wearing the habit that evening, I encountered someone—a self that I didn't realize was missing. Who is it I became? Was it as simple as simple as "being of use" as my mother put it? Or did the habit have its own power?

I got into bed in a haze. I had just spent the evening helping a doctor I hardly knew perform an abortion on a woman I didn't know at all. I pretended to be a nun and gave fabricated benedictions during an illegal procedure that, in itself, merited excommunication. What an unlikely evening for a good girl like me.

I was familiar with the blood mysteries of women—the onset of menstruation, birth, and the end of the bleeding time. But this mystery—this sacred tension between life and death—wasn't referenced in any of my books. This was an initiation into something ancient and elemental. I was both exhausted and as awake as I had ever been. I lay my head on the frilly pink pillow and willed myself to go to sleep. I didn't think I feared Hell, but my nightmare found me on a small boat with Charon, the Greek ferryman of Hades, paddling frantically on the river Styx between the catastrophes of the monster, Scylla, and whirlpool, Charybdis. There was blood in the water, and I woke trembling.

It was not a good night.

I rose early. I put on my street clothes because the habit seemed too momentous. I looked in on Françoise. She was still sleeping, her mouth slightly open, golden hair in a cloud around her face. Dr. Levy was in the kitchen smoking and drinking coffee. I declined his offer of breakfast. He said I should go back to the school and get some rest.

The ten-minute walk back to the school bore no resemblance to my walk the evening before. I was not the same. The girls were with Mathilde at the park, and Danielle was at the market, so it was just me in the house. I made a cup of tea and lowered my creaky body onto the old chintz-covered chair in my tiny bedroom. As I drank the tea, I considered my nightmare and found, to my surprise, that I wasn't feeling scared or ashamed about my part in Françoise's abortion. I contemplated the black robes sticking out of the top of the brown leather satchel. What once seemed like a costume was transformed into grace.

I wrote many pages in my diary about that experience, but I don't need to refer to them to remember the details of the night that changed everything. The night when abortion became inextricably braided into my life.

CHAPTER 10

MON ANGE

Occupied Paris, August 1940

Mathilde didn't ask what had happened at Dr. Levy's, though I suspected she knew. By then we were already breaking so many laws that I assume she thought the less said, the better. It fell to me to attend to our new charges and to do as much teaching as possible. Little girls were passing through our school on their way to safety armed with temporary names and biographies so they could pass muster by anyone demanding papers.

"That night," as I thought of my evening with Dr. Levy and Françoise, seemed like a movie about someone else. After a week, I got another call from Levy. Another request that I wear my "uniform" and meet him for brunch. I thought it wasn't a coincidence that Mathilde uncharacteristically insisted on taking the girls to the park that morning.

It was a beautiful day, much cooler than usual for the end of summer. Dr. Levy was already at the bistro when I arrived. He jumped up and pulled out my chair as if I were someone important. We ordered breakfast. As soon as the coffee was served, he began to talk so rapidly and earnestly that I was surprised.

"Françoise hasn't stopped talking about you. It makes my contribution to the whole thing seem quite minor. I suppose I should be insulted," he said with a wide smile. "She says you are her angel. Her parents want to meet you. I hope it is all right that I didn't explain that you are not precisely a nun."

"That's ridiculous! It is one thing to fool a confused young girl and quite another to fool her parents," I said, taking a sip of coffee. "How do you think you are going to get away with that?"

"It will be easy. I have already told them you are American, so they will not be surprised by anything you do." Another broad grin. "They have told me they have something they want to give you. I couldn't dissuade them and, believe me, I tried. They are convinced I saved her life, but *you* saved her soul." He tore into his chocolate croissant with vigor.

"Oh, my. I don't see how I could accept anything from them."

"But doesn't Mathilde need help? Couldn't you just give whatever it is to the school?"

Drat, he knew what to say to me. "Of course. But do I really have to meet them? Can't you give it to me?"

"They have insisted on thanking you in person. They will be at my apartment in thirty minutes."

So much for my concerns. And my breakfast. We hurriedly finished eating, and he paid the check. Since the café was just a block from his house, we were inside and up the elevator in a moment. Levy took a big key ring from his pocket and unlocked the front door.

"I have some papers to gather for Monsieur Bouvier. Will you make the tea? I think you will find everything quite easily," he said, pointing to the kitchen door. Amazing how quickly I could go from being an angel to being kitchen help, but it was a relief to have a job to do. Within ten minutes he was answering the door. I carried the tray with cups and saucers, lemon, sugar and cream, and some biscuits into the study. He ushered Françoise and her parents in. I barely had time to set the tray down before Françoise ran to me, took my hand, and curtsied! She looked much better than the last time I saw her.

Dr. Levy said, "Monsieur and Madame Bouvier, may I introduce you to Sister Jane."

Françoise's father was very tall and slender. His bald head, glasses, and whiskers made him look like a bureaucrat, which, it turned out, is exactly what he was. He smelled like my father's pipe which made me trust him. At first his expression was serious, but then he smiled, clicked his heels together, and made a slight bow. Wow, I was being treated like a very important angel!

"Je vous remercie, mademoiselle," he said. Dr. Levy had neglected to mention that Françoise's parents spoke very little English. My French was good enough for seven-year-olds, but I figured I'd just do my best.

"Ma plaisir," I said, hoping I had it right. "Votre fille est très aimable." I hoped I had told him it was my pleasure and his daughter was very sweet.

Madame Bouvier was short and plump. She had blonde hair in ringlets and wore a blue brocade jacket with a black pencil skirt that made her look more like a teenager than the mother of a nineteen-year-old. She kissed me on both cheeks, and laughed nervously during our entire encounter. They finally sat down. Meanwhile, Françoise had taken the space next to me on the couch and was holding my hand.

"Maman," she said. "Elle est mon ange."

"Oui, chérie. Je sais."

The Bouviers thanked me effusively, and they got right to the point about a gift. I glanced around when they came in, expecting to see a basket of fruit or bread—or even a chicken. Since they weren't carrying anything, I concluded that they were going to give me money—or even better, food coupons.

That would have come in handy, especially when we had so many children and no one to pay tuition. I knew how much it would mean to my aunt who was supporting the school with her own funds, so I resolved to get over myself and say thank you for whatever they had for me.

I had difficulty following conversations in French that were not slow and deliberate. Monsieur Bouvier spoke rapidly, and I wasn't even getting the gist, but I knew Dr. Levy would fill me in on the details. I was waiting for something physical to change hands, but the conversation seemed to be about the "paysage" and a "couvent" and "cinq hectares." I had no idea what any of those things were, except that there were five of something. I smiled and nodded in appreciation. Noting my dazed look, Levy came to the rescue. "It's a convent," he said under his breath. "They are giving you an abandoned convent that is in the country on their family estate. Smile and say yes!"

So I mustered up my warmest smile and said, "Vous êtes très gracieux. Merci beaucoup. J'espère que tout les anges vous gardez."

I knew that was really cobbled together. At least I refrained from kissing them on the foreheads when I said I hoped the angels would watch over them. They handed Levy some papers, and he showed me where to sign. Then Monsieur Bouvier stood and ceremoniously proffered a huge wrought iron ring with several ancient keys dangling from it. I stood to face him. He gave me the keys and kissed me on both cheeks. I felt as though I had just received the keys to the city. Two more cheek kisses from Madame, a hug from Françoise, and they were gone.

Neither Dr. Levy nor I had any idea if such a transaction would be recognized in Occupied France, but the gesture was made. And so I became, in the hearts of the Bouviers, the Prioress of Notre Dame de la Miséricorde—Our Lady of Sorrows.

CHAPTER 11

NOTRE DAME DE GRÂCE PERPÉTUELLE

Countryside Outside Occupied Paris, August 1940

Mathilde obtained a special permit to drive, but it took a week to find the fuel to visit the property. We loaded the 13 girls in our care into our rickety bus and ventured out, following hand-written directions from the Bouviers. They apologized that they let the caretaker go months before, so I did not know what to expect.

The countryside outside of Paris always amazed me. A cool August blessed us with a breeze that seemed to make all things possible. Poppies, my favorite flowers, bloomed everywhere. It was like driving through a Monet painting. As we got further and further into the country, we passed fewer and fewer farms and dwellings. Mathilde and I felt unsure about our destination, so we started the girls singing a rousing round of "Frère Jacques," which made us all feel jolly. At last, we arrived at an enormous set of black wrought-iron gates.

"Mon Dieu! Can this be the place?" Mathilde asked.

"Easy to find out."

I brought the bus to a stop, found the larger of the two ancient-looking keys, strode to the gate and turned the key. With an enormous creak, the gates parted, and we saw the house at the end of the driveway. It was glorious. I got back into the bus and hugged Mathilde. The girls jumped with excitement, although they didn't know why we were so happy. We hadn't had any cause for happiness in a long time. As we approached the building, we saw its age, though on that day nothing could have dampened our enthusiasm.

A large fountain sat in the middle of the circular drive. A portico to protect coaches from the weather dominated the entry. It was not a castle, but bigger than a mansion. As we got closer, I noticed the fountain had dried up and was covered in algae. On the left side, a rose garden had gone wild. On the right, a large arbor covered in vines gave the promise of grapes.

We let the girls get out of the bus to play with the balls and badminton sets we brought with us. We agreed that Mathilde would stay outside to monitor the children, while I determined the condition of the building. As I put the key in the front door, I felt a small hand in mine. Lucie, of course. I started to send her back to play with the others, but changed my mind when I saw her expression. She had been having bad dreams, and shadowed me whenever possible.

"Allons-y. Ready for a big adventure?" I asked. "We'll stay together and watch where we step. Okay?"

She smiled. "Okay."

The convent was enormous. Clearly, it had once housed a substantial community, but it appeared to have been empty for ages. One of the back windows was broken so dirt and leaves had blown in. After we explored for a while, I realized the building was in the shape of a cross. It was made of stone, in some spots deeply worn by the footfalls of the years. The entry was in the front, kitchen and refectory on one side, offices across the way, and there were twelve rooms, six on each side of a long corridor. There was a small chapel just off the entry, and a larger chapel with built-in wooden pews. The dank smell of wet stone hung in the air. There wasn't any working electricity, but wall switches and light fixtures revealed it had been wired. I left the front door wide open to give us light.

After exploring the inside, we went out a side door beneath a covered walkway swathed with grapevines. An overgrown path lined with smooth river rocks led to a clearing. We heard the laughter and cries of the girls playing on the other side of the building. Lucie reached up and took my hand again as we emerged into the bright sun. I hesitated when I realized what we were approaching, but there was nothing sinister in it, so we continued on.

"Mam'selle, is this a churchyard?" she asked, looking up at me.

"Yes, my darling, it is. Many years ago, nuns lived here. They were cloistered. That means they lived here by themselves and prayed and sang hymns. When they died, they were buried right here. Can you read any of the names?"

We searched the small white headstones buried under the dirt.

"Look at this one," Lucie called to me. "It has a name."

She brushed the leaves from the stone, and read out loud, "Sister Marie-Eugénie de Chantal, gone to our Lord September 13, 1930. That is ten years ago," she said proudly.

I put my hand on her head. "You are my little mathematician," I said, also proudly.

We walked around to the front and joined Mathilde and the other girls.

"It's safe. Aunt Mathilde, it is huge. Go on in and look, but there are no lights, so leave the door open."

I took over as badminton coach to give Mathilde time to inspect the building. When she came back out, we enjoyed a lovely picnic on the lawn.

Then we were all back on the bus, again singing "Frère Jacques" at the top of our lungs. Mathilde and I smiled the children. We talked as I drove.

"That is quite a gift, chérie. You certainly impressed them," Mathilde smiled.

"Do you know why they would call it Lady of Sorrows?" I asked.

"The name refers to the sorrows of the Virgin Mary."

"You weren't Catholic growing up, were you?"

"No. Episcopalian. I missed school for a month because I got scarlet fever. My parents hired a private tutor, Sister Michael, a member of the School Sisters of Notre Dame. I loved her. She is the reason I became Catholic. Even though my school is not associated with the Church, I designed our uniforms to match her habit."

"I have always wondered about that. Doesn't the Church object?"

"I teach their children, so they overlook it. But I remember Sister Michael talking about the sorrows of the Virgin."

"At a time like this, we need to do better than sorrows."

The network of people who loved Mathilde or owed her a favor allowed us to continue to repair our school and provided us with food. They gave us gasoline long after most people were required to surrender their vehicles. We returned to the convent once or twice to clean cobwebs from windows, gather roses, and imagine the building in its glory days. But for the time being, the convent remained a dream of the future.

The one thing I did was to have a large brass sign made and posted on the gate. It read: Couvent Notre Dame de la Grâce Perpétuelle—Convent of Our Lady of Perpetual Grace. One day, that building would house a new chapter in my life and the lives of many other women. But that is a story for another time.

CHAPTER 12

JANE SMITH TELLS A LIE

Occupied Paris, August 1940

The man who came to the door of the school that afternoon was tall—even taller than I am. It wasn't that he was thin—he was made of pure sinew. He wore a uniform so clean and sharp that I wanted to tuck my dusty black robes behind me. I invited him to take a seat in the sitting room. He declined my offer of refreshment and introduced himself as Wehrmacht Captain Klaus Schmidt.

Have you ever seen one of those movies where they shine a spotlight on the accused? He had a gaze that made me want to shade my eyes. At first, he addressed me in German, then in French. When I replied, he shifted to a British-accented English. I found that more disconcerting than anything. As if he could accost me no matter what exit I used to escape.

Thankfully, Aunt Mathilde was away with the girls. In the midst of our interview, Danielle started to come into the room from the kitchen, wiping her apron, but wheeled around and disappeared once she saw who I was talking to. Or, to be more accurate, who was talking to me.

Even a year into the Nazi occupation, Mathilde's close contacts, from the mayor of Paris, to the archbishop, to the Italian ambassador with ties to the Vatican, had kept us safe. Being an American still seemed to count for something. Endless numbers of children needed to be rescued. We'd put them in a school uniform, Marcel would squeeze one more cot into the dormitory, and our students would welcome one more secret guest. Mathilde would obtain the best-forged documents possible, and as soon as we could, we would meet a volunteer from the Resistance who would transport the child to a boat or to hide in a hay wagon. They would take the girl to a border, there to be taken to another border until she was somewhere safe. Or at least safer. We didn't ask any questions, and no one asked us any questions.

Until today.

So, it was up to "goody two-shoes, cannot tell a lie, Jane Smith," to answer the Nazi's questions. My first impulse was to pretend that I was deaf. Or that I couldn't speak. Then I wanted to burst into tears and run out of the room.

But I did none of those things. The captain asked to speak to the headmistress. I swallowed hard to get some saliva in my mouth. I told him she wasn't in, and I didn't know when she would be back. I asked if I might be of any help. I was expecting him to demand to know why so many little girls were going in and out of the school, or to request the names of our contacts in the Resistance, so I almost missed it when he asked if the school was of good quality. He told me his commander had charged him with finding a suitable educational institution for his ten-year-old daughter. I nearly yelped in surprise. Then I blushed. My brain darted from one answer to another.

Eventually I said, "I hate to tell tales. The lady who owns this establishment fancies herself a headmistress, but she is nothing of the kind. This is a place for misfits. The students, if you can call them that, have been rejected by their parents, and for good reasons. There is no real teaching being done here. The building is in disrepair, and the food is terrible. I am only working here because of a family obligation. Believe me, I'll get away from this place as soon as I can." I remember hearing that if you are going to tell a lie, keep it close to the truth. I was able to say that last part with great sincerity.

"I had been told otherwise," he said formally.

"Well, I have been here for more than a year, so I am only sharing what I have observed. Perhaps the school was once good, but that time has passed. If I cared about a child who was stuck here, I'd get her out of here as fast as possible."

The German stood and clicked his heels together. "I must thank you," he said. "You have saved me from a big mistake. If I had spoken with your headmistress she might have taken me in. But I recognize honesty when I hear it. I am in your debt."

"It is my pleasure to assist you." I ushered him into the entry, and we nodded good day to each other. I closed the immense wooden door firmly behind him and slid down onto the floor. I don't know how long it was before I felt someone trying to push the door open. I jumped up and pushed back. My frantic mind told me he had returned with an army. At last I heard voices calling, "Jane? Jane?"

It was Aunt Mathilde and Danielle! I pulled the door open and threw myself into Mathilde's arms, to the surprise of the little girls standing behind her in two straight lines.

"Nom de Dieu, Jane." Mathilde kissed me on the forehead.

We got the children into the house and to the sunroom where Danielle sat them down with a snack. Mathilde, Danielle, and I went into the sitting room.

Danielle was beside herself. "Mademoiselle Jane, I am so sorry. When I saw who had come to the door, I didn't know what to do. I looked in Marcel's closet for the revolver, but I listened outside the door and when I realized the soldier wasn't here to arrest you, I ran to find Madame Mathilde."

"That's all right, Danielle. If he had meant me any harm, I'd have rather you saved yourself, anyway. Thank you for wanting to defend me." I patted her on the knee, happy that she didn't shoot anyone.

Mathilde said, "I can't forgive myself for not being here, Jane. What did you say to make him leave?"

I recounted the entire story, adding, "I am so sorry, Aunt Mathilde. I would never want to harm your reputation. I couldn't think of anything else."

"Nonsense, mon trésor. How brilliant! What is my reputation compared with your life? All our lives? I don't give a tinker's dam about other peoples' opinions. But you must have been terrified. Jane, you are still shaking. Come here to me." My aunt enfolded me. "I never want that to happen again. We mustn't stay at the school alone. When we are taking the girls out, we'll go together."

I agreed with a great sigh of relief. I loved them so: Mathilde, Levy, Danielle, and Marcel. It meant everything to stand shoulder-to-shoulder fighting for what I believed in with such good people. With my friends, at last, where I belonged.

CHAPTER 13

MIMI

Occupied Paris, September 1940

I had almost relegated my night with Dr. Levy and Françoise to a strange dream. I wasn't the kind of person who had experiences like that. The only evidence of my encounter with abortion was a black wrought-iron keychain with keys of various sizes that I kept on my dresser, and a pile of gynecology textbooks that Dr. Levy had sent over. Like a dutiful student and certified good girl, I had actually studied them and then put them in a corner covered with a black scarf. They looked like a woman at mass.

I might have been done, but Dr. Levy was not. After our visit with Françoise and her parents, he called again, and I helped him again and again. We worked with mature women who brought their children with them, and young women who cried. Some of them were wealthy and wore furs when it got cold. Others were poor and lived in the ghetto. I learned how to provide support, which was part of abortion care being safe—bringing out my habit and the spiritual comfort of Our Lady of Perpetual Grace whenever she was needed.

One night at about eleven, Mathilde knocked softly on my door, and opened it a crack. I wasn't asleep. I had been sitting in bed reading Grimm's fairytales in search of stories for the girls. It wasn't a good source. All the female characters were either eaten, turned into something, or bled to death.

"It's Doctor Levy," she said solemnly. "He needs you. Pack a bag. He wants you to come in the habit."

I motioned for her to come in and we sat together on my bed.

"Aunt Mathilde, it's after curfew. I could get stopped, and that might bring unwelcomed attention to the school."

"I have a solution for that. Don't worry."

"You are aware of what he wants my help with, aren't you?"

"Yes, chérie. I am," she answered.

"Are you all right with it? I mean, as a Catholic?"

"I am a woman first, and a Catholic second, it seems." She paused. "I must confess, that is why I suggested he ask for your help rather than offering mine. I believe in what he is doing, but I don't think I could get over my catechism to help him."

"But you think I should?" I asked.

"Ah, you have more courage than I."

I shook my head slowly. "I have no idea where you got that impression. I am not brave. I am even terrified by a classroom of seven-year-olds!"

"Well," Mathilde said, smiling broadly, "that is entirely another matter!" and we both laughed. "Truly, Jane, you have been wonderful with the girls. I realized Madame Rochand was strict, but I thought she was a good teacher. Now I am not so sure. The girls blossomed under your care. Especially Lucie. And you are marvelous with our little guests." Her face grew serious. "Levy is at his apartment. I believe you know the way. Stop in my office so I can give you a letter from the Church permitting you to be out after curfew."

Even though I was happy about Aunt Mathilde's praise, a sense of dread followed. I dressed, and put some clothes and a toothbrush in my satchel. Mathilde's office door was open. She pressed an envelope into my hands. "Keep this permission to travel with you at all times," she said. "It may not save you forever, but for now the Bishop still has sway." I pushed the envelope deep into the pocket of my robes.

The night was cool and rainy. The smell of loneliness was in the air. I put a black cloak on over my habit, pulled an umbrella from the closet, and made my way to Levy's apartment. The visit from the commandant really spooked me. Despite my "get-out-of-jail-free" letter, I stumbled on the wet cobblestones, swiveling my head from side to side to make sure nobody was watching. The streetlights, covered in wartime blue fabric, cast an eerie shadow. When I got to the apartment building, Levy's concierge was nowhere to be seen. I was glad, because they were all expected to spy on the people in their buildings. An "out of service" notice was posted on the elevator, so I walked up the stairs to the third floor. The door opened even before I knocked.

"Good evening, Sister," Levy said, more loudly than necessary. He leaned in and whispered, "I saw you from the window. Thank you for coming. We must hurry."

I left my wet umbrella in the foyer, and the doctor took my dripping cloak and hung it on the bentwood hall tree. Over his shoulder, I was surprised to see our first patient, Françoise, sitting on the couch looking anxious. Next to her, wearing an examining gown, was a pale young woman with stringy brown hair, perspiring profusely. Françoise gave me a weak smile and a little wave and then turned to the woman.

"Mimi, this is the Sister I told you about. She is an angel with Our Lady of Perpetual Grace. I'm sure she will help you, too."

I nodded to the two young women, then Levy pulled me into the adjoining room. The examining table, instruments, and sterilizing machine were all there, by now seared into my memory.

"Quick, scrub your hands. This woman is a friend of Françoise's. Some scoundrel tried to "help" her, and I am afraid she is septic," he said as he washed his hands vigorously.

"I don't..." I began.

"Of course you don't. I am so sorry," he said as he jammed his arms through the sleeves of his white coat. "What I mean is that someone—some *boucher*—a butcher—has jammed something dirty into this girl in an attempt to procure an abortion. She has a raging fever and an infection. I may not be able to save her."

"I know what septic means," I insisted, a bit insulted. "I read the textbooks you sent me. I was going to say that I don't know how I can help."

"Oh. Of course." In spite of himself, Levy looked impressed. By then, I was washing my hands as he instructed. I must have stopped for a moment, and he motioned me again to hurry.

"It's these barbaric laws that send young women into the hands of the ignorant and the vultures. She's in terrible pain. I haven't taken her vital signs yet, but her blood pressure may be too low to give her morphine. I'm sure there is tissue left behind in her uterus. We'll have Françoise try to keep her calm, and you may need to hold her down."

"Hold her down?"

"I don't like this any more than you do, but she has nowhere else to go. Bring them in."

I returned to the living room and put on a fake smile of reassurance. It was only Dr. Levy's sense of urgency that kept me from running out of the apartment and not stopping until I was back at the school.

Françoise looked terrified. "Will she be all right?" she whispered to me.

"I don't know," I whispered back. "Let's get her onto the table and I'll take her blood pressure." We guided Mimi into the room, and with one of us on each side, we hauled her onto the table. She was limp. Dr. Levy came in. I strapped the cuff of the Baumanometer onto her upper arm and reported a blood pressure that I thought was too low to be correct.

"Merde. I'm afraid that is accurate," Levy said, beginning a futile search for a vein to give her fluids.

"Merde," he said again, under his breath. "Quickly, put her legs into the stirrups," he barked. He moved over to sit on a stool at the end of the table.

As Françoise and I spread Mimi's legs onto the knee rests, I nearly gagged at the stench. There was blood streaked on the inside of her thighs.

"Look at this," Levy barked again. "Jane, look. You need to see."

I had averted my eyes from the source of the blood and the stink.

"She is rotting from the inside," he said in English. He needn't have worried that Mimi would understand him. Her head was lolling to the side as if she had lost consciousness. I looked as he demanded, and I saw a blood-soaked rag hanging out of her vagina.

"He must have stuffed this cloth into her to cause an abortion. If I remove it, she may go into shock, but if I leave it inside her, her body will continue to reject it because it is a foreign object. I have no ability to provide a blood transfusion. I can't take her to the hospital. She would be arrested, and I would be as well. My only chance—her only chance—is to remove whatever this is and to attempt a curettage to empty the uterus."

I couldn't tell if he was talking to me or to himself.

"Hold her, Sister," he said. "You need to drape yourself over her." I could hardly see any reason to put pressure on her limp body, but I did as he said. The moment he grasped that rag with his forceps and started to pull, she bellowed and bucked with such force that I feared I would be knocked to the ground

"Help me!" I called to Françoise, who had been holding Mimi's hand and suddenly looked faint herself. "Go behind and take her shoulders." She shook herself and moved to hold Mimi's shoulders.

"Mon Dieu. Mon Dieu," Levy cried out. "Incroyable. This is not some fabric inserted to create an abortion—this is her uterus in prolapse! It has turned inside out and it tears like tissue paper. I am not prepared to do the surgery she needs. The uterus must be removed. It is killing her."

I was still splayed across Mimi who was thrashing less since Levy had released his instrument. Her heart was beating wildly under my heart. Then I felt beneath me, one giant breath in, and one out, and Mimi was still.

None of us moved for an eternity. Finally, Levy pulled off his rubber gloves and dropped them onto the floor on top of the pile of bloody cloths. He stood and pressed his fingers under Mimi's jaw.

"She is gone," he said.

I was astonished to see this man, whom I had only experienced as a commanding presence, collapse back onto his stool and dissolve into great, gasping sobs, holding his head in his hands. Françoise looked aghast.

I reached out and took her hand.

"No. Ce n'est pas possible!" she blurted. She looked at me. "You can help her. You must! She is just a girl—she is a good girl," she sobbed.

In a motion I had only seen in a film, I reached over and closed Mimi's eyes. By then Françoise had joined Levy in tears, and it was left to me to move the girl's legs off the rests and cover her with a sheet. How could I be so calm? It was as if someone had flipped a switch in me, as if some kind of machine had taken over. It would be hours before my tears came, and then hours before I could stop them.

"Dr. Levy, what do we need to do with her?" I asked. I surprised myself with the matter-of-factness in my voice.

Levy straightened up. He turned to Françoise.

"Does she have friends or family who will look for her?" he asked. She didn't respond. "Françoise!" he snapped, in a tone sharp enough to shake her.

"Yes, yes," Françoise answered. "Our parents are dear friends. We have known each other our whole lives. We kept this secret. We thought she would get better. But she wouldn't stop bleeding and she was so hot. If only she had come to me first. Is it true? Is she really dead?"

"Yes, ma petite," he said gently.

"Her parents will expect her to come home soon. She is devout. She never let a boy touch her, except that one time."

I looked at Levy and said, "Her family will be disgraced. The Church won't allow her to be buried in consecrated ground if anyone finds out what has happened."

Levy sighed. "You are right, of course. And the police could be involved and investigate all of us. Even you, Françoise." He looked at his feet. "And me."

I bit my lip. "I have an idea." I looked at Levy. "Remember when Paulette had appendicitis and you were afraid that you were too late?"

"Bien sûr," he answered, understanding dawning on his face.

"Could we do it? Could we make it appear as though she was ill and Françoise brought her to you, but her appendix had already gone bad?" I asked. "You would be the physician trying to save her, and the one to make the report of her cause of death."

Levy looked exhausted. He sighed deeply and answered, "We might be able to do it. It seems like a sacrilege, but the death of a young woman—the unnecessary death—is already a sacrilege. Will you help me?"

"Of course," I answered, still numb.

Françoise looked back and forth between us.

"I don't understand," she said.

"Françoise," he said kindly, "you don't need to understand. Go into the powder room. Wash your face. Sit in the study. The Sister and I will take care of this. We will tell Mimi's family that her appendix ruptured and that we couldn't save her. If we are successful, no one will ever learn what really happened. They will mourn her and bury her with the blessings of the Church."

"But how…?" Françoise sputtered.

"I think maybe you don't want to know everything," Levy said. "Go on. We'll join you soon. Then we will call for an ambulance."

Françoise whimpered as she took a last look at the inert body on the table. She turned and left the room, closing the door behind her.

I glared at Levy. "You lied to me," I hissed. "When you asked for my help, you told me this was safe."

"It *is* safe. It should be safe. You saw how quick and easy it was with Françoise and all those others. But when someone who is ignorant about the human body attempts an abortion—someone who doesn't understand the need for instruments to be sterilized—someone who is preying on vulnerable women to make money, then it can be deadly, as you see. That's why it is up to people like me to help as many women as I can. But I cannot save the ones who have already been harmed without putting myself in jeopardy. Even my influential patients can't protect me if there is a death. If I go to prison, that is one fewer haven for women."

"How can it be so easy for you, but in other hands, it turns out like this? I don't understand." We talked as we cleaned up the instruments and bloody cotton everywhere.

"Outside our bodies, germs and bacteria are not very dangerous to us. But within our bodies, we are vulnerable. They can quickly cause infection. A woman's uterus is vascular, filled with blood vessels. Germs or bacteria introduced into the uterus spread quickly, so what might otherwise be a local infection affects the entire body."

"That's why Mimi was septic?" I asked.

"Likely, yes. Besides introducing germs from instruments or implements that are not sterilized, many abortionists use sharp objects to attempt to dislodge the fetus. They can puncture the wall of the uterus, which can also lead to infection."

I must have grimaced a bit, but he continued.

"Some women ingest herbs or toxic substances in an effort to kill or dislodge the fetus. This can harm or kill the woman, and I am not aware of any that are dependably effective. Quinine doesn't stop the pregnancy but often makes the baby deaf. Any of these approaches can lead to heavy and prolonged bleeding and retained tissue. This is the term used when some of the placenta, or even some fetal tissue, is left in the uterus. Once the pregnancy is no longer living, this tissue is foreign to the body and can cause a variety of dangerous responses, including the patient's blood losing its ability to clot, resulting in almost certain death."

I was chastened. "Thank you for explaining. So how is it so different when you do it?" I asked, because I wanted to mend our trust.

"When I do an abortion, I wash my hands thoroughly. I sterilize the instruments. I know how to estimate the size and shape of the uterus, and to take care not to puncture it. And I say no when the woman is unsure of what she wants or is being pressured by someone else. Or when she is too many weeks pregnant, or when she is in ill health. That policy allows me to be available to help other women. It is difficult to say no, but you must understand that you cannot help everyone. You cannot save everyone."

I was trembling. "I'm sorry I said that you lied."

"I understand. This has been a terrible and frightening experience for you. For me too."

"But Dr. Levy—" I hesitated. "How can you get away with this? With being Jewish yourself, and making out health certificates for all the girls who pass through the school. And doing illegal abortions? Why don't they arrest you?"

Levy sighed. "I believe I told you that I have cared for a number of Catholic families over the years as well as for so many of my Jewish neighbors?"

"Yes. You said Françoise is from one of those families."

"C'est ça. It so happens that these are the families of the mayor, and the councilors, and many of the dignitaries of the Catholic Church. They depend on me, and they care more about their families than they do about any laws."

"But the Nazis?"

"They need doctors, too. And my influential patients recommend me. I keep all their secrets—too many secrets for them to bother me. Besides, I am a French citizen. They are going to harass the immigrants, but not the French. You'll see."

Dr. Levy would live to realize how wrong he was, but that night, I just smiled wanly.

"Every day, I realize how naïve I am about power and how it works." I sighed. "Now, back to our task here. Am I picturing our next step the same way you are?" I asked, trying to sound brave.

"I think so. An incision and stitches in the area of the appendix. A bit of Dr. Frankenstein."

"And to be safe, you will have to reverse the prolapse," I suggested.

"Yes. Yes, of course. And you will help?"

"Of course."

Levy opened the cupboard to find the scalpels and suture and other instruments he needed. He started to scrub again but hesitated. Then, even though he realized that Mimi no longer required his scrupulousness, he washed his hands and arms. "She deserves that," he said. As I helped him into a fresh pair of gloves, I nodded in agreement.

A few days later, Levy and I slipped into the back of the church during the funeral mass for Mimi. The cathedral was enormous, and almost every pew was filled, so her father must have been important. The afternoon sun filtered red and blue through the stained glass windows. Dark woodwork added to the solemnity of the occasion. Françoise gave a tiny wave from the front row, and I recognized her mother and father. Mimi's parents were sitting next to them. It was heartrending to see Mimi's mother in tears and her father looking stoic, but we had spared them a far greater sorrow.

"This sadness is very painful," Levy said. "But it is the shame that is insupportable."

"I think I understand," I said, taking his hand. That day our friendship began.

CHAPTER 14

AFTERMATH

Occupied Paris, September 1940

Though Mimi was already dying when Françoise brought her to us, I kept wondering *What if? What if she had asked Françoise where to go? What if she had come to us right away?* She was only twenty, a young woman as green as the spiraling tendrils of the pumpkin plants that had taken over our garden.

Then something bad happened to me. The Nazis bragged about their well-behaved soldiers, but even Nazis can't control everyone.

I saw many things during the war that I have tried not to remember. They are seared into that oddly shaped little part of my brain whose name I can't recall. This neural lockbox is too small to withstand the horrors we humans store in it, so they leak out in nightmares and memories.

In those days in Paris, we all learned to see, and not see. Helplessness in the face of atrocity can drive you mad. And every day, the most mundane of life's comings and goings were like navigating a minefield. I'm not going to tell you any stories about babies, or blood, or bayonets wielded by cold-blooded German soldiers. I'm not going to convey the unspeakable agony of the shrieks of mothers who have been forcibly separated from their children. I am not going to attempt to describe the unimaginable horror of genocide. I am not going to tell you about what hunger looks like from the outside, or feels like from the inside.

The story I am going to tell you is of a day in Occupied Paris, just a normal day in a world that had lost its mind. I was walking with a five-year-old as fast as it is possible to walk with a five-year-old. Her name was Naomi. She was big for her age, and she refused to be carried, a bit of a relief because she was quite heavy. She had thick black hair and pink cheeks that a grandmother should have been pinching enthusiastically. In retribution for some act of the

Resistance, her parents had been executed with a dozen other innocent people in the town square. A neighbor hid her and sent word to Mathilde.

I had never been sent to fetch a child so young. The older girls understood about taking on a new identity, but I had no idea how to convey the idea to a little one. Sitting in the neighbors' parlor, I tried to make it a game.

"Do you know how to pretend?" I asked her.

She looked up at me with her lower lip trembling. "You mean like if I act like a kitty and go meow, meow?" she asked.

"Just like that!" I answered, wondering how she would possibly comprehend the importance of this particular game. "Today, we are going to pretend that your name is Catherine Bernard. Can you remember that?"

She looked doubtful.

"Try to say it. Who are you today?"

She glowered. "I want my mama."

"Of course you do, darling. But right now she wants you to play this little game of make-believe with me."

"She does?"

"Yes, she really, really does."

We practiced her new name a few times, but the neighbors were anxious for us to leave their house, so insufficient had to suffice.

Five is old enough to ask incessant questions in a very loud voice, but not old enough to understand the need to be quiet.

"Where did those men take my mama and papa, and Mrs. Goldberg, and Mr. Stein?"

"I don't know, sweetheart. But right now we must be very quiet and hurry to the school where we can be safe." I whispered. "There are other little girls there who can be your friends."

"But if we go away, how will they find me?"

"Shh. We must hurry!"

"But…"

I stopped abruptly and knelt down, my face even with hers. I put on my most serious grown-up expression. "Child, we must hurry, and you *must* be quiet," I hissed.

As I stood up, I saw them. Three German soldiers with rifles slung over their shoulders, crossing the road toward us. I can still picture them so clearly. In my mind, they approached in slow motion. The first was tall and distinguished. The second one scowled. And the third one was no more than a boy. *Please,* I said, to whom I cannot say, *please let this be all right.*

Just before they reached us, I bent down again and said to Naomi urgently, "Remember, in this game you are called Catherine." Then I pushed her behind my robes.

"Good afternoon, Sister," the tall one said, in surprisingly good French. "Your papers please."

That wasn't a problem. I was one of the few people who actually *had* a legitimate passport and visa. Mathilde had given me passable fake papers for the little one. I removed our documents from a pocket within my robes, trying to stay calm. He examined our papers carefully. The one ogling me as if he had never seen a woman before stepped behind, trapping me between them.

"These appear to be in order. But an American? What are you doing so far from home, sister?" he asked unctuously.

"I am here on a mission to teach children," I said, my voice quavering in spite of my best efforts. "We are on our way back to the school."

It shocked me when the frowning soldier behind me said, "Damned Roman Catholics think they are better than all of us," and spat on the ground. I understood very little German, but I understood that.

I never corrected people who assumed I was a nun. I hoped it gave me some sort of protection or authority. His acrimony disabused me of my naivete.

"No, Officer," I said breathlessly, turning my head to look at him. "I don't think I am better than anyone. Please, just let us go to the school," I begged, speaking as calmly as I could manage. It was never easy to tell what tone to take with them. Defiance often led to violence, and I had to protect the child at all costs.

"And who are you, little girl?" The tall soldier bent down to talk to Naomi. His French was good enough that I feared she would understand him.

She looked up at me uncertainly, and I nodded at her. "I am Caffin. I live in Paris. I am this many," she answered, holding up her pudgy fingers. I had stopped breathing entirely by then. I realized that the fictional Catherine Bernard would not survive another question.

I tried to fold Naomi inside my robes to make her disappear entirely. "I have money, just to pay for your inconvenience," I said, putting my hand into my pocket.

The tall one stood up and looked at me in a way that made my stomach drop. He said, "We have no interest in your money. But we are far from home and lonely. And you are pretty enough. You understand? We would love to get to know you better this fine morning. Kurt, tend to the brat. We have business with our dear American sister."

The boy took Naomi by the hand and glanced at me with a look that I could only interpret as an apology.

There was not a soul on the street I could cry out to. I knew that resisting would not save Naomi. Left by herself, the child was doomed. So I did the only thing I could. I followed the two of them around the corner into the alley behind us.

I don't want to tell the rest of this. You can imagine it, but please don't let it be seared into your memory as it is seared into mine. You can picture the alley where they took me. I thank whatever God there may be that they didn't force the child to watch. I had never been with a man before, but that was incidental. The alley—the stone building—my face pushed against the wall as one of the soldiers held me. My robes bunched up—my underwear torn away. My forehead bruised and skinned against the stone. My tears. When they had each had a turn and left me in a heap, I heard them arguing in their guttural French.

"What about the brat?"

"What about her? Leave her with the bitch."

They laughed and ordered the one named Kurt to bring the child to me.

I clung to Naomi, faint with relief, as they marched away without a backward glance. I held on to her so tightly that she tried to squirm away.

"Are you all right, Mam'selle?" she asked sweetly.

I wanted to scream. I wanted to cry. I wanted to die. I wanted to disappear off the face of the earth. But here was this child whose life was somehow, by some miracle, saved. Somehow, I found my voice. "Of course, chérie. I just tripped and fell," I said, trying to catch my breath. "I'll be up in a minute and we'll be on our way. I just need to sit here for a little while." I was numb. I was lost. I didn't know how to find myself again, so I relied on what had always helped me.

"Why don't you come down right here beside me and I'll tell you a story. I'm afraid it is a sad one."

"I don't like sad stories," she said.

"I don't either. But this is one I must tell you." I felt a painful throbbing where I had been violated, and the unpleasant sticky wetness trickling down my legs, but I tried to ignore the sensations. Still shaking too hard to stand up, I pulled Naomi down and close to me and began a story that I had already had to tell too many little girls.

"Once upon a time, in a kingdom not so very far away, the king and his soldiers acted like mean boys, and they wanted more land and riches for themselves. They were so mean that they decided to steal their neighbors' lands. They marched across the border with their big guns and the neighbors were so frightened that they gave the king whatever he wanted."

"I don't like this story," Naomi said in a small voice.

"I know. I don't either." As I told the terrible story of men who would do anything for power, Naomi burrowed her head even deeper into my shoulder.

"And the mean soldiers took people away from their families," I finished.

"Like he took my mama and papa?" Naomi whispered.

"Yes, my darling, just like that. But your neighbors hid you so the mean soldiers wouldn't take you, too. And now we will go to the special school and soon I hope we will find a new home for you."

"I don't want a new home. I want my mama and papa," she whimpered.

"I know, chérie." I held her even tighter as she cried.

"What is the end of the story?"

"For you, the end of the story is a wonderful new family who loves you and who lives in a country where the mean soldiers do not come."

"And for my mama and papa?"

"For them…" I hesitated. I had more answers for a twelve-year-old—this child was so young. I decided that the truth was more merciful than hope.

"For them, my sweet one, there is a beautiful Heaven."

She pulled her head away from my shoulder and looked at me. "Where my Bubbie is?" she asked.

"Yes, that's right." I smiled at her and she gave me the tiniest smile back.

We sat there until I was able to walk. The tearing between my legs ached, but I managed to hobble along, Naomi telling me all about her beloved Bubbie.

Perhaps you can see why I didn't want to tell this story. I am no hero, lest you are thinking that. I bartered what I had to save Naomi's life and my own. In my mind, I made a good bargain. When Mathilde asked about my bruises, I attributed them to clumsiness. With the chaos we faced every day, there was honestly no one looking very hard, even my devoted aunt. The last thing anyone needed was someone else to console, so I took care of myself. How does one attend to individual victims when humanity and even civilization itself are under attack?

I fell into a space of sadness and silence. Only Levy knew why. Like little animals, the girls in my care sensed my emotions. They were careful with me. While the rest were napping, Lucie sneaked out of the nursery and brought me biscuits. Her expression begged me to be all right. I wanted to, but I couldn't. Aunt Mathilde took the girls to the park in the mornings. Marcel carved a little blue bird and left it on my windowsill. Danielle cooked my favorite foods. Levy called every day.

It was a complicated time for me. It was not only Mimi who had died. It was Jane as well. The Jane I had known for twenty-five years. The Jane who sat up straight and ate her vegetables. The Jane who told the truth. The Jane who pledged allegiance to the flag and trusted that policemen were her friends. The nice Jane, who never got angry. The innocent Jane, who only wanted to be good and to make a difference. The unbroken Jane. The Jane who always asked for permission and colored inside the lines.

In the months that followed, Levy and I sometimes stopped in the cathedral to light candles for Mimi. I lit one for myself as well. I didn't care if tapers lit by a Jewish abortionist and a broken atheist from Connecticut had any purchase in a Catholic church. The matches I struck served a dual purpose. My prayers were in sorrow for everything Mimi never got to experience, as well as for my own future. I yearned for my father. When I was a child, he'd sometimes pick me up and carry me to bed, murmuring something my child-ears heard as a name—Moe Kushla. As I got older, I understood it was Gaelic—Mo chuisle. "My pulse."

In time, I began to feel like myself again. I lit a candle for the self I was becoming. I recognized this new Jane reflected in the windows of the school's conservatory when the angle of the sun was just so. She was broken, but not ruined. The plainness, which had always distressed my mother, transmuted into steel.

During those dark weeks, I wondered whether I was in a dream, or if I was the essence of transformation, like a caterpillar devouring itself in a cocoon for the sake of beauty. The cellular understanding of my impotence in the face of male violence terrified me. I was ashamed. All these things shaped me. Fury grew within me. It fueled my yearning, my unquenchable thirst for justice.

On the nights when I was paralyzed by fear, too afraid to step out of the school to take girls to the safe house, I summoned that fury like an obedient electric charge. Then I could do whatever was required. On the mornings when we grieved the disappearance of yet another trusted ally, fury dried my tears before they were shed. Fury let me stand, unblinking, producing fraudulent documents for one border guard after another.

That fury has propelled me to give abortion care to women in need, in sanctuaries they deserve, for three-quarters of a century. The gift to me, the blessing next to the wound, is the white-hot anger that has lasted all these years, a renewable energy source like the sun. Are you uncomfortable when I tell you about my anger, so unattractive in a woman? Fury has been my trusted friend. If more women were furious, it would be a better world.

CHAPTER 15

DO WE *HAVE* TO TELL HER?

Occupied Paris, November 1940

One afternoon, Mathilde looked grim and said she needed to talk. I followed her into her office.

"It's about Lucie's father. I had a letter from one of Dr. Fastion's colleagues in Russia."

I moved papers off the chair next to her desk and sat down hard.

"And...?" I asked.

"It is terrible news. The Jewish scientists were taken from the laboratory in Moscow and executed in Kiev. The envelope was torn and dirty. The date was hard to make out, but I'm guessing it was sent weeks ago."

"Oh, no! Why were they executed? By the Germans or the Russians?"

Mathilde shrugged her shoulders. "Impossible to say."

"What was Lucie's father like?"

"I met him only once. He was a gentleman. He brought Lucie to me shortly after his wife died. She was the first new student in my school, so she has always been special to me."

"Oh, Mathilde. Her best friends are gone. How will she bear it? Do we have to tell her?"

"My dear, of course we do. I dread it as much as you do. I should tell her now so that she can come to you in the middle of the night if she needs to."

"But I'm not supposed to..."

"Don't be silly. That was old Madame Rochand's regulation—probably made to justify her laziness because she couldn't be bothered to get up. I am well aware you have been breaking that stupid rule since you got here. Grâce à Dieu."

"How will you tell her?" I asked.

"I don't know," she said. "Lucie won't accept anything less than the truth, and she shouldn't. But there is so little information. I think I must tell her he died as a hero. We'll likely never learn any more about what actually happened. At least she won't be alone. So many of these girls have already lost brothers, fathers, and uncles in this war."

"Oh, Madame, I won't know what to say to her."

"Yes, you will, chérie. Follow your heart."

It was already cold that bitter winter, so we were bundled up in extra sweaters and lap blankets. Mathilde asked Lucie to go to her office while I engaged the girls in a game of charades. We played the names of their favorite characters from the stories I had been sharing every night. Charades was new for ten-year-old Babette.

"Mine has two words," Babette said.

Of course, we were acting out names, so that didn't take a genius.

"Babette, we play this game in silence, remember?" I said. "You must act it out."

"Okay," she said, and she brandished two fingers.

The other girls cried out, "Two words!" Babette looked at me in triumph.

Then she held up one finger, now remembering how to do it.

"First word!" they cried. She nodded and scrunched up her face as if in thought. She raised two fingers again tentatively. She didn't remember the symbol for syllable. But she had some help.

"Two syllables!" Renée called out.

Babette started to say yes, then put her hands over her mouth. I had to appreciate how hard she was trying.

Hopefully, she held up one finger.

"First syllable?" Lydia asked.

More excited nodding, and she pointed down.

"Rug—carpet—foot?" She shook her head vigorously.

"Floor," one of the girls said.

"Yes, yes!" she cried out. My stern face sent her back to nodding as if her head would fall off.

Lydia looked at her sympathetically. "First syllable, floor."

Babette beamed. Just then Lucie came back into the parlor looking pale, her eyes red. The girls broke off the game and crowded around her, so Florence Nightingale remained forever a mystery.

"What's wrong?" Katia asked amid the murmurs of concern.

"My papa has been killed in Russia."

"Oh, no," the children chorused. None of them bothered to ask why, since there were no good answers to that question. They all had family members in dangerous places, so Lucie's news might have been any of their news. I gathered Lucie to me and wrapped my arms around as many of them as I was able to reach. I had been thinking all afternoon about what to say, but words left me when faced with fourteen little girls, in no rows at all, crying their eyes out.

CHAPTER 16

REACH FOR THE STARS

Occupied Paris, Winter 1940-Spring 1941

That terrible winter we didn't even try to observe La Toussaint, the traditional day of remembrance of the dead. Everything closed as usual for the November first holiday, but few chrysanthemums were placed on the graves. The dead had to take care of themselves.

Christmas arrived as a hollow ghost of the joyous holiday we had celebrated in years past. We each saved a bit of food to give to each other for presents. Mathilde managed to get new mittens that actually fit for every girl.

Danielle brought some candles into the dormitory. I thought it was a lovely Christmas decoration, but worried there would be a fire. I was relieved when I saw that the older girls were taking charge of lighting them. They lit the candles, adding one each day, saying a prayer in Hebrew. I asked Mathilde about it, and she gave me a cursory explanation of Chanukah. I am embarrassed to say that Lucie Fastion was the first Jewish person I had ever met.

By the New Year I could not hide my worry. "Aunt Mathilde, some of these girls have been here for weeks. When will we get them to safety?" I asked.

"I am afraid I do not know, chérie. We do not have legitimate papers for them. It is harder and harder to pass. The documents I have been able to get until now are not good enough. They must be perfect."

"Well then, let's get the papers! Who makes them for us?"

"Ah, if it were only that simple. The person who has been helping us no longer has access to the materials needed. Identity cards and passports are on paper that cannot be duplicated. The forgers use hard-to-find discarded documents so that the paper is authentic. The process is precise and demanding. There is great danger to everyone involved," Mathilde sighed. "I have not shared everything with you. At any time, one of us might be taken and questioned. Information you do not have, you cannot reveal."

"I would never reveal anything."

"Of course you would not mean to. I would not either. But I am an old woman and I would not do well under torture. Inevitably, some of us will be arrested. Each of us knows only what we must. We can only hope to weave a web of protection wide enough and strong enough that they cannot catch us all."

"All these months I took it for granted that if we found a bed and some clothes for these girls, the papers would appear as if by magic. I never thought about it. Everything—*everything* comes from someone who risks their life for people they don't know. I am so ashamed I didn't see."

"My darling, in these times we all do whatever we can. We do whatever we are brave enough to do. But do not be ashamed. I shall not allow any of us to take on the shame that belongs to these evil men. Never."

I held Mathilde, and we both wept. Neither of us noticed Lucie crouched behind the door listening intently.

By the time I had tucked them into bed, I was as frightened and uncertain as the children. We needed a story of a woman who lived, as they did, in impossible times.

"Mes enfants, how shall we end our evening?" Of course, they all answered that they wanted a story. I knew I had chosen the right tale when a small girl named Henriette answered last. Even though she said she wanted a story, she looked unsure.

"It is all right, chérie," I said to her. "Here with each other, we are safe." I hoped it was true, although I recognized that any moment storm troopers might break down our doors and take us all away.

"Once upon a time, not so long ago, there was another place with much sadness and injustice, like today in our beautiful Paris. This story takes place in America, where I was born. It is the story of a brave woman who lived in terrible times, who helped many people. She was enslaved, owned by another person, like a horse or cattle. Men stole her ancestors from Africa and brought them to America to be sold. African slaves had dark skin. Darker people were thought to be less than human and often treated worse than livestock, but you know that is not right. Some of you have blue eyes and some have brown eyes, but the color doesn't matter. In the Southern part of America, the slaves did all the work to grow cotton on farms called plantations. The men who owned the plantations became wealthy because they didn't have to pay the people who tilled the land, planted the seeds, and harvested the cotton."

Lucie was wiggling her hand urgently. There was no point in trying to ignore her.

"Lucie, I can see you have a question."

"Oui, Mam'selle. How did they get from Africa to America? That is very far. I have seen it on the globe."

"You are correct, Lucie," I answered. When was she not? "That is just one of the dreadful parts of the story. From the time my country started, slavers brought people like freight on enormous ships—not like the ocean liners you see in pictures—they were cargo ships. They packed people into the ships the way you would pack—" I searched for an image they would understand. "The way you would pack herring into a jar. The ocean voyage took several months. Many of them died on those voyages, and the ones who survived the journey were sold."

"What about the children?" Lucie piped up again.

"I don't think they took many children, mostly grown men and women." I gave her a look that said *Let me continue.* "When they got to America, laws prevented them from speaking their own languages or practicing their own religions. They weren't allowed to marry or even learn to read and write. The slaveholders forced many to become Christians. And the children they had were often taken from them and sold to other plantations."

Lucie looked at me defiantly this time. "How could they have children if they were not allowed to marry?" she asked.

I hated it when I was caught between reality and what grown-ups taught children.

"They just did," I said. "May I continue with the story?" Lucie nodded soberly.

"I am going to tell you about a woman who called herself Harriet Tubman."

"Harriet? C'est Henriette, n'est-ce pas? Elle a le même nom que moi?" Henriette asked, looking delighted.

"C'est ça! Yes, dear one. She had the same name as you! She was born way before any of us, around 1800, in a place called Maryland. Now in those days, some people thought they had a right to own slaves—mostly the ones in the Southern part of the country on the plantations. Fortunately, other people thought owning slaves was evil and should be against the law."

Lucie broke in. "It should! It should be against the law!"

"Yes, dear one. Of course it should. And now it is. But it took a lot of work and courage, and a long time to make that happen."

She looked mollified and allowed me to continue.

"Most of the people who opposed slavery lived in the Northern part of the country. Many of them were a special kind of Christian called Quakers. The ones who wanted slavery to be illegal tried everything they could to change the laws. They also helped slaves escape from plantations and get to places where they would be free. They created something that they called "the underground railroad" where slaves could go through the countryside at night and then hide in people's cellars or barns."

"They built a railroad?" Miriam asked.

"No, petite, not an actual railroad. That's just what they called it. People had to walk for many miles at night so no one would see them. Sometimes they might get to ride in a cart or wagon covered with hay so they wouldn't be discovered."

"People helped them hide so they could get away?" Henriette asked.

"Yes, mon tésor, they did. And of course, Harriet Tubman didn't want to be a slave, so one day she escaped. She had to travel 90 miles, about 150 kilos, to a place called Pennsylvania."

"And then she was free?" Lucie asked hopefully.

"Yes. But there is more. Harriet wasn't happy just being free. She wanted to help other people. She went back to the South many times and guided other people to the North. That took a lot of courage because even though she had once gotten to freedom, the law gave something called a bounty, like a prize, to anyone who captured slaves. If she were caught, she would be sent back to her owner. There were lots of men with guns looking for escaped slaves, especially ones who had become well-known like Harriet."

"They were like the Gestapo?" Lucie asked.

"Yes, ma petite."

I turned to Henriette. "Harriet Tubman was sometimes called the Moses of her people. Do you know why?"

I could hear the gasp as the girls drew in their breaths, terrified at the mere mention of the forbidden name.

"I'm sorry, més enfants. I didn't mean to scare you. When we are all here together, it is all right to remember these names."

Lucie sat up, ready to tell me about Moses, but I gestured to her to give Henriette a chance. With her eyes closed as if summoning information from a long distance, Henriette said, "Moses took his people, the Jews, on a hidden railroad to go away from the Pharoah."

"Exactement," I said. "It takes a lot of courage to escape to freedom. And it takes a lot of help. We are lucky that we have both of those, and I hope that all of you will escape to freedom, just like Harriet Tubman, someday very soon."

Then I remembered a quotation I had learned years before.

"That brave lady said something meant just for you. She said: 'Every great dream begins with a dreamer. Always remember, you have within you the strength, the patience, and the passion to reach for the stars to change the world.'"

I motioned we were at the end, and Lucie and I intoned, "They had their good days and their bad days, and they took care of their problems the best they knew how."

"And with that," I said, "it is time to go to sleep and have dreams of reaching for some stars of your own." I tucked the girls in and gave each one a kiss on the forehead, with an extra one for Henriette. I told them the angels were watching over them, hoping that one of those angels was the venerable Harriet Tubman herself.

CHAPTER 17

GOOSE AND GOSLINGS

Occupied Paris, Spring 1941

A few weeks later, Mathilde called me into her office, looking heartsick. "I have more terrible news. Levy just called. His wife, Leah, is missing, and her family suspects she has been killed. I'm going over there right now. Will you please stay with the girls?"

"Of course," I answered. "He has been so worried about her. What happened?"

"I don't know anything yet. I hope I will learn more when I see him."

"Please tell him I am thinking about him," I said.

"Of course I will."

It took several days for Levy to learn the full story of his wife's death. She was shot while defending her grandfather who refused to leave his home in Alsace. I tried to get him to tell me more about it, but he brushed me off.

"So many people need our help. There is no time for this talking," he said. I understood about putting feelings to the side.

But his feelings were too strong to hide. Even if he wouldn't talk to me, his grief took a toll. His face had angles I had never seen before and his shoulders caved in around his heart. I had to prompt him more than once to the next step of our work. I couldn't imagine how he was even functioning. I did my best to be supportive, but I understood that working helped him shut out the painful reality.

That spring Dr. Levy and I helped many women. Young women. Older women. Women who said they wouldn't bring a child into a broken world. Women who were convinced we would lose the war, who chilled me with their dire predictions. Most of them were sure of what they wanted and didn't need Our Lady. But whenever a woman was in turmoil, I played the role. Levy and I did our best to make each of them feel safe, repeating the simple steps that became so familiar.

One evening, after we'd seen all our patients, we sat at the table in his colorful kitchen. Bright plaids next to stripes next to polka dots in blue, red, and yellow gave it a more playful feel than the rest of the apartment. After a couple of glasses of whiskey, we had both relaxed our usual professional guard.

"Dr. Levy, I love this room."

"Leah designed it."

"I thought so." I looked deeply into my empty glass.

"What is bothering you, Jane?"

"I have had some bad dreams. Even the smallest embryos tug at my heart. When patients are more advanced, it is hard to see those tiny limbs—though I have no doubt the abortions are needed. How did you come to terms with this? With ending life?"

"Part of it I attribute to my wife. Maybe because she was Jewish, Leah always focused on the life of the patient with her own story, her relationships, her dreams. I came to see that a woman's life and dreams take precedence over a life that is not fully constructed. I don't think I am saying this right."

"I understand."

"I remember the first time I did an abortion. The girl's name was Raquel. She was just fourteen. Her uncle had interfered with her. The family was in shambles. Her father was furious, her mother was distraught. They begged me to help her. I had known Racquel since she was a child. I was almost as upset as her parents. I'm embarrassed to recall my rudimentary technique. I had only a cursory idea of what to do. I gathered what instruments I was able to, and went to their house. When I saw the girl, I almost started to cry. She was pale and drawn and she wouldn't even look me in the eye. I told myself I would only do it that one time. Leah was with me, and she helped by holding Racquel's hand. Before we started, Leah asked if she wanted to have a baby, just to be sure she wasn't being forced. Our patient shook her head and wailed. I did my best to end the pregnancy without hurting her."

"Were you afraid?"

"Honestly, I was. Thank goodness she was all right."

"Then you decided to continue?"

"I didn't really intend to, but others came. I don't know how they found me. At first, I thought I would only help the most compelling cases—or the ones who had been taken against their will. But I came to doubt my attitude of superiority. Or, rather, Leah set me straight. Now I am grateful that I can save these girls from the kind of ignorant hack who killed Mimi. That's enough for me. Are you troubled by it?"

"A little. I had a nightmare after that night with Françoise. But it was all just so new and unexpected. Years ago, I overheard my grandmother say something about how abortion should never be spoken of. That has haunted me. But I don't have judgments about anyone else." I smiled at him. "I am very grateful to you. Now that we are friends, I can tell you that after Françoise, I wanted to help you again. I just didn't know if it was right. It is a kind of killing, isn't it?"

"Oui, bien sûr. That is why I take it so seriously. But I always remember there are two. When a woman knows she cannot care for a baby, an abortion honors both lives. I'm glad you came back."

"I realized what it would mean to have a baby under impossible circumstances. And I wondered what it would do to a baby to be born with no one to celebrate its life. Every time we do an abortion, I tell the baby, 'I'm sorry it is not the right time.' I don't believe a spirit can be destroyed, so perhaps it returns later?"

"That sounds like something Leah would say."

"I wish I had known her."

"Ah, Leah," he sighed, exhaling his fragrant cigarette smoke. "She made me a better man. I miss her every day. You would have liked each other." He cocked his head to the side. "You remind me of her. She would stand in front of a car to protect the goose and goslings crossing the road."

"That sounds more like Lucie than me," I said, smiling.

"Yes, yes, I guess that's true," he said. "Like Lucie, she was too brave and stubborn for her own good. I begged her not to go to Alsace, but her grandparents needed help. The French and Germans have traded that part of the country back and forth for hundreds of years, so Germany just marched in and claimed it like a lost glove. The Nazis took over last year and Leah wrote to me that Jews were being shipped to the South. When her grandfather confronted the police with his rifle, she ran in front of him and they were both shot. No more guilty than the goose and goslings," he said, wiping tears from his eyes.

CHAPTER 18

BRIGITTE

Occupied Paris, Spring 1941

When I pestered her again about getting the papers we needed, Mathilde helped me understand the forger's problem. "You can print all the twenty-dollar bills you want, but if they are not on the right paper, they won't pass muster." We didn't have the right paper, so the girls piled up, and we did the best we could. We weren't starving, but we were hungry. All of Paris was hungry, except the soldiers and their sympathizers who had lights, food, and entertainment. Even bordellos, according to Marcel. After Socorro and Paulette were whisked off to Switzerland, I worried about Lucie, but though she was only eight-and-a-half, she had decided to serve as a hostess for our guests.

It was warm for April, which was a godsend after a freezing winter, and we took a walk in the park—me and my twenty little friends. We had too many children, so some of the girls wore summer uniforms, light blue striped cotton pinafores with white blouses and blue cardigans. The others wore our winter uniforms, dark green plaid wool skirts with navy blue sweaters and blazers. Some of the garments fit. Almost. Praise God for safety pins. Since we had been miserably holed up during a week of rain, we were all giddy and delighted with the nice weather. I was grateful for a beautiful day and had found the prettiest park we could walk to without passing Nazi checkpoints. The Jardin du Luxembourg had a pond surrounded by apple trees in full bloom with their heady scent. The Mallards quacked and splashed, and the girls laughed and shared crumbs from the leftovers of our lunch. Finally un-caged, they were chasing each other and giggling frantically, falling down, breathless. I ran with them—my robes flying. And together we sang a little French song about ducks. It was lovely. Yet even here, our happiness was a bit like mania—random and undependable.

It began to get overcast, and I was concerned that the girls who didn't have jackets would get cold. I was about to corral them for the long walk home when I turned around and locked eyes with—Brigitte.

Brigitte, the Nazi-loving housemaid whom Mathilde had fired.

Brigitte, who wanted to rid France of the undesirables.

Brigitte, who so disliked me.

Brigitte, who was supposed to be in the South of France.

I froze.

"Good afternoon, my dear Mademoiselle Smith," she said in a voice that sent chills down my spine.

"Good afternoon, Brigitte. How are you? I didn't realize you were in Paris." For a moment, I considered trying to shield the children, but to no avail. One woman, even a very tall one with long black robes, cannot block out twenty little girls laughing and throwing breadcrumbs.

"I am very well. I moved back to Paris because I am needed here. The Nazis have deputized citizens to monitor their neighbors and report illicit activity to the Gestapo."

"Yes," I said. "I know."

Brigitte moved very close to me and spoke in hushed tones. She curled her lip and said, "You think you are better than me. You think that because you are an American, you can do whatever you want. Well, this is not your country, and you are not as smart as you think you are."

I winced and blushed head to toe, my heart on fire.

"I can count, mademoiselle. And I have done the dirty work for Madame Mathilde's spoiled brats for long enough to recognize them. Apart from the disrespectful Lucie, I do not recognize any of these creatures. Who are these urchins with the mismatched uniforms? Not one has the blond hair and blue eyes of Madame Mathilde's students. What am I to do with this troublesome information?"

I stumbled and dropped the food hamper. Oranges, biscuits, and linen napkins fell on the ground in front of me. Church bells rang out in the distance, and for a moment, I hoped an angel would fly off with all of us.

As I scrambled to gather our lunch items back into the basket, Brigitte continued her sinister tirade. "I wager that is why she got rid of me—to put her leftover school uniforms on these parasites. Juives." She spat on the ground next to my foot, and I jumped back reflexively.

"You think they are harmless because they are children. But children grow up. This lot has been feeding off the French state for years." Her face was so close that I smelled shrimp and garlic.

"Brigitte," I began, in a voice so faint that I could hardly hear it. I cleared my throat and started again. "We have a common goal. We are doing everything we can to get these children out of France, ridding the country of what you call 'undesirables.' Can you… would you be silent as long as I can promise you that?"

"You can promise the vermin will be gone? To be the problem of another unfortunate nation?"

"Yes. I promise."

Brigitte wiped her glasses on the hem of her skirt and looked me squarely in the eye. "What would I get for my trouble?" she asked.

Ah, Brigitte. Her loyalties had always been more about herself than anything else. My brain whirred. I guessed what would appease her.

"I have money."

I dug into the pocket of my robes for my battered leather purse and held it out to her. She pushed open the metal clasps and rifled through the bills inside—money intended for the following week's groceries. I didn't know how much was in there, but her scowl softened. I hoped we might be all right when she snorted. "What else do you have to save the lives of these..."

I didn't want to hear her next slur.

"My ring," I said, pulling it off my finger. "You always said how well it suits you." I held it out to her. For the first time, I saw the shadow of what passed for a smile. She took the ring and slid it onto her finger. She cocked her head left, then right to let the light catch the facets.

"It is quite beautiful on me," she said, still smiling.

"It's yours," I said, "If you can forget you ever saw us."

We both recognized that she held all the cards. I didn't even want to imagine what would happen to the children. To Aunt Mathilde. To me.

"It is very good with my warm skin tones," she said. "Thank you for this kind gift, chérie." I had never realized how "my dear" would sound emanating from the mouth of a snake. "You should never have come here, you know. I don't mean to this park. You should never have come to this country. You should have taken the example of that fellow Lindberg. He knows this war is a matter for us, not for your meddling. Leave Europe to Europe."

It wasn't safe to demur. I had to be sure that what I had given her was enough. "So, with these gifts of friendship, you will turn a blind eye?"

She pursed her lips and said, "Blind, for now." She laughed and started to go, then stopped and swung around. "Please give my regards to your dear aunt." She turned on her heel and walked away. I prayed I would never see Brigitte again.

The girls saw from my expression that something terrible had happened. They asked what was wrong, but I clapped my hands sharply and got them back into their lines. I kept Lucie next to me, holding my hand. I know it is not appropriate for an adult to use a child for support, but it was the only way I was able to keep going. I didn't say anything on the walk home, but I gripped her hand to save my life.

When we got back to the school, I told the girls to go into the kitchen for an afternoon snack. Lucie followed me into the conservatory and put her hand on my shoulder as I dissolved into tears.

"Mademoiselle Jane," she said, more formal than usual, "What is wrong?"

I didn't want to put my burdens on her—I knew it wasn't right—but I did it anyway. I told her what had happened with Brigitte, and how scared I was that she could harm us, and how afraid I was to tell Mathilde.

Lucie looked me in the eye and said, "It is best to say what you need to say, mademoiselle, and get it done." These were almost the exact words I had told her a few days before when she was having an argument with one of the other girls. I laughed and said, "Thank you, oh wise parrot." She looked at me as if she had no idea what I meant, and I shooed her off to the kitchen to get her snack.

I entered Mathilde's office, moved a pile of papers so there was a place to sit down, and told her the story. By the end, I was furious. "Can you believe the nerve of that terrible woman? She extorted my ring from me! And she took our grocery money for next week."

Mathilde shook her head. "Thank you for your quick thinking, Jane. Instead of a lost ring and some francs, we could all be on a bus getting shipped to a camp. You saved us."

"Maybe. But for how long? With more girls coming every day, and no way to get them to safety, it is just a matter of time until Brigitte or some other collaborator turns us in."

Mathilde gave a "what is there to do about it?" shrug, and we went into the kitchen for some café au lait.

CHAPTER 19

THE TRAIN

Occupied Paris, Spring 1941

After my unfortunate encounter with Brigitte, I was more frightened with each day that passed. It was essential to get Lucie out of France. Because we could no longer get papers, it appeared it might already be too late. I was inconsolable.

Mathilde was adamant. "You cannot stay, Jane. You must sail for the U.S. while there are still boats to sail on."

I was no less adamant. "I will not leave without Lucie. We will find a way. Surely the forger will find the materials he needs soon. I can't go without her. I won't."

"What would your parents say? They trusted me to take care of you," Mathilde replied.

"It isn't your fault that the world has lost its mind and lost its heart. And they don't know Lucie. If they did, they would agree with me. We must find a way."

With nothing resolved, we resumed our trips to the farm for fresh vegetables and scraps of meat that supplemented our tiny flower-box vegetable garden. We could no longer get fuel for our bus, so we took the train from Paris to the outskirts of town and had a long walk from the station to the farm. Thank goodness Mathilde could still obtain what she called "local papers," good enough to get us through the checkpoints that had popped up all over the countryside.

Up to that time, I was not a participant in the underground. Mathilde did everything she could to shield me from her activities, but I was aware of quiet meetings, late-night telephone calls, and, of course, the girls who came to us. Our small dormitory was more crowded than ever. Instead of ten little girls, that day on the train we had twenty-five. After my run-in with Brigitte, we didn't dare leave anyone behind.

In a normal world, that would have meant we had a bunch of unruly kids on our hands, but terror had rendered these children old and silent overnight.

On that day, I had to work hard even to get the girls to sing. The only song they all knew was our old favorite, "Frère Jacques." Lucie taught them how to sing it as a round. It was damp and cold, even for April, so everyone wore winter coats. A few of the garments fit, and many were miles too big or too small, so we brought along a supply of lap blankets to keep us warm.

The miracle that changed our lives came on the return trip. Not long after we boarded, the train came to a screeching halt. Three armed German soldiers strode down the aisle and ordered us to be silent. When they walked past me, my stomach caved. It took everything I had not to see three other soldiers. I willed myself back into the present—into the small train—a big black engine, a passenger car with Mathilde and me, our girls and a few farmers, and two cargo cars.

Mathilde stood up to protect the children when the soldiers walked past. I whispered to her, "What is wrong? Is there something on the tracks?"

She whispered back, "I don't know. A cow perhaps?"

One of the farmers looked out the window. "Someone has stolen the track in front of us. The train cannot go forward." I thought I detected a note of pleasure in his voice.

At that moment, one of the soldiers came back and barked in horrible French that we should all be quiet. The soldiers argued with each other in German, which Mathilde understood. She whispered that they were fighting over whether to leave us on the train or force us to march into the closest town. Two of them wanted to eat and spend the night in their favorite hotel. They didn't want to babysit a bunch of children. Then she said that all three soldiers decided to leave!

In their poor French, they ordered us to be quiet and wait onboard until they returned in the morning with what they needed to repair the tracks.

We were flabbergasted. It had been so long since we had been free from the ever-present eye of soldiers. Once the Germans left the rail car, we explained to the children what was happening, and our girls broke out in a little cheer. Lucie passed around the bread and chocolate and cider that we had packed in a large wicker basket. I stood up to offer some to the farmers sitting in the back of the car, but they were huddled in an urgent discussion. I stepped toward them to overhear, when suddenly the engineer raised his voice.

"They were supposed to force the passengers to march into town. It was their orders. How did I know they would leave these damned children? What do you want me to do about it? We cannot miss this chance!"

He looked sheepish as the others hushed him, and I couldn't hear the rest of the conversation. Mathilde bustled down the aisle of the train, her black robes sailing behind her. "Emile Durand!" she exclaimed. The engineer turned around and his scowling face broke into a wide smile.

"Mathilde! It is you? These are your students?" he asked.

"Ah oui! Certainement! Qu'est-ce qui se passe? What is going on?"

He pulled her into the circle of men and they lowered their voices again so that the conversation was muffled. I thought it was my responsibility to keep the children occupied, so I vainly attempted to get them under control and tried to get them singing again. The absence of the soldiers seemed to have unleashed pent-up energy. They were climbing over the seats and trying to open the windows. When I turned around, I was horrified to see the door of the railcar wide open. "Restez ici! Stay here!" I commanded, as I ran down the steps to corral any of the girls who might have gone outside. Little Miriam stood at the bottom of one of the cargo cars looking up at—oh no!—at Lucie who had climbed up the ladder to the level of a small barred window. Lucie reached in, then scrambled down and ran to me, holding out a tan booklet. On the front it said "Republique Française" with the emblem of France and a large red letter "J." Inside it said "Nom" with Bernheim written in neat script. Below said "Prénom: Charles."

A French passport.

"The car is full of them! And other papers. This is what we need. This will save us!" Lucie cried. Before I could even ask what she knew about it, a deep voice behind me said, "She is right." It was Emile, the engineer. He took the passport from my hand. "These have been collected from Jews taken to camps. The Nazis send them back to Berlin for their records. We have been waiting a long time for this shipment. These documents will save many people." He explained they had assumed the soldiers would take any passengers into town when they went to get materials to repair the tracks. The farmers had planned to convince the Nazis to leave them behind to guard the train, giving them time to roll the cargo into a barn and hide it.

"That's ridiculous!" I blurted out. "It will be obvious that you took the documents."

"Not if the plan goes as it is supposed to. We will get onto the train and back up to a spur that goes into a village," Mathilde explained.

"I am familiar with that spur. I have seen it every time we ride by here. It is as broken as the tracks in front of us," I insisted.

The engineer interrupted. "My nephews might have a bit to do with that. They are coming right now with the parts to repair the track behind us." He turned to my aunt. "Mathilde, this plan is dangerous. We are going to set some fires tonight. We never expected there would be children on the train. We cannot carry out this plan without risking all our lives."

Mathilde's mouth was firm. "Without this plan, these girls' lives are already forfeit," she said. She turned to me. "We have asked them to keep too many secrets already, but the girls will have to act innocent in front of the soldiers. If they give us away, we will all be shot. Do you think they can do it?"

What other choice did we have? "Yes. Yes, I am certain they can," I said. I hoped my voice wasn't shaking as much as the rest of me.

Emile nodded solemnly. "Then hurry, we have no time to waste. It's likely the soldiers will spend the night in town and not return before they have had their fill of food and wine, but we can't be certain. Please, get back on board." Mathilde motioned me to come, and swept Lucie and Miriam in front of her up onto the train. In moments, the engine made a deafening noise, and we moved slowly backward, delighting the girls who were still giddy with the unexpected turn of events. We had to trust that the nephews were doing their job. As we chugged along, I could see that the reconstruction of the track must have been successful because we were pulling backward into a small village. The train came to a stop in front of an old barn.

Mathilde stood and clapped her hands. "All right, girls. We've got to hurry. Let's get to work." As we piled out, the men pried open the doors of the cargo cars to reveal hundreds of boxes and piles of documents. We made a fireman's line outside the barn, our girls and the farmers passing papers along to Mathilde, who covered them with an oilcloth. The men left a thin layer of documents on the floor of the boxcar and covered it with dry straw. By the time we got back on board, it was getting dark and we were all exhausted. The girls rested against each other and fell asleep as the train chugged forward once again. Even Mathilde snored gently, her head resting against the window, a little girl on her lap. One of the farmers stood at the front of the car and said, "Thank you all. You have been very brave and worked very hard." But by the time he spoke, only Lucie and I were awake to hear. She sat next to me and tugged at my sleeve.

"Am I saved, Mam'selle?" she asked, her eyes shining.

"I hope so very much, my darling. I hope so."

When the locomotive was back in place, we woke the girls and got out and the men set the fire. The boxcar in flames was a source of fascination for Lucie, but the other children were afraid. It took all we had to calm them down. Mathilde and I told them we had made the fire to keep us warm. Our biggest concern was making sure they understood that the entire enterprise had to be a secret. I knew I needed to tell a bedtime story like none I had ever told before. Their silence told me that they had intuited my fear. We gathered away from the tracks under the shelter of an old oak tree.

"Girls, it is time for a very important story," I began. "Hold hands." Coats rustled as they reached out to each other. "There is a community of angels who carry knowledge of what makes us human. Each day, they rebuild humanity in secret by renewing goodness to fight against evil so that life can continue. Everything that has happened on this train is part of their work. And everything that happened tonight must be kept secret. This is a promise we make to each other and to the angels." The girls were glassy-eyed with exhaustion and overstimulation. Only Lucie nodded. I had more work to do. "The grains of sand that sparkle in the sunlight are their home. They carry our secrets. They hold our lives in their hands.

"The drops of water that sparkle in the moonlight are their home. They carry our secrets. They hold our lives in their hands.

"The dust of ash that burns in the night is their home. They carry our secrets. They hold our lives in their hands.

"Now girls, this is your part. After I say 'Will you tell?' you say, 'I will not,' as a promise."

I began. "The grains of sand that sparkle are their home. Will you tell?"

"I will not." At first, there were only a few confused voices. Lucie stood up and made it a declaration. "I WILL NOT!"

"The drops of water that sparkle in the moonlight are their home," I intoned. "Will you tell?"

"I will not." A few more understood and joined in with Lucie.

"The dust of ash that burns in the night is their home. Will you tell?"

"I will not."

We repeated this incantation until their voices grew strong, they were all standing, and they were no longer children. And I was no longer afraid. We made nests of the coats and blankets and curled up on the hard ground against each other to wait out the night. Mathilde came back to where I was sitting and leaned to embrace me. She whispered, "Incroyable, chérie. Incredible."

The soldiers returned the following morning to find the empty boxcars black with soot, and a ragtag of silent little girls, along with Mathilde and me and assorted farmers, huddled by the side of the road. They were beside themselves with fury, but the engineer patiently told a long story about an explosion in the engine throwing embers into the cargo cars. His acting skill, along with the residual evidence of burned documents, convinced them. I trembled as I considered the risks we had taken.

CHAPTER 20

GUTENBERG

Occupied Paris, Spring 1941

After our train adventure, Mathilde agreed I could be more active in the Resistance, even though it was against her better judgment.

"How would I explain to your father if anything happened to you? I am responsible for you, just as I am for these children."

"But I am not a child. My father and mother would want me to help. This is my chance to do something important. Mathilde, you must let me!"

They gave me a job as a courier. On the days when I saw a shirt hanging on the clothesline at a particular house, I carried data for the forger to a specified intersection in the guise of a grocery list. An old woman in black widow's weeds with a lace veil and only one eye took the list to the baker, where she got instructions on what to do next. Things went smoothly until one day the widow didn't show up. When she didn't come, I started counting the way I did as a child. *One Mississippi, two Mississippi…* First I bargained with myself that I would go in her stead if she didn't come in 100 Mississippis. Then 500. Then I found that I couldn't keep the numbers straight. And I couldn't breathe. No one else showed up to go to the bakery and ask for any "old bread left for the orphans." At last, I decided I had to take her place.

As usual, the queue outside the boulangerie was long, and filled with women fussing and gossiping, ready to fall silent if a soldier should appear. A year since the occupation, everything was scarce, because the Nazis sent the bounty of French produce to Germany. Lines were serious business. I stood and fidgeted and moved up slowly. When I got inside, I stumbled on the code, saying, "The orphans need old bread." The man behind the counter looked frightened, but he took my coupon card and used the scissors hanging from a string around his neck to clip out a section. He reached down and handed me a stale baguette. I took the bread around the corner to a dark alley that smelled like rotten sausage. The loaf was so hard that I had to hit it on the ground to break it. A small piece of paper fell out with instructions and the code phrase for the day. I was shaking and took several wrong turns before I found what I hoped was the forger's headquarters. A boy stood in the doorway.

He couldn't have been older than ten or eleven. He looked at me suspiciously, but I asked the correct question. "Can you tell me where the post office is? I must mail a letter to my mother."

He gave the correct answer: "I have some stamps inside. I can help you mail your letter." I followed him into a small stationery shop. He nodded to a woman behind the counter and beckoned me to pass through a curtain into a room in the back. The walls were lined with shelves laden with boxes of paper. He looked around and pulled on a shelf which swung open to reveal another large, windowless room with a long wooden table with stools around it. The table was covered with papers and tools—magnifying glasses, lights, and bottles. In the corner was a printing press. My heart was racing, but at least I was sure I had found the right place. I gave him the coded information from inside the bread. Then I worked up my nerve.

"Is he here?" I asked timidly.

"Who?" he said.

"The man who does these miracles," I answered. "I would like to meet him and thank him myself."

"You have found him, and no thanks are needed. I am only doing what I can do, the same as you," he said. "My name is Michel, but you can call me Gutenberg."

I laughed at the nickname. "But how…?"

"My mother worked in a laundry that catered to wealthy clients. I helped her from the time I was very young. I can remove almost any kind of stain or ink you can imagine, including the red ink on a passport that designates that the bearer is Jewish. My father was a printer. This is his press." He gestured to the machine. "And these are the same typewriters they use. If I can get the authentic paper, I am able to create almost any document. So far, my work has gone undiscovered. Because I am only a boy I have a lot of freedom to come and go."

My mouth must have been hanging open. "But where are your parents?"

"They are Communists, sent to a work camp. I live upstairs with my grandmother."

"I am so sorry. You have saved hundreds of people who will never be able to thank you. But I can. I was there when they liberated the documents from the train."

"Then I believe it is I who must thank you. We have been waiting weeks for those papers."

I thanked him again and let him get on with his work.

As Lucie predicted, the documents from the train were literally a miracle. Over the following days, I gave our forger information to make papers for many people. One by one, the girls left us, traveling in hay carts or by foot to the boats. Then it was time for Lucie and me.

I thought it would be just Lucie for whom I needed papers, but then Dr. Levy's apartment was "requisitioned" by the Nazis. They had already taken over the best hotels, and many of the apartments that were left empty when millions fled the city. As they brought in more and more secretaries and bookkeepers and bureaucrats, they needed more and more space. The doctrine of lebensraum, "room to live," was enacted on a small scale as they stole the apartments, art, and belongings they wanted, just as it was being enacted on a large scale as they stole entire countries. Levy moved in with some friends in a crowded flat in the Marais district.

One morning at the school, Levy told me how it happened. We sat across from each other in the dining room at the enormous wooden trestle table marked by years of loving use. Danielle poured us two cups of the chicory brew that had taken the place of the coffee we loved. I was distraught and more frightened than ever for his safety.

"They pounded on my door and announced that my apartment is now the property of the Third Reich. They gave me an hour to collect my things. What was I to do? I'm lucky they just threw me out and didn't arrest me."

"That is so frightening. Dr. Levy, do they have you on their list? Will you be detained? And your beautiful apartment… all your art and rugs? Your medical equipment? All taken?"

"It was arrogance to think I would be spared. I am not the first to lose everything and I am afraid not the last."

"Won't you please come to America with me and Lucie? I've been told we will be safer if we are traveling with a man—as a family."

"How can I leave my country? How can I leave the people who need me?"

"What good will you be to them if you are sent to a work camp?"

Several conversations like this one, and Mathilde's encouragement, finally convinced Levy to go with us.

One early morning I had a most curious experience. I was in my street clothes standing in the usual interminable line. I had my coupon book clutched in my hand, waiting to get whatever little bit of milk and cheese was left. I glanced behind me to see the line of people still in their dark winter clothes, flowing down the street like a river. My knees nearly gave way when I recognized the tall man behind me. He was the inspector with the fractured English who interviewed me. What was his name? Lavigne. I still had his card in my drawer. I snapped my head forward, praying he had not recognized me. How could he have? He only saw me once, and I was wearing my habit. I tried to shrink—to be as small as a woman who is six-feet-tall can be. Yet my heart caved in as I felt a hand on my shoulder, his breath in my ear. Time stopped.

"Merci, Mademoiselle Smith. Thank you for your courage."

I swiveled my head around to see him, but he had already disappeared into the crowd. What did it mean that a French policeman knew what I was doing? That he was thanking me? When I shared the story, Dr. Levy told me it was a sign that the Resistance was everywhere.

Our forger promised that the papers for Lucie and Dr. Levy would be ready quickly. Since I already had my authentic papers, we'd be Dr. Smith, Jane Smith, and our daughter Lucie. I wouldn't be able to sleep until the new passports and visas were in my hands.

On the day I picked them up, I said to our boy savior, "You are rescuing me and some people I love very much."

Leaning against his father's printing press, Michel said, "I am so glad. Even though my documents have worked so far, you will have to be very careful. Be ready. They will scrutinize you. Anyone found with forged papers will go to the death camps. Act like an American at each border check."

"What do you mean? I *am* an American," I answered.

"I mean, act entitled, annoyed at the inconvenience, surprised that you should have to prove yourselves. You know—an American."

I couldn't help but laugh. "That's not true. I think you are describing the quintessential French man! Where did you get your information about what Americans are like?"

"Films, of course. My cousin runs the cinema," he answered earnestly.

"Ah, our beloved cinema. Thank goodness, both entertainment and training for the Resistance," I said.

We both laughed, surprised that we could still laugh.

CHAPTER 21

I TASTED IRON

Occupied Paris, Spring 1941

On a beautiful day, Dr. Levy was giving all the girls health exams, so I walked to the market by myself. I thought it was a sign of my healing that I was able to wander down the street without reliving that terrible day with Naomi. On the way home, I enjoyed the aroma of the fresh baguette and croissants that were in a bag slung over my shoulder. In the distance, the faint, lilting melody of the song "J'attendrai"—*I will wait for you, night and day*—wafted in the air. It had become the anthem of Paris, expressing a longing for whomever or whatever we had lost to the terrible war—innocence? Our family? A lover? Our childhood? The feeling of safety? We had all lost so many things. As I passed an all-too-frequent sight—men and women tied together being herded into an alley, I glanced guiltily at the prisoners. I never wanted to look, but I always did. Oh, my! One of them was Brigitte.

At first, I was confused. Wasn't she more likely to be *guarding* the prisoners? Even after I was sure, I almost walked away. What was I to do? Her hair was filthy, her glasses broken, and she was wearing tattered clothes. She bowed her head in an uncharacteristic posture of surrender. Could this be the Brigitte who had haunted my thoughts since our fateful meeting at the park?

I moved in front of her and whispered, "Brigitte, what has happened?"

She didn't raise her head. Her voice was hoarse and flat. "He isn't really Jewish. Only his mother. He didn't tell me he was a Communist. But I don't care. He loves me. His neighbor reported us and soldiers arrested us. They sent him to a work camp. I am not like these other people. Where will they send me?" She looked up at me. "Sauvez-moi, Mademoiselle Jane. Help me."

What could I possibly do? Before the occupation, Mathilde was friendly with everyone from the dog-catcher to the mayor, but none of them had authority anymore. And I didn't know if I even wanted to help this wretched woman.

Mathilde. How scared I had been of her! As the image of my formidable aunt bloomed in my mind, I ran my palm over the fabric of the uniform that made people assume I was a nun. I stood up tall, and let my long black robes billow out the way a bird puffs its feathers to stay warm. As I summoned my inner Mathilde, I tasted iron. I dropped the bag of croissants on the ground and sought out the commandant. He was short and stout, with a pale complexion, and a food stain on his uniform shirt. He was not one of the beautiful Aryan specimens who first marched into Paris to impress us. More likely a reserve officer called up as the ranks dwindled and soldiers were sent to Russia. When he pointed to give an order, a silver medal on a chain poked from underneath his collar. St. Christopher. My lucky day.

"Offizier." The power of my voice startled me. "Sprechen sie Englisch?" My tone made it obvious that a negative answer branded him a cretin.

He looked up at me. "Ja, meine Schwester. Yes, Sister, I speak English. How can I help you?"

I pictured him as a chubby, insecure altar boy in Bavaria. A boy who feared nuns, and grew into a man who feared nuns. The church said, "Get them by the time they are five and we'll have them for life." I counted on it. If only I had a wooden ruler, I would slap it hard across his open palm to remind him who was the Bride of Christ, and who was nothing but a sinner.

"You have blundered." The implied opening was *You Fool.*

His face paled. "My apologies, Sister."

Good. This is just where we need to be. I put on my hardest Mathilde face. "One of your so-called prisoners is a loyal supporter of the Reich. Release her before I alert your superiors to this fiasco."

He paused, so I repeated my order with more urgency and added, "Do not keep der Priester waiting." Maybe I had remembered the right word for the priest. I was hoping it didn't turn out to mean butterfly.

That got his attention. "Right away, meine Schwester. Which one is it?"

I almost cried that I wasn't able to save them all, and that my one best chance meant saving the deplorable Brigitte. I pointed at Brigitte and marched briskly away, my black robes billowing behind me, lest he stop to reconsider. As I glanced behind, I saw him untie her. Brigitte was smart enough to curtsy and cross herself before she bent down to retrieve my bag of groceries. Then she ran after me.

I marched along, not looking back. In some ways, I hoped she wasn't there. I had not visualized the second act of this farce. When I was out of breath, I went down three steps into a café, and she followed behind me.

"Your pastries," she said, proffering my bag.

"Thank you." The acrid smell emanating from Brigitte told me she had been in a very frightening situation for a long time.

I scrunched my nose and said, "Let's have a coffee."

We sat down and ordered. In deference, I thought, to my being a nun, the waiter ignored Brigitte's bedraggled appearance and took our order. I resolved to make the interaction as short as possible.

Before I began, Brigitte said, "Mademoiselle Jane, I can never thank you enough for saving me. But I will not change my opinions," she said. "Take me back there if you expect me to."

"I am not asking you to." The waiter served our café au lait with some beautiful croissants. Brigitte stuffed one into her mouth nearly whole. I was embarrassed not to have anticipated her hunger. I pulled off a flaky piece and tried to figure out what to do next. Somehow it seemed that my inner Mathilde had deserted me. "But I *am* asking you to change your behavior. I want you to promise three things." Why did I pick three? I felt like a troll in a fairy tale—asking her for three wishes.

"First, never report on anyone else. Second, never again use cruel words against anyone. And third, um. Third… well, find a way, at some time in your life, to stand up for someone who cannot stand up for themselves." There. I was proud of myself. "I don't think this is asking too much."

I couldn't have imagined how that last request would come back to haunt me. But that is a story for another time.

Brigitte was still eating. She took a sip of coffee and stuffed a croissant into her pocket. "I can make those promises. As soon as I can, I'm taking the train back to my family's home in the south. I will never come to Paris again."

She lowered her head in an unspoken "thank you" as I gave her the bag of pastries I had been carrying. We parted ways outside the café with a nod.

Back at the school, Danielle was serving lunch to the girls, so I found Mathilde in her office and told her the whole story.

"Jane, what can I say? You never fail to surprise me. I understand what you did and why. I don't know if I would have had the courage, or the stupidity—I honestly can't say which it was—to do it."

"I don't know either. I've been trying to teach the girls right from wrong, but in these times it is so hard to tell the difference. I hope I didn't make a terrible decision."

A few days later, we were surprised when a delivery man brought us a large carton of hard-to-find groceries. Nestled next to a head of lettuce was a small, square jewelry box. I smiled before I even opened it. My ring.

CHAPTER 22

FINALLY, I COULD BREATHE

Le Havre, Occupied France, May/June 1941

I was frantic until the papers were ready, and frantic after that to find a way out of France. By a miracle, my mother's Unitarian friends, Mr. and Mrs. Ford, who helped so many, allowed us to join a group of twenty-nine children and their adult chaperones taking trains from Marseille to Lisbon. From there, we'd board the last remaining ship sailing to the United States. The Fords had obtained visas for the people in their group, but we still had to depend on our own papers. We would travel from the Vichy "unoccupied" section of France, and go through Spain to the port of Lisbon. That meant I had to return to our forger and request Spanish and Portuguese transit visas. My friend Michel saw the panic in my eyes. I had nightmares that they wouldn't be ready, but he got them done in time.

Mathilde didn't come to the train to say goodbye. We all agreed that she should keep a low profile. She and I spent the evening together the night before we left.

"Ma chérie, I am so sad to see you go, and yet so happy that you are going now. I can't predict the future, but I am afraid things will get much worse." She embraced me in her ample bosom and held me for a moment.

"Mathilde, you are so brave. Are you sure? Are you certain you will not come to America with us?"

"I am certain. My place is here. Be safe. Take care of our darling Lucie and the brave Dr. Levy."

Lucie and Aunt Mathilde had said their goodbyes earlier. Lucie proudly showed me Mathilde's parting gift, a silver charm bracelet with a tiny Eiffel tower. She didn't know whether to be happy or sad. Very confusing for an eight-and-a-half-year-old girl, no matter how precocious.

We were scheduled on an evening train, so after dinner I changed into my navy-blue blouse and blue straight skirt with a front pleat. My blazer was red gabardine with wide lapels, blue buttons down the front, and substantial shoulder pads. My mother had helped me pick it out at the Tall Gal's Shop in New York City, what seemed more like two decades than two years before.

Mathilde gave me a jaunty little red hat with a grosgrain ribbon and a matching clutch to go with the outfit. If I hadn't been out of my mind with apprehension, I might have felt almost pretty.

I hung the black robes and tunic in the wardrobe and folded the veil and wimple into the small bureau. I felt a tenderness as I bade farewell to the garments that had brought Our Lady of Perpetual Grace to so many women. I wondered if I would ever see the convent again, or if it would be left to decay into rubble? I wondered if anyone would notice that "perpetual sorrow" had been transformed into "perpetual grace"?

On our way to the train station, I said goodbye to Paris, which the war transformed from the City of Lights to the city of muddled gray. Goodbye to the traffic jams that had almost disappeared in favor of horse-drawn wagons. Goodbye to the discordant chimes of Notre Dame, not heard since the day the Nazis entered Paris. Goodbye to the fashionable Parisiennes, who now stood in lines waiting for not-enough-of anything. Goodbye to the memory of three German soldiers. Goodbye to the young woman I was when I first met Lucie.

The breeze around my legs was unfamiliar, and I felt vulnerable without my robes. Levy was quiet. I felt ashamed of my selfishness when I realized that, while I was saying goodbye to my beloved Aunt Mathilde and my adopted city, he was saying goodbye to his country, his practice, memories of the home he shared with his wife, and everything he had ever known.

We boarded the train to Marseille, each of us wearing an American Friend Service identification tag provided by Marcie Ford. The trip was not an easy one. The smell of engine oil was suffocating. They scrutinized our papers as we got on, even though we were with a group. The trip of 400 miles took over two days. The train stopped several times, and soldiers reviewed our papers over and over. I said a silent thanks to Gutenberg every time we passed muster.

I didn't mean to be ungrateful, but we were all quite miserable. The provisions and sanitation on the train were wholly inadequate. Fortunately, Danielle had prepared an enormous basket of food. The problem was how to eat with the eyes of hungry children looking at us. We shared as much as we could.

We finally disembarked in Canfranc, a railway station in the Spanish Pyrenees. There we would connect with the train to Lisbon. We had slept in our seats, covered by our coats and sweaters, and we arrived cramped and aching. What a relief to stand up and haul our baggage out onto the platform. Fresh air! Mercifully, the station offered food and water. Our train to Lisbon was due to arrive in an hour, but, like everything else in wartime, it was delayed. So we snuggled up on the benches and against the walls inside the station house. Lucie talked a bit with some of the other girls, but not much. She wasn't usually so shy, but all the children seemed subdued, as if someone had drugged them. Everyone on that trip was scared and exhausted.

It took forever, but the train to Lisbon finally arrived with a loud screech. It was larger and a bit more modern than our first locomotive. I hoped the bathrooms would stand up better to so many people. It wasn't much of an improvement. After two more uncomfortable days on the train, the announcer called out our arrival in Lisbon.

Traveling with a group gave us cover and provided transportation to the port from which we'd sail on the SS Souza-Cardoso to New York. At the dock we entrusted our meager baggage to a porter. In these tumultuous times baggage was stored to the side, with the certain knowledge that not everyone would be permitted to board the ship. Even though we were part of the Ford's group, we had to queue up like everyone else. We joined a long line of old men and women, people my age and, of course, the children. A very pregnant young woman tried her best to corral her two toddlers. My armpits were soaking and my blood was cold as we waited.

A disturbance broke out in front of us. A young man who was not part of our group said, at first quietly, and then so loud that everyone heard him, "You cannot forbid me to board. My papers are in order. I paid for my ticket."

A man in uniform took him roughly by the arm. He said, "No theatrics, sir. We will sort this out. You must come with me."

The look on the young man's face terrified me. It was the look I would have if they rejected our papers. Then it was our turn. As we had agreed, Dr. Levy proffered our documents, as any good paterfamilias would do. Lucie and I stood behind him. The bald, middle-aged man who held the key to our freedom examined the papers and the tickets, looked us up and down, smiled at Lucie, and said, "Have a pleasant journey." He turned and motioned to the porter to load our luggage. And just like that, we were saved.

Although I wanted nothing more than to faint or shout hooray, I did neither. I held Lucie's hand tightly—I'm not sure whether to keep her from talking or to remind myself to be quiet. I managed to walk decorously up the gangplank.

Once the initial terror wore off, I was overwhelmed by what I saw of the Souza-Cardoso. The boat was enormous, but what I noticed was how different the ship was from the elegant vessel that had brought me to France just two years before. Lucie and I were in a cabin one-quarter the size of the one I had on my trip over. It was four floors below deck and smelled of diesel. There was one bathroom at the end of the hall for six women and their children, two in diapers. They separated the men and women for maximum efficiency, so Dr. Levy had a cot in what I could hardly recognize as the ballroom. I can't even guess how many men slept there. It must have been hundreds. Heavy canvas bags covered the lights on the deck and along the railings that had made the Queen Elizabeth so splendid at night. We ate in shifts according to our last names. The pushed-together dining room tables resembled a monk's refectory. Everyone was in a somber mood. Each morning, the captain shared news of the war through the loudspeaker system that had once announced hula lessons and shuffleboard competitions. And on every face was the very present but unspoken fear that a U-boat could attack, and even sink, our ship.

Lucie's eyes had been wide from the moment we arrived at the dock. As horrified as I was, Lucie was equally delighted by every aspect of the ship, even in its crowded, unkempt condition.

"Mam'selle!—I mean, maman!"

We had discussed the importance of maintaining our charade throughout the voyage, but in the excitement I occasionally became Mam'selle.

"Maman, the ocean is so big. Does it go on forever?" she asked as we stood near the railing. She was so excited I don't think her feet touched the ground.

"I hope not forever, chérie, or we won't get to New York," I answered, smiling and bending down to button her coat. The ocean breeze made it cool even for spring.

"Will you show me again where we are going?" she asked, taking my hand.

"Of course." We walked together onto the deck, where a huge globe surrounded by step stools awaited us. Lucie climbed up so that her head was even with mine. I was terrible at geography, but I found Europe—and then France. I pointed to Paris.

"See Lucie? This is where we started. Can you find Portugal?"

"Yes, I see it! We have already traveled so far! And where are we going?" she asked.

I put my finger on the globe and said, "Let's follow the ocean and we will find New York City."

Lucie leaned way over and put her finger next to mine on Portugal; then traced through the cerulean blue that represented the Atlantic Ocean. I've always been glad that globes and atlases fabricate the color of water for oceans and seas. It would be too depressing to make them their actual color. Too much black. Together, we traced what I guessed would be our route.

"Here is New York," I said.

"That's where we will see Our Lady of Liberty?"

"That's right. Remember we studied about her? She was a gift from France to the United States in 1885—many years ago."

Lucie gave me a little uncertain smile. She had stopped squirming and had become still.

"Can I come and look at this again?" she asked.

"Of course, my dear. Be careful, though, since it is high."

"I will be very, very careful," she said.

I stepped away from the stool, but she took my hand again. She had traced her finger back to France and looked earnestly for something else. She moved her hand far to the right.

"That's Russia, isn't it?"

My heart sank. I already knew why she was asking. The loudspeaker that morning had announced Hitler's invasion of Russia. I nodded.

"That's where my papa died." It wasn't a question.

"That's right." I gave her a hug. I couldn't think of anything else to say. There had been quite a few adult conversations about censoring the morning announcements to protect the children, but it was reluctantly decided that these children had as much right as the adults to know what was happening. In those times, childhood, like the elegant ocean liner, was a casualty of war.

Levy and Lucie and I ate together. The rations were simple, but the ship staff found some wine and excellent stinky cheese left over from the ship's glory days that they shared among all the passengers. On this voyage, at least, a happy consequence of chaos in our world seemed to be the elimination, or at least diminution, of class differences. I hoped that America's relative class-lessness would appeal to Dr. Levy.

He was very quiet on the trip. We usually had long, deep conversations about medicine, abortion, politics, art, and history. Yet even when we sat together after dinner, he only wanted to sit on the deck wrapped in a blanket and stare at the very black sea in total silence. I tried to make light with him.

"Good thing you are on board. Did you see that woman with the two little kids? She is so pregnant that I'm sure you'll be asked to deliver her before we reach New York."

"What? Oh yes. Of course I would do so if I am needed," he said seriously. His mind was somewhere else.

"Are you thinking of Leah?"

"How can I not? She should be the one getting saved. I don't deserve it." There was nothing I could say to make it better.

One night, after a couple of glasses of wine, Levy seemed so sad that I tried again. We sat next to the railing bundled in our plaid blankets. The moon was just a sliver, and the star-studded night sky over the ocean outdid its usual splendor.

"What are you thinking about?" I put my hand on his arm.

"Jane, complaining would be a poor repayment for all you have done for me."

"Oh, Bernard," I said. I never called him Bernard, even though he had asked me to a thousand times. "We have been through enough things together to value honesty above all. What good is any of this if we lose that?"

He smiled a little—the first smile I had seen on his face in days.

"I can't stop thinking about Leah and that she gave her life to protect her grandfather, and here I am, running away. Of course, it was only a matter of time before they arrested me. But I am afraid this makes me a terrible coward. Not only am I not helping the Resistance, but our people require medical care. What kind of man leaves when he is so needed?" He wiped his eyes on his sleeve. Once again, I did not know what to say, so I just sat with him. He was my rock. Seeing him so distraught tore at my heart.

The same questions haunted me. Although I had no doubt it was right to save Lucie, I knew that my small, brief time in the French underground had primarily benefitted me and the people I loved. But I tried hard not to dwell on myself. I turned my thinking to Lucie and her new life. The courageous Unitarians who had helped us find passage on the ship had also found people who wanted to adopt her. Dr. Hymie Goldfarb and his wife Sadie lived close to my parents. From their letters, which I had shared with Lucie, they seemed like lovely people. They had no children of their own, and they were young enough to enjoy and keep up with an energetic, soon-to-be nine-year-old. Mrs. Ford shared photographs of them and their house and their cute little cocker spaniel, Rosie.

One night when I came in late to our tiny berth, Lucie had fallen asleep with her head on the desk. I saw a sheet of paper filled with drafts of her new signature:

Lucie Fastion Goldfarb
Lucie Goldfarb
Lucie F. Goldfarb

She was practicing her new identity. I had told her she could use her last name, Fastion, as her middle name. Some signatures were large and swirly. Some were small and sharp.

I picked her up and carried her to the berth. She stretched and turned over onto her stomach. I perched on the edge of the bed and put my hand on the small of her back. With each breath, I knew she wasn't a little girl anymore. More to the point, she wasn't *my* little girl. Her life was about to change. As much as I hoped she would love her new family, I was bitter that I would not see her every day. I wondered again if I could have kept her with me. My selfishness took my breath away. She deserved more than the best I could give her. I knew I had to let her go. Mo chuisle. My pulse.

On our third night, Lucie ate dinner and played with her new friends, so Levy and I found ourselves alone—if you could call sitting at a makeshift table with twenty men, women, and crying children—alone. As we ate the bland, watery stew that was the standard fare for our journey, Levy leaned over and thanked me again.

"Really, Levy. Stop it. It is I who should thank you. Without you, I might never have been able to get Lucie to safety."

He nodded. "I am very glad about that, too. I sometimes wonder about the future," he said, looking out the window at the inky sky and the vast ocean. "It has been hard for me to be so alone. And for you?"

"Well, I guess I have never had anyone special, so it's not the same for me. Besides, I have you and Lucie, and in a few days, I'll have my parents as well. Speaking of them," I hesitated, "I hate to ask this, but would you please not tell them about the abortions? My mother would not approve."

He nodded. "I understand." Then he put his hand on mine. "We have been such a good team. I wonder, Jane, if you might see anything in the future for you and me?"

It took a moment for his meaning to become clear, and I blushed.

"I am very flattered if I understand what you are asking." I put my other hand on top of his. "I love you dearly, but I don't have those kinds of feelings for you—romantic feelings. I have never had those for anyone. I'm afraid I am destined to be a spinster."

I experienced an old, familiar shame. When other girls dated in high school, my mother said, "You are just independent, dear." When my college classmates got married, she said, "You are just waiting for the right one to come along." But I feared it was something else entirely. The rest of our dinner passed in awkward silence, and he never broached the subject again.

The fourth day of our voyage found us a little over half way, and there was tentative agreement that we were safe. Although the morning's news of war was still grim, by evening some passengers broke out fiddles and accordions; the men pushed cots up against the walls and did a bit of impromptu dancing in the ballroom. Polyglot singing filled the room. My father would have called it peasant music, with a lively tempo and much kicking and jumping. It was fun to watch and made us all feel happier. Even Levy seemed to cheer up.

The next morning in our little cabin, I thought I'd better have a conversation I had promised Mathilde.

"Chérie, can we talk?"

"Of course, Mam'selle—maman."

I smiled and sat down on the bed next to her. "It's all right to call me Mam'selle when we are alone. Soon we'll be home and we won't need to pretend."

She looked up at me. "Is something wrong?"

"No, petite." I tousled her hair. "I just...." I shifted a little. "You know, you will be nine soon."

"Almost grown."

I wasn't sure if it was a declaration or a question. "That's right. You are old enough to understand that the past couple of years have not been normal."

"What do you mean?"

"It is not normal to live in the middle of a war. To have all your friends move away. To be afraid. To lose your father. To sail to a new country pretending to be somebody's daughter. None of that is normal."

She thought for a moment. "But that is my life. Perhaps I don't know what normal is."

"That's what I mean. I... You have had to keep so many secrets. You have taken care of all the girls we helped, and me and Mathilde as well. You haven't had a chance to be a child."

She gave me that Lucie look, her little brow furrowed.

"What I am trying to say is that you have been entirely too good. You haven't talked back, or gotten into trouble, or been mean, or selfish or even messy. You have had to act like a grown-up, and that's not fair. I hope you will feel safe enough in your new home to act like a child."

"Mam'selle, you are telling me to misbehave?"

"Of course not. Well. . . I just want you to be confident that the grown-ups in your life will love you even when you are not perfect. Do you understand?"

"No."

"I'm sorry. I probably don't have it right."

"Are you telling me not to pretend all the time? That I don't have to?"

"Yes! Exactly. That is, after we get off the boat. Until then, stay perfect!"

The merry mood increased on the morning we arrived in New York. When Lady Liberty came into view, a roar of excitement came from the deck, crowded with every age and sort of person. We spontaneously shouted for joy in a dozen languages. A few minutes more and we docked. My parents were behind the wire fence waving madly at us. I pointed them out to Levy and Lucie, and we waved back. As awful as so many things were in the world, we were going to be safe.

Lucie was going to be safe.

Porters handled our luggage, so we collected our coats and gloves and our precious documents as we got in line. It seemed strange that the officials wanted to see our papers again—as if we could have parachuted onto the deck. But the war had changed everything about everything. We crept along in the queue down the gangway. My heart was in my throat. As we got closer to the man in uniform scrutinizing documents, I forgot to breathe.

Levy put his arm around me and whispered, "It's all right. We are going to be fine. Calm down. You are frightening Lucie." And sure enough, her face looked as stricken as mine. So I beamed at her and took her hand. "We're almost home!" I said. And she smiled back, which made everything better. At least the man's uniform was blue, he worked for the ship's company, and he wasn't Gestapo—so many things to be grateful for. Finally, it was our turn. I smiled breezily at the ticket inspector. "Beautiful morning to dock, isn't it?" I said, as if I owned the ship. He smiled back and nodded. He hardly glanced at our documents and waved us through.

"Just hold on there," I heard from a short stout man in uniform who came running up to us. "We can't let her into the country." My sunny smile evaporated, and I trembled as I frantically began to explain that he should allow my daughter to enter the country because of my citizenship.

"No, ma'am. I mean to say that we can't let her in without giving her an American flag made right here in the Garment District of New York." My ears were buzzing as he grinned and handed Lucie a small flag attached to a wooden stick. "Welcome to the United States!"

Lucie was taking her cues from me. All the blood had left her face until I burst out of my shock to join Levy in effusive thank yous. Seeing our faces, she managed a wan "Thank you" that sounded more like a question.

Levy shook the man's hand energetically and said, "Apologies, my friend. My girls were terribly seasick. They are not quite themselves." The fellow chuckled and gave us a sympathetic wave as he consulted his list and trundled off to find the next child who needed a flag. It was only then I could see that the writing on his jacket said *Barney Mitchell, American Welcome Committee.*

As we inched toward the gate, Lucie glanced back and waved at her little friend, Israel, who was disembarking. But instead of giving him an American flag, they shuttled him and his family off in another direction.

"Where are they going, Mam'selle?" Lucie looked worried. I asked the porter where they were being taken.

"They are immigrants. They will go by barge to Ellis Island to be inspected."

"Inspected?"

"Yes. If they are diseased, feeble-minded, or can't work, they will be sent back. But most of them will be allowed in." He tipped his hat at me and pushed his luggage cart away.

Most of them.

I would like to tell you I was brave. I would like to tell you I spoke out to make sure that Mrs. Rubin's ancient father wouldn't be sent back to France; or that I demanded they not reject sweet eight-year-old Israel because he was, what they called then, "simpleminded;" or that I stood in front of the officials and stopped them from sending mothers in one direction and children in another. But I did not. Instead, I commanded Lucie and Levy to face front, stay in line, and keep moving. In case you think morality is easy, remember life often sends us impossible situations.

I hardly had time to experience relief when my mother wrapped me in her arms. My father reached his hand out. "You must be Dr. Levy—Harry Smith here." Levy shook his hand firmly.

My mother released me and stepped back. She crouched down with her arms wide open. "And you must be the wonderful Lucie we have heard so much about."

Lucie fell into her arms as if they had known each other forever. And finally, I could breathe.

CHAPTER 23

I PROMISE

Connecticut, Summer 1941

After we had been home for a couple of days, the Goldfarbs came over for dinner at my parents' house to meet Lucie. Lucie was shy, as we had all expected, but dinner went well. As I was tucking her in, she cried a little bit, but said she thought they were nice. That was a good beginning. My parents, Levy, Sadie, Hymie, and I sat in the living room and talked about Lucie's future. There were three months until her new school started. We decided she would stay with us until at least the middle of August, with lots of visits from the Goldfarbs.

Sadie changed to a part-time schedule at the library during this transition, so she spent mornings with us. Hymie came every weekend with chemistry books and experiments that fascinated Lucie. My mother made sure that they brought the cocker spaniel, Rosie. That was the easiest conquest. How Lucie loved that little dog.

We had written to the Goldfarbs that lavender was Lucie's favorite color, and they took us at our word. They made her a room that was everything a little girl could want. The walls were papered in lilac, lavender, and blue flowers. There were twin beds with lavender gingham bedspreads so that a friend could stay over. I still have a picture in my mind of Lucie lying on her bed with her long red hair spread out on an oh-so-lavender pillow.

Early on she had nightmares, but they seemed to diminish. I worried Lucie would have a hard time adjusting to a new family and a new culture, but the Goldfarbs were everything I could have hoped for. There was a community swimming pool, and within a month she had made friends. In July we celebrated her ninth birthday at a local petting zoo. We had ten little girls, in no lines at all, shrieking with delight at the tiny ponies; hugging pigs, goats, and bunnies; eating too much; and laughing and crying, just as little girls do.

By the middle of August, Lucie asked if she could live at the Goldfarbs' house so that Rosie could sleep on her bed. Voilà. Transition. I put on a brave face, and we packed the car with her clothes, toys, and books, and helped her settle into her room at the Goldfarbs.

That night, I sat alone on the floor of her bedroom at my parents' house, and cried.

School started in the middle of September. At first Lucie called me every night, excited to tell me about her new teachers and friends. She shared her amazement at riding the big yellow bus that picked her up and dropped her off at the Goldfarbs' house. She wasn't just the new girl in school—she was the new *French* girl—and she enthralled the other children with her accent and her stories. After a couple of weeks, she called on Sundays before bed. Then it became up to me to call. I felt ashamed and didn't want to interfere with her new life.

I had to learn to live without her.

As for me, I unpacked my trunks and kissed my parents. And then, to tell the truth, I didn't know what to do. Levy was living in our neighbor's garage apartment, so we walked together almost every morning. We shared our experience of the letdown after having lived in a pressure cooker of fear and adrenalin for so long.

"A car backfired as it was passing my apartment last night. I crouched behind the sofa," Levy said, grimacing.

"I keep forgetting it's all right to open the curtains, and I have been having those nightmares again—about losing Lucie."

He put his hand on my shoulder.

"Maybe it is only natural for us to need time to get used to not being in danger," I said, kicking a stone to the side of the road.

Levy lit a cigarette, took a long drag and blew the smoke out slowly. "I am haunted by it. By the ones we left. The ones still fighting, and the ones already taken. What am I to do here? I cannot practice medicine—none of my credentials will be accepted. Am I just to play pinochle with your father every night for the rest of my life? I must be of use. I think perhaps I must go back."

"Levy, you cannot. That would be suicide."

"I know. I know. But I have to do something."

"Have you talked to the Unitarians?" I asked. "I heard they need someone to find housing and work for the refugees."

"Hmm. I like that idea. I will talk to them. It would be so good to feel as though I am of use." He stubbed out his cigarette and put the butt in his pocket, as I had taught him to do. My mother was a fanatic about not leaving trash behind, and I had adopted her philosophy.

"I have been feeling the same way. Do you think I could get into medical school?"

"When did you get that idea? Of course you could, but that means many years of study before you could be a physician. Could you wait that long?"

"No. Just like you, I want to do something right now."

"But Jane, are you serious about medicine? You would be excellent. You are smart, you remember everything I teach you, and I have never seen anyone better in an emergency."

"I'm not sure if becoming a robot counts as being good in an emergency."

"Whatever you call it, I depended on it."

"I can't afford to go to medical school, anyway. It was just an idea."

Not long after that conversation, Levy became the administrator of the Unitarian Service Committee, working with refugees and coordinating with agencies all over the world. I continued to fritter my days away with no direction at all, and no plans on the horizon. I felt generally useless. As I look back, I try to forgive myself by realizing that I was overwhelmed.

It seemed that everything was going well for Lucie, so I was dismayed in October when Sadie phoned, asking if she could come over to talk. We sat in the kitchen as my mother filled our cups and heated up some coffee cake.

Sadie looked worried. "She is handing homework in late, and she's having nightmares again. She cries out, and then wakes disoriented. I sing to her until she falls asleep. When I ask her to tell me about her dreams, she says she doesn't remember them. I can only imagine what she has been through. Even with new friends, everything is so unfamiliar to her. She misses you terribly, Jane."

My mother furrowed her brow and served us each a slice of iced cake. "Darling, let's have Lucie come back and stay with us for a little while. What do you think?"

"No. No, Mother. She's had nightmares before. They will go away eventually. She can't depend on me—I mean, she has to get used to her new family. It will just be worse and confuse her more if we are not consistent."

Sadie put her hand on my arm. "Jane, could you at least talk to her? I know you are busy, but she would love to spend time with you."

"Of course, I'll come over tomorrow when she gets home from school."

The sad truth is that I was not busy. It was just that I had constructed a brittle shell around my heart that Lucie could shatter with a glance.

The next afternoon found me sitting at a picnic table in the Goldfarbs' yard with two glasses and a pitcher of lemonade when the school bus dropped Lucie off. She walked toward me carrying a pile of books, her hair in braids, her blue sweater tied around her waist. So independent. She reminded me of the children's book character, Pippi Longstocking.

"Can we talk?" I asked.

"No. I'm mad at you," Lucie said, scowling.

"I can see that. Do you want to talk about it?"

"No." She turned her back. "You can't bribe me with lemonade. I don't even want to see your face."

"Okay. I'm just going to sit here on the grass. If you want, you can sit behind me, back-to-back. You don't have to look at me."

I sat on the lawn. Lucie paced around a little bit. Then she put the books down, and I could feel her little back pressed against mine.

I waited for a moment, then asked, "Qu'est-ce qui se passe? What's going on, chérie?"

"Nothing." Silence. Deep sigh. "Mam'selle?"

"Yes, petite?"

"I feel like you don't like me."

Damn.

"My dear one, I love you *and* I like you."

She scooted around to face me.

"But you never call me. You never come to see me. I am all by myself."

I shrugged my shoulders. "All by yourself with the Goldfarbs and Rosie and your five best friends."

I could feel her agitation. "It's not the same." She sniffled. "Mam'selle, remember what you told me on the boat?"

"Which thing?"

"You told me not to be so good—to be a normal kid. I'm just doing what Linda and Barbara do. Their mothers are always yelling at them, but they are just being normal, right?"

"Is that what you want? For Mrs. Goldfarb to yell at you?"

"No. I don't really like being normal. I am doing it for you."

"I am so sorry. I did a terrible job of explaining. I wasn't saying you should copy someone else. You just don't have to be such a good girl."

"But I *am* a good girl."

There was nothing to do but laugh. Here we were, two good girls.

"Lucie, I love you to the moon and back."

We had a hug, then got up and sat at the table. I poured us each a glass of lemonade.

"What about the nightmares?" I asked.

"I can't help those." She fiddled with the end of her braid.

"I have them, too."

"Will they ever go away?"

"I don't know. What is your worst one?" I asked.

"I have fallen down into a hole and I am all alone."

"I hate that one. Next time you have it, imagine I'm in the hole with you."

"All right." She looked me in the eye. "What is your worst one?"

"Hmm. I have lost someone."

"Is it me?"

"Maybe."

"But you don't *need* to lose me, Mam'selle. The Goldfarbs have been so kind to me, but I miss you. Why couldn't I just stay with you? *You* could be my mother."

Tears came without permission. I'm sure other people had wondered why I didn't take care of her. I wiped my eyes on my sleeve and took a breath. If only.

"I miss you too. You know I love you so much. But it wouldn't be fair to you when you could have a real family with a mother and a father."

"It *would* be fair. Doctor Levy could be the father, just like on the boat."

I smiled. "We were a lovely family, weren't we? But that was just pretend. Dr. Levy must be allowed to have his own life."

"And you?"

"Maybe one of these days I shall have a life. In the meantime, it is you we are talking about. You like the Goldfarbs?"

"I love them. They teach me about things and they listen to me as if I am someone important."

"You are the *most* important."

"Will you come see me more often?"

"Yes, I promise."

In my mind I thanked my lucky stars, or God, or the angels, or Munchkins, or whatever fortune watched over my darling Lucie and gave her wonderful people to love her.

CHAPTER 24

MY SHERO

Connecticut, Winter 1941-Fall 1942

On December 7th, the Japanese attacked the United States base at Pearl Harbor. So much loss and terror. Everything changed again. My country was compelled to join the struggle to save our world from evil. Even after that, I was lost. I filled my days with food drives; helping Levy with the Unitarian Church's refugee program; attending my mother's book club; rolling bandages for the Red Cross; having nightmares of Brigitte throwing Lucie off the ship; walking dogs for a few dollars a week; spending time with Lucie and her new friends; listening to endless episodes of Ma Perkins on the radio; and packing cigarettes and books and candy to send to the boys overseas. Nothing that made me feel like I was doing my part.

Hope was a stranger to me. I was a stranger to myself.

The following fall, we received a blow that sent me reeling. An airmail letter that looked as though it had been through a war came to me with a Swiss return address I didn't recognize. Because of the cost of airmail, the letter was written on very thin onionskin paper. The ink was so splotchy and faded it was almost impossible to read. This is what we could make out:

My dear Miss Smith,

I hope this will reach you through my friend in Switzerland. I am desolated to inform you that les salauds murdered dear Madame Mathilde. She went with some Quakers to take food to the Vélo-drome d'Hiver, where they rounded up and imprisoned thousands of Jewish men, women, and children for days without water or food or sanitation. They shot her as she was trying to help a young man who was scaling the wall to escape.

The rest was illegible, except for Marcel's signature. Mother and I sat at the kitchen table, reading and re-reading the letter, trying vainly to decipher the last paragraph, wet tissues scattered around us.

"Can you reach Bernard?" my mother asked. Dr. Levy was in Washington, D.C., attending a conference on immigration.

"I know what hotel he is staying in. I'll call him tonight. Mathilde was one of his oldest friends. He'll be devastated."

Mother wrung her hands. "Oh, Jane, your father will be so upset. You know how much he loved his older sister. I'm going to wait to tell him when he gets home from work. But we don't have to tell Lucie, do we? She adores Mathilde. She has shown me that Eiffel Tower charm a hundred times. She is so young, and she has been through so much—so many losses. Her father— all those little girls—surely we can wait until she is older?" my mother pleaded.

I shook my head. "Mom, this is Lucie we are talking about. I've never been able to keep a secret from her. And besides, when would we tell her? When she is fifteen? Twenty? What would be an appropriate age to learn that someone you love has died? And when she asked how long we have known, do you think she would forgive us for not telling her? Mathilde insisted we be honest with Lucie when her father died, and she would say the same thing now."

So we called Mrs. Goldfarb with the sad news and asked her to bring Lucie over after she got home from school. When Sadie Goldfarb's black Ford coupe pulled up in front of the house, Lucie ran into the kitchen, leaving the front door wide open.

"What's wrong? What's happened?" she demanded.

Sadie scurried in after her, looking disheveled, closing the door behind her. "I'm sorry!" Sadie said. "She guessed you had bad news."

Lucie plopped down at the table and glared at me.

"Let's all sit down," I said. And we did.

"My darling, Madame Mathilde is dead." Lucie burst into tears. I showed her the letter and helped her work out the parts that were legible. She kept staring at the last paragraph as if she could break the code.

She turned to me. "Why did they take them to the Vel d'Hiv? Isn't that a place for sports?"

"Maybe they needed a big place where they could lock the gates."

Lucie looked thoughtful. "It was the Nazis?"

I sighed. "Yes. And the French police as well, I am afraid. It happened in July. I read about it in the paper. They sent thousands of people to camps. Mathilde was trying to help, as she always did."

"Why didn't Marcel tell us right away?"

"This happened in the middle of July, so it took three months for Marcel's letter to be smuggled to his friend in Switzerland, and mailed here."

"She saved all those girls, didn't she? The ones who came to our school?" Lucie asked.

"Yes, darling, she did. She was a splendid woman."

"Madame Mathilde is the bravest person I know. She was a... what is the name of the person who stands up to the bullies?"

"A hero?" my mother suggested. Lucie nodded her head.

"Yes, petite, Mathilde is indeed a hero," I agreed.

"But not a 'he.' Madame Mathilde was a she. . . Mam'selle. Madame Mathilde is a s-he-ro. A shero!"

I folded her in my arms, and we cried together.

Later, we baked cookies, and talked more about Mathilde.

"I remember when my papa first took me to Madame Mathilde's school. When my maman died, Papa couldn't take care of me by himself," Lucie said, licking dough off her fingers. Sadie took the measuring cup and wooden spoon to the sink and began to wash them. My mother was pre-heating the oven.

I talked as I dropped globs of chocolate chip cookie dough onto the baking pan, the scent of vanilla filling the kitchen. "You were only six, and it must have been a confusing time for you. You were Mathilde's very first student after she bought the school. She told me you were as silent as a mouse and hid behind the furniture when anyone came into the room."

"I was silent?" Lucie asked. We all laughed.

"Mathilde often had insomnia, as you did. Some nights after your teacher, Madame Rochand, had put you all to bed, Mathilde tiptoed in and took you by the hand into her office. She read to you in English—your mother's language."

"Oh yes! I remember one book. *The Secret Garden*—it is a book about a little girl who lost her parents, just as I had lost my maman. I loved it. It's one of my favorite books."

My mother, Sadie, and I all nodded our heads. It had been a favorite for each of us, too.

"What do we do now?" Lucie asked.

"What do you mean?" Sadie asked.

"You know—the naming!" She turned to me. "Like that big hall named for the railroad man you showed me in New York?"

I must have looked blank, but my mother chimed in, "Carnegie?"

Lucie nodded her head. "And the bridge named for the father in the country."

I laughed, "You mean the father of the country, George Washington?"

Lucie nodded again. "So what shall receive Madame Mathilde's name?"

I took Lucie into my arms and said, "I think, for now, we'll keep her name in our family. But what about writing a report about Madame Mathilde to share at school?"

"Yes, I want to."

We gathered a pad and pencil, my mother's dictionary and thesaurus, and glasses of milk to drink with our plateful of warm chocolate chip cookies. Then we sat around the table helping Lucie find words to describe the indescribable Madame Mathilde: redoubtable, indomitable, fierce, gregarious, warm-hearted. At the top of the page, Lucie wrote a title, "Madame Mathilde Smith, My Shero." We laughed and cried as we shared some of our favorite memories of a woman who gave her life for justice.

CHAPTER 25

CALL ME

Connecticut, Fall 1943

In the fall of 1943, I called Dr. Levy in a panic. I read in the news that a French woman named Marie-Danielle Giraud had been guillotined because she had performed abortions. GUILLOTINED! They called her *une faiseuse d'anges*—an angel maker.

"Did you see the article in the *Times* about Giraud? The Vichy government executed her over a month ago. Levy, that could have been you! And me!" I couldn't catch my breath.

"I would like to tell you that you are exaggerating the danger we were in. But I cannot."

"I remember you told me that the Nazis oppose abortion for Aryans…"

"And Pétain is insane about forcing French women to act as obedient housewives and increase the population. But I never imagined it would come to this," he said. "We got out just in time. Another thing to thank you for."

Suffice it to say, regardless of my former dedication, I never imagined that I would be involved with abortion again.

But I had to do *something*. Ever since Pearl Harbor, I had felt guilty for not finding a better way to contribute. At the end of another day of nothing much, my father sat me down in his study. I loved the smell of leather and pipe smoke that always lingered in that room. But it was not the story-reading Papa who sat across from me. The business-like expression on his face told me he wanted to talk about something serious.

"Daughter," he began. There was bound to be trouble when he started that way. I was in no mood for a lecture, so I gave as good as I got.

"Father," I said, and held my head up.

He didn't appear amused. "I understand you have been through a great deal," he said, "But I want to know what you plan to do with your life?"

I had no idea how to answer. It was embarrassing that he had, once again, found me at the "loose ends" that had occasioned my trip to France.

"I'm not sure, Father. I am considering a number of things—I had a crazy idea about medical school—or maybe getting a teaching degree. But nothing has really called to me."

"Not called to you? Not *called* to you?" he said indignantly. "Do you imagine banking somehow *called* to me? My dear, life is about obligation, not calling! Aren't most of your classmates already married and settled down? Many of them with children? This war is going to be over one day, and life must go on."

I sighed. So it was going to be one of those conversations. I guess he had forgotten all about how much he loved reading me *Peter Pan*.

"Papa," I said. "I can see that you and I have a fundamental difference of opinion in these matters. As it regards marriage and motherhood, I am afraid I believe that being *called* is the only way to do them." I kissed him on the cheek and went to bed.

My discomfort with that dangling discussion is why I was so excited when I saw a poster in the window of a Navy Recruitment Office. The photograph was of an attractive, smiling woman in a snappy blue uniform with a matching hat. The poster read: "Make a difference, become a Navy nurse." Underneath, in smaller lettering: "Join the Navy for a free two-year nursing education resulting in an R.N. degree. Support our troops."

When I went into the office, the man behind the counter looked me up and down and asked, "Do you have any medical experience?"

"A little," I answered. I blushed, but I doubt he noticed.

"Have you been to college?"

"Yes. I graduated several years ago," I said, relieved to have a straightforward answer.

"Great! We need smart cookies like you. The Navy offers a free accelerated nursing education and a chance to travel to countries where our boys need help. Come back tonight at seven. We're having an orientation and a few of the gals who have completed the training will be here."

"Okay. Perhaps I will," I said.

And I did.

I didn't tell anyone where I was going. I don't know why I felt so awkward about it. That evening at the enlistment office, I was excited about something for the first time in years. There was a plate of Lorna Doone cookies and a pot of coffee with china cups and saucers on the table. Milling around were half a dozen potential recruits, and three women in uniform as sharply dressed as the girl on the poster. In fact, one of them *was* the girl on the poster. She turned and smiled as if she recognized someone. I looked over my shoulder, but no one was there. She was smiling at me!

I was flustered and blurted out, "You're on the poster!"

She laughed and ducked her head. "Oh yes. The poster. That was my father's idea. Why did I ever agree to do it? Now people greet me everywhere I go, as if they know me." She stuck her hand out. "I'm Betty. Betty Marston."

Something about her stupefied me. Was it her perfume that smelled like a thousand flowers? Was it her crazy smile? Those dark eyes? After all these years, I still can't explain it. I shook my head to get out of my fog and said, "Hi, I mean, hello."

"And *your* name?" she said, laughing again.

"Oh, sorry, I'm Jane Smith."

She tilted her head to look up at me and said, "Well, Jane Smith, are you going to join us? It's a great group of girls. Loads of fun, and loads of work. Are you up to it?"

Before I could answer, a sailor tapped on his coffee cup and asked us to take a seat. It surprised me that Betty sat next to me. The sailor made a few remarks about the Navy and this wonderful opportunity to help the troops. Then he moved to the back of the room and started a projector.

The movie was grainy with dramatic music in the background. It showed uniformed women raising their hands in a classroom, patients being tended to in crowded hospitals, and a formal graduation ceremony. Just before the film was over, Betty put her hand on my shoulder. "You'll love us," she said, and left her chair to go to the front of the room.

"You'll love us?" She must have meant "You'll love it," I thought.

As I tried to figure out what was happening to my breathing, Betty began to talk, and I was transfixed. I'm pretty sure that her brief remarks were less enthralling to anyone else in the audience than they were to me. When Betty finished, she sat down behind the table at the front of the room with two other women who spoke after her. I could swear she smiled at me the entire evening. The meeting wrapped up with a sailor saying, "Sorry to rush you out, but we are due at our base at 2200 hours–that's ten p.m. to you civvies—so we have got to run.

As they were leaving, Betty handed me her business card. "Call me," she said.

I didn't call her. I was mortified to think that I had acted like a schoolgirl—that's how I saw it. I didn't call Betty, but I did feel *called*, and I enlisted.

Before I signed the formal papers, I sat down with my family—my parents, Lucie, and Levy—to tell them my plan. My mother worried that it could be dangerous, but she beamed at me. My father smiled and said he was happy that I had found something important to do.

"I'll miss you princess—*mo chuisle*." Tears came to his eyes. Papa always made a joke after being vulnerable. "I knew we wouldn't be able to keep you home once you had been over there," he said. "Remember that song from the Great War?" He sang, "How we gonna keep 'em down on the farm, after they've seen Paree?" We all laughed at his rendition.

Levy said, "You did it! That's fantastic. You'll be so good!" He made me smile.

"Thank you, Levy."

Lucie asked, "How long will you be gone?" in a plaintive tone.

I turned to her. "Oh Lucie, it won't be for too long. The program doesn't start until September, so I'll be here for a few more weeks. It only takes two years, and I will come home to visit. And, of course, I'll write. Will you write to me?"

"I'll write every day!"

"Of course you will, my darling!" I said, and I swooped her up into my arms.

CHAPTER 26

NAMETAPES

**Connecticut and California,
September-October 1943**

The next few weeks were a whirlwind of buying textbooks, uniforms, and the basics for my quarters. It was like preparing for summer camp. I didn't have to sew a nametape into every garment, only the most intimate ones. Orientation was set to begin at the end of September. Our classes started in October with a memorial planned in December in commemoration of those lost a year before at Pearl Harbor. My mother asked several times why they would select those dates to start.

"It means that all you girls are going to miss Christmas with your families. Why on earth doesn't it begin in January like everything else?"

Of course I had no answer, but I would come to observe that the Navy did what the Navy did with very little explanation, and sometimes no discernible logic.

Even though I was leaving weeks before Halloween, I got an obligatory preview of Lucie's costume.

"I'm going as *you,* Jane!" she exclaimed. "Mama Sadie helped me read about nurses, and I chose Florence Nightingale. So my costume is you!" She practically jumped up and down. "Read the nametape on my smock!"

I crouched down to look at the breast of the apron that covered a severe, long-sleeved brown dress. The small white tag read "Jane Smith." So that was why Sadie had insisted on helping sew those danged tags on my unmentionables. Lucie grinned at me—so cute under that little white cap that I could hardly bear to be leaving her. Then she hugged me and her tone changed.

"Mama Sadie told me that Halloween is like La Toussaint," she said. I had forgotten that the French don't have Halloween, and even in the States, sugar rationing had reduced Trick-or-Treating to a quest for apples and peanuts.

"The girls in my school told me ghosts come on Halloween," she said so quietly that I had to bend forward to hear her. "Do you think…?"

Why hadn't I realized how confusing it must be for her to have people talking about being scared, when she *yearned* for ghosts? She had already lost too many loved ones—her mother, her father, Mathilde.

"Oh, my dear, that is just for fun. There aren't any actual ghosts. But your maman and your papa and Mathilde are always in your heart. You don't have to wait for a holiday, you can find them there whenever you want."

Lucie hung her head. "But I don't remember what they look like," she whispered. I had never met her parents, and I didn't even have a photograph of Mathilde to show her. I pulled her close, and we stayed there for a few minutes until her breathing evened out. Then I kissed the top of her head and stood up and said, "I'll be seeing you soon, Nurse Nightingale."

She looked up at me and grinned again, "I'll be *being* you soon, Nurse Smith!"

My parents, Levy, and I drove into the city for my first ever airplane flight, from New York's Idlewild Airport to San Francisco, California. Mother insisted we shop for a suitable outfit at the Tall Gal's Shop. It was silly, since I'd be in uniform most of the time for the next two years, but she was determined. I wore a pale green boiled-wool suit with a matching hat, suede shoes, and dark green kid gloves. I must admit, I looked very stylish. I cried as I waved goodbye at the airport.

The nursing program operated in Alameda, California, at the huge new naval base. Once I had stowed my gear in my quarters, I walked to the NEX, where they sold almost everything, and they had rows of cubbyholes for our mail. Surprisingly, there was a letter in my box—from Lucie!

Dear Mam'selle,

SURPRISE! I bet you didn't think you would get a letter so soon. Mama Sadie said it takes a whole week for you to get something in California, so we mailed this a week before you left!

I know I said I would write to you every day, but Mama reminded me that you will be very busy in school learning to be a nurse, so we decided I would only write once a week. She bought me a whole box of pages and envelopes that have these pretty flowers on them. She's going to help with spelling.

Don't be too scared on your first day of school. You are really smart and you will be a really good nurse.

XXXOOO (Mama told me this is how you make kisses and hugs)
Lucie

I printed my reply so Lucie would be able to read it herself.

Dear Lucie,

What a wonderful surprise! You and Mama Sadie are very smart. Once a week will be perfect. And when you get busy, don't worry if it is less often. I keep a photograph on my bedstand of you and all the girls from Aunt Mathilde's school standing in front of the Eiffel Tower, so you are in my thoughts every day. Write to me about what you are learning in school.

XXXXOOO to you,
Mam'selle

p.s. See, I bought a box of pretty stationary too.

My classes were intense, but at least I didn't have to tow a victim 220 yards and swim 440 yards in 10 minutes, as the flight nursing students did. I couldn't imagine the courage those girls had. All I had to worry about was working on a busy ward. They would go to hospital ships, sailing to parts unknown.

It wasn't easy to cram four years of education and experience into two years, but they needed us in so many places that we rolled up our sleeves and worked like crazy. There were forty-two girls in my class, and I adored them all. They were swell—gutsy and funny and just the best people you could ever want to meet. I was in my element.

During the day, we had our classes, and in the evening we took shifts at the base hospital. We started out doing the most basic things: emptying bedpans, changing sheets, and giving sponge baths. During one very tense moment, I took charge when a sailor's blood pressure suddenly plummeted. I impressed the administrators so much with my composure in the face of an emergency that they decided I should have more complicated duties. Soon I started and discontinued IVs, inserted catheters (never my favorite), and responded to all kinds of emergencies.

We brought much more than our nursing skills to the men in those beds. We brought our smiles, our gentle hands, and sunny outlooks. What we said to them and how we said it mattered as much as the bandages and ointments we provided. Some of them needed extra attention. My roommate, Sally, sang to the sailors as she changed their dressings. It was unusual to see a dark face on the base. She must have realized there were some who didn't accept her being there. But her deep, warm voice, and the gospel hymns she sang, touched all of us. Sally was about ten years older than me, but still one of my

best friends in the class. As far as I could tell, she was the only Negro at the
Naval Nursing Academy. We talked about it one time.

"I don't think they could tell from my photograph that I am Negro. And I
have always been told that I don't sound colored, whatever that means," she
told me.

"You had to send in a photograph?" I asked. "I guess I didn't have to do
that because I enlisted in person."

"There were no enlistment offices anywhere near me. There was an ad in
the newspaper for a free nursing education, and I knew it was my only chance
to be an R.N. I called for an application and sent it in with the requisite photograph, then did an interview over the phone. The decade I spent as a practical nurse in the hospital impressed them. By the time I arrived here, I was like
a bottom-feeder you didn't mean to take home in your bucket. It was impossible to throw me back!"

I felt terrible that she saw it that way, but I didn't know what to say.

Edna and Clarice were my other two buddies. Fortunately for me, Edna,
or Eddie, as we called her, was about my height, and a total tomboy. Her
mother had sent her off to nursing school with a wardrobe of lovely things
Eddie said she was "never, ever" going to wear. So when I needed something
pretty, as I surprisingly would, it came from her closet. We made a great team,
so they often assigned the four of us to the same shifts. We even managed to
switch with some other students to get a suite together, sharing two bedrooms
with a bath in between. A gorgeous magnolia tree stood outside the window
of the room I shared with Sally. In the afternoon, the light shone golden
through the tree.

In the little time we had before bedtime, we would talk. Sally told me
what it was like to grow up in Gadsden, Alabama, as the grandchild of a slave,
and I would tell her what it was like to grow up in Stamford, Connecticut, as
the grandchild of a teacher. As different as our lives were, we were like sisters—or sometimes more like mother and daughter. Sally taught me to have
humility when it came to working with people whose lives were different
from mine.

"We can be friends, even love each other," she said one night after we
were tucked into our little twin beds, "but you can never see from my per-
spective. The best you can do is recognize that your viewpoint carries more
weight than other people's."

"What do you mean?" I asked. "We are all the same. We all just want to
help our patients."

"See, you don't understand. We are by no means 'all the same,' and if
you don't recognize inequality, you won't be able to do anything about it.
When you look at your work as helping other people, they will always be your

inferiors. It just makes you the 'nice lady,' which is what I suspect you want to be."

That hurt my feelings. "What's wrong with being nice? It's what my mother taught me. Aren't you being a little unfair?" I asked in a pitiful voice.

"Maybe. But sometimes the truth is uncomfortable. I think you have the capacity to be different. If you can approach this as a partnership instead of doing a good deed, then other people will see it differently, too. The bottom line is that none of this is about you feeling good. It is about them—the people who you are caring for—their lives and hopes and dreams, and *their* perspectives."

"But don't you think I understand what other people are going through?"

"Let me illustrate it this way. Have you ever hung a picture on the wall?"

"Of course I have," I answered, trying to keep the defensiveness out of my voice.

"How did you do it?"

"What do you mean? I just did it."

"Did you hang the picture at eye level?"

"Of course," I answered again, getting a bit impatient. The entire conversation was waking me up just when I was trying to fall asleep. "That's how you are supposed to do it."

"So, when you hung pictures at eye level, what happened when all the other people in your life who are not six feet tall came into the room?"

I was silent.

"Jane, are you still awake?"

The enormity of my assumption that everyone would see the same way I do, and want the same things that I want, descended upon me. Perhaps it was just because Sally was such a good friend, or because it was so late at night, but I heard her without getting defensive.

"Sally, I think I am—I think I am awake. Thank you," I said. "And now I am ready to go to sleep. Sweet dreams."

"Sweet dreams, and bless you, my dear friend," Sally said.

My mother and I wrote to each other faithfully. I told her about my classes and my new friends and bragged about my good grades. At the end of each of her letters, she wrote, "Your father sends his love." I don't think she ever knew that on the first of every month until he died, I received a Hallmark card from my father. Inside it read, *I miss you Princess, love, Papa.* And inside there was always a crisp five-dollar bill.

Lucie also wrote to me, though not every day. I could imagine Sadie sitting her down at the kitchen table Sunday evenings. Sadie addressed the envelopes, and at first gave Lucie stationary with lines across the page. I recognized the paper from my own early forays at penmanship.

Dear Mam'selle,

I hope the Navy is fun. I like my school. My new friend is named Monica.

Love, Lucie

I wrote to her every week as well. I have decades worth of correspondence from my mother and Lucie in an inlaid box I bought in Paris. Precious beyond words.

There was one thing that I couldn't talk to anyone about. I got a mail-order book that I had heard about in my Abnormal Psychology class—*The Well of Loneliness*, by an English woman named Radclyffe Hall. It's a story about a girl ambulance driver in WWI, oddly enough, named Stephen. She falls in love with another girl named Mary. It's not a happy book—I guess the title gives that away. Stephen has terrible thoughts about herself. I imagined there would be some sex in the book, but the furthest the author goes is to say, "and that night they were not divided." Hmm. The copyright was dated 1928. I imagined that even getting a book like that in print must have been quite a feat back then. It didn't answer any of my questions. I hid it under my mattress. I sometimes wondered if Edna might have a copy of *The Well of Loneliness* hidden under her mattress, too? But of course we never talked about such things.

CHAPTER 27

DR. NICK'S BEARD

Alameda Naval Base, California, November 1943

Early in my studies, I caught the eye of one of my favorite professors, Dr. Nicos Ariti, whom everyone called Dr. Nick. He was tall and slender, only a few years older than me, with a shock of black hair and an olive complexion. He was a terrible flirt, and all the girls were crazy about him. I took his Advanced OB-GYN class for a semester. I think the quality of my questions impressed him, thanks to my work with Dr. Levy. Nick surprised me by asking the powers-that-be to have me assist him in his Women's Care Clinic.

Because the school adjoined a naval base, our women's clinic cared for the wives of officers and sailors, and the nurses themselves. Dr. Nick navigated the red tape and also set up a twice-a-week free clinic for indigent women—most of them seasonal farmworkers from Mexico who worked the cotton fields and almond groves a few hours away. They came to us by bus, some of them travelling half the day. There was nowhere else for them to get care. We did routine Pap smears, colposcopies, breast exams, prenatal care, and occasionally a delivery for the sailors' wives and our nurses. But many of our Mexican patients had never seen a doctor before. They came with fistulas, breast tumors, complicated pregnancies, ovarian cysts, and social diseases. They came only as a last resort, because they couldn't afford to lose time in the fields or orchards. None of the nursing students spoke Spanish, so I fumbled along with my French. Our best interpreters were the women's children who attended school sporadically in the off-season and spoke some English. They reminded me of little bilingual Lucie helping when my college French failed me.

Most of the migrants had more problems than it was possible to address. The first day we opened the clinic we had a long line. They jammed our waiting room. The first woman I escorted into an examining room wore a bandage. When I asked her about her arm, she said, "No more babies," in a way that seemed carefully rehearsed. I heard that exact phrase repeated at least half a dozen times that day, and more during the following clinic sessions. I didn't know who taught them how to say it, but it was always said with great urgency. We did what little we could with condoms and diaphragm fittings. In my halting Spanish, I asked, "Cuándo fue su última regla?—When was your last period?" But it was not enough. I didn't know if they were aware of the most rudimentary approaches to preventing pregnancy.

Dr. Nick requisitioned a Spanish-English dictionary and that helped a lot. Many of our patients came from Mexico as "invitees" through the Bracero program that started during WWI. Our government invited Mexican farm-workers into the country because there weren't enough American men to work the crops in Texas and California during the war. These patients were bitingly poor, and from what I could tell, worked for almost nothing. Yet they were proud and had a hard time asking for help.

Dr. Nick and I became comfortable with each other. There is a special working shorthand that doctors and nurses sometimes develop. Dr. Levy and I had it, and until Dr. Nick, I had missed it. It is a camaraderie that can only happen when there is equality. I think that is why it is so rare.

My roommates teased me that Nick gave me special treatment, so when he asked me to have dinner with him I was nervous. I didn't want to say no, although I felt some trepidation. As I was getting ready, my three pals gave me a terrible time about going on a "date" with Dr. Nick.

"It's not a date!" I protested.

"You know he likes you," Sally said coyly.

"He does not *like,* like me. We are just friends," I protested again.

But I did put on my nicest dress—or rather Edna's nicest dress—and I allowed Sally and Clarice to fuss with my hair and apply a little makeup. Nick picked me up at the dorm. I felt apprehensive, although I can't say exactly why. Surprisingly, Dr. Nick also seemed nervous. He stayed cool and calm through every emergency—something we had appreciated about each other. Yet this evening, he stammered as he said hello and told me how pretty I looked.

On the drive to the restaurant he was uncharacteristically quiet. A few times I tried to talk, but he just grunted a non-reply. I gave up trying to engage him. It was as though I was a teenager at one of those awful mixers my mother always made me go to. We finally arrived and parked. Dr. Nick came around to open the door for me.

He had chosen a French restaurant. It was elegant, with low lights and white tablecloths. The tuxedoed host seated us and gave us menus. When our waiter asked if we were ready to order, just hearing his accent made me home-sick for Paris. I resisted the urge to show off, and anglicized the pronunciation of one of my favorites, Boeuf Bourguignon. I hoped it would taste even a bit like the magical dish served up by Danielle's skilled hands. Dr. Nick ordered Coquilles St. Jacques, which I considered a bold choice, and a bottle of very expensive and prized Bordeaux. The waiter left bread and fancy unsweetened butter on the table.

"Dr. Nick, how can they still get French wine?"

"The Bordeaux wines seem to have been spared the ravages of the Occupation. They are smuggled into the country—not unlike people, I imagine. But dinner isn't worth a damn without wine, is it?" he answered, smiling.

I blushed at the mention of smuggling people into the country, but it was impossible that he knew anything about my Paris exploits. Nick buttered a piece of the crispy baguette. The unpleasant Brigitte had always said, "The French don't butter their bread," in such a condescending tone that I smiled as I slathered butter on mine. The waiter poured some wine into Nick's glass and waited, his white towel over his arm.

I gave him a little nudge. "He wants you to taste it."

Nick shook his head. "Of course. Of course. Sorry." He took a sip of wine and nodded. The waiter filled our glasses and then backed away in the best French-waiter style. I took a small sip. I hadn't had wine since coming back to the States. The flavor rocketed me back to my first year in France. I closed my eyes and experienced the unmistakable sounds and smells of Paris: the clop-clop of horses' hooves, the whistle of the gendarmes, the coo of pigeons, the smell of baguettes fresh from the boulangerie, and the tangy scent of piss ever-present on the sidewalks.

This time, Dr. Nick broke my reverie.

"Janie," he began… he was the only person I ever allowed to call me Janie. "There's something I want to ask you."

He sounded so serious.

"Are you interested in having a boyfriend?"

I flushed. "We're so busy with classes and the clinic, it really hadn't crossed my mind."

"You are swell. You are smart, and nice, and adventurous…"

I realized my friends were right. I should have listened to them when they warned me that this was going to happen. I interrupted him.

"Nick, please don't. I'm sorry I didn't tell you already, but it seemed so presumptuous. I like you very much—but I don't have those kinds of feelings for you—romantic feelings." The night on the ship with Levy flashed before my eyes. "I haven't ever had those kinds of feelings for any man."

Dr. Nick stared at me and then burst out laughing. I must have looked as insulted as I felt because he stopped laughing and put his hand on mine.

"Oh, Janie, I am so sorry. I am not laughing at you. It's just… I really trust you."

Now I'm sure I just looked bewildered.

"I trust you, too," I said. And I did, although my trust was being tested by this strange conversation.

"It's just that not everyone could handle what I want to tell you. And I have a huge favor to ask."

"My God, Nick! Now you are scaring me. Please don't tell me you are a spy!"

"No. Nothing like that." He took a deep breath. "But far from revealing romantic feelings for you, I need to tell you that I bat for the other team."

By now, I must have looked more than bewildered. "I have no idea what you are talking about. You men and your obtuse sports references!"

"I am a friend of Dorothy."

"Is that one of the nurses?"

He sighed. "I sing in a different choir?"

I shook my head, still not understanding.

"I am not romantically inclined toward women," he said at last.

The clouds in my brain parted, and the light shined through. Dr. Nick flirting with all the girls but never asking any of them out—how comfortable it was to be with a man who wasn't always on the prowl. It suddenly made sense.

"Do you think me a fiend?" he asked.

Now it was my turn to laugh.

"Of course not! You are splendid," I answered with a broad smile. "I don't mind at all. But I understand now why you were so afraid to tell me. I'm guessing it is not at all fine with the Navy."

"That's right. Not at all. They would drum me out if they knew. There isn't anyone else I trust enough with this." He sighed. "I have been wanting to tell you for a long time. You can't imagine what a relief this is."

I smiled and put my hand on his arm. He was tearing up.

"So now you have told me, and I am fine with it. But what is the favor you wanted to ask?"

At that moment, they served our salads, so we stopped talking until the waiter finished brandishing the pepper mill. Nick nodded a thank you to dismiss him. Then he began a story.

"I realized what I am when my parents sent me to boarding school in England."

I interrupted, "Ah, that explains the accent I sometimes hear."

"Right. And it explains other things that I won't go into. Anyway, there are a lot of boy crushes in that kind of school. Most of the fellows get over that phase and move on to marry lovely young ladies, making their parents proud. I was sure that would not be my future. In my junior year, there was an incident, as they called it. One chap broke up with another boy and then bullied him relentlessly. The others called him a pansy, even though most of them had already had their secret love affairs. I kept my distance from him as if the shame were contagious. Just before the end of the year, he hanged himself in the school library."

"Oh my goodness, Nick. How awful!" I interjected.

"It *was* awful. I had a breakdown and went into a hospital for several months. It turned out to be the best thing that ever happened to me. There was another fellow there who had the same affliction. He told me about the Greeks and other cultures that honored love between men. And he taught me how to hide in plain sight. I got out of there much stronger. I finished high school and college with no trouble. After graduation, I started medical school. There I found a woman who could be my friend, confidant, and also my protector. Are you familiar with the term 'beard?'"

I felt very naïve. "No…"

"It is a woman who protects a homosexual man from scrutiny by pretending to be his girl. That's what Katherine did. You remind me of her. She was one of the few women accepted into my medical school class—and twice as smart as I'll ever be. Kitty agreed to be not just my friend, but my girlfriend, and later, my fiancée. She accompanied me to all the dinners and social events that were expected, and no one questioned my normality."

"What a wonderful arrangement. Where is she now?"

"In the spring of 1939, she traveled to Poland to help her family get out. I have never heard from her again."

"Oh, Nick. I am so sorry."

"I miss her every day. Ironically, her loss gave me cover for a time—you know, 'Poor old Nick—he lost his girl.' But once I got to this naval base, people started asking why I wasn't married. The old 'I am a confirmed bachelor' line doesn't seem to hold much sway. Lately, a few of the officers' wives who are friends of my parents have been trying to fix me up on blind dates. And then there is the swarm of nurses. I think my air of unavailability attracts them."

"Nick, they are attracted to you because you are attractive!"

He shrugged that off. "Anyway, perhaps you can see where I am going with this. Would you consider helping me that way? Being my lavender date?"

I smiled. "It is my honor. But I will not wear lavender!"

We laughed. And with that, our entrees arrived. My first forkful assured me that the Boeuf Bourguignon was everything I dreamed of. We had a delight that was new to me—flaming Crêpes Suzette for dessert. We talked about our patients, our hopes for the clinic, our drive to help people who had so few resources, and our need to find a translator.

I enjoyed the evening, but as we drove home, I realized Nick had told me one more thing I could never tell another soul. I had always prided myself on being scrupulously honest, and here I was with one more secret to add to my already formidable list:

- Illegal abortions in Paris
- Smuggling girls out of Paris
- German soldiers in the alley
- Documents stolen and forged
- Smuggling Lucie into the United States
- Smuggling Levy into the United States
- My confusing feelings about Betty
- The *Well of Loneliness* hidden under my mattress

And now this.

Yet, as I sensed the weight on my heart, I recognized that most of them had been choices of conscience. I smiled as I pulled my wrap around me and listened to the purr of Dr. Nick's sports car.

With secrets come lies. It hadn't occurred to me that agreeing to Dr. Nick's request included creating a charade for the nurses, including my roommates. They were waiting up for me.

"We told you he's sweet on you, '*Janie*,'" Edna said smugly.

"Where did he take you for dinner?" Clarice demanded.

When I told them, Eddie made pretend groaning sounds and grabbed her stomach. "I have heard about that restaurant, but I never imagined I would know anyone who ate there. Can I touch you?" She laughed so hard at her own joke that she nearly fell off the couch.

"It's not that funny, Eddie. It is just a restaurant. And yes, you did all tell me, and I am sure he likes me because of the way you did my hair, Clarice. And before you even ask, no, there wasn't any hanky-panky. Despite his constant flirting, Dr. Nick is a perfect gentleman. Now can we talk about that horrible Organic Chemistry test?"

That put an end to the "Nick and Janie" discussion, but only for the moment. Nick did a good job of acting friendly with all the nurses, while being especially solicitous of me. He had experience walking that fine line. We spent a lot of time together, both during and after work. My roommates sometimes said they missed me, but, of course, they understood that age-old reality of women abandoning friends when they fall in love.

CHAPTER 28

I ALREADY HAVE

Alameda, California, December 1943

With the pressure of our work, I hardly noticed Christmas come and go. The Navy didn't provide holiday leave, so my family and friends had to make do with Christmas cards. Only Lucie got a gift for Hanukkah. Sadie suggested *A Tree Grows in Brooklyn*, by Betty Smith. She had a copy mailed to me as well. Lucie and I both loved it. Lucie sent a thank-you letter.

Dear Mam'selle,

You sent the perfect book! Francie is eleven—almost my exact same age. We both love the library and read all the time. Mama Sadie lets me take almost any book I want out of the grown-up section.

I am not finished reading the book yet and I am afraid the ending will be sad. Francie's family is so poor that they sometimes pretend they are all right when there isn't any food. The grown-ups tell us every day that there are children in Europe who are hungry. Thank you for rescuing me.

I love you as much as infinity. We just learned about that.

XOXO, Lucie

I loved that child more than I can ever say, and I missed her with all my heart.

I had become friends with one of the janitors named Felix. When I mentioned we needed a Spanish translator, he told me his wife would love to work with us. Marisol became our translator and much more. Her sunny disposition brightened up the clinic. She came in every day with what she called "words to live by." I don't know the source of her wisdom, but we all learned a lot from her. One very hard day, she came up to me and said, "Nurse Jane, you look so sad. 'Al mal tiempo, buena cara.'"

Of course, I gave her a blank look. She translated, "A bad time needs a good face," which made me smile.

One of her favorites that we all learned was "No hay mal que cien años dure"—"There is no evil that can last one hundred years." We repeated it like a charm, as if it might bring an end to the war. Our patients and their children loved her, and I regularly thanked myself for becoming friends with Felix.

One day, Marisol came into the staff room looking upset. Nick and I were just finishing lunch.

"I need to take a break," she said with a sigh. "I was just working with that woman who came in from Berkeley."

"The one with the bruises?" I had seen her in the waiting area with three small children.

"Yes. Her name is Lana. She started telling me about all the times she had fallen, and her oldest boy said, 'You did not fall down. Papa hit you,' and we continued the discussion from there. Her husband works on the docks. He gets drunk on payday, then comes home and hurts her. She has no friends or family here—no one to protect her. She doesn't speak English, she has nowhere to go. And she is pregnant again."

"Oh, no."

"She beat around the bush until she finally asked where to get an abortion. I told her it was illegal, and I didn't know of any place. It's a shame," she said, pouring a cup of coffee. "I wish I didn't know how hard her life is, since I can't do anything to help her. 'Ojos que no ven, corazon que no llora'—If I didn't know about it, I wouldn't cry about it."

She finished her coffee and returned to work.

At first I didn't say anything, but then I ventured to Nick, "It really is terrible that a woman like that has to be forced to deliver another baby. Terrible for the woman and terrible for the baby. I wish they had another choice."

Nick looked at me steadily. "I agree. Would you ever want to work in a place that provided abortions?"

I thought about how much I trusted Nick and whether to take a risk. I looked him right in the eye and answered, "I already have." I proceeded to tell him about my work with Levy in Paris. His eyes widened as I described providing illegal abortion care in the midst of the Occupation.

"We were already outlaws in so many other ways that adding one more thing didn't seem to matter—especially when it was so important. They would have executed us if they had found us out. Just last year, the Vichy Government guillotined a woman for doing abortions. But we were breaking other laws, so what was the difference? It was the most important work of my life. It's what inspired me to come to nursing school."

"That explains why you know so much about gynecology," he said. "I always wondered. But Janie, would you ever think it was worth the risk to do abortions here—for these women? It has haunted me that we give them condoms that we suspect their husbands will refuse, and then there is nothing more for them. When I think of my oath to 'do no harm,' I am ashamed."

"Is that something you want to do?"

"Yes. I believe it is wrong to force women to have babies they don't want and can't take care of. When I was in medical school, I worked at a clinic in a very poor neighborhood. The husbands wouldn't take no for an answer and the wives had one baby after another until they were worn through," he said. "It would mean a lot to me to provide abortion care, but I'd need help."

"I would like to be able to help these women, too. But how could we do it under the nose of the Navy?"

"You would be surprised what is possible if you have the right connections," Nick answered, smiling. "Or rather, if you know the right people's secrets. Like your doctor in France, I am already out on a precarious limb, so why not do the right thing?"

And so it happened that Dr. Nick got a grant for a special study on "menstrual irregularity." We moved into a small clinic separated from the rest of the base and began to provide care two days a week for women who were "missing their periods." We provided abortion care, as I had said, "right under the nose of the Navy." I fit my classwork around the clinic, which became the center of my attention.

I didn't intend to involve Marisol in our new endeavors. I assumed she was Catholic, as most of our Spanish-speaking patients were, and I didn't want to put her in an uncomfortable position—or worse, create a situation in which she felt the need to inform the higher-ups. But one day Nick and I were in the main clinic talking about a patient, and she overheard us as she came into the break room. I mumbled something about a woman who was in the hospital, or some such nonsense. Dr. Nick just stood there looking stricken. Regardless of his claim of impunity, his entire career—mine too, when I think of it—as well as our freedom from criminal charges—rested on keeping the work a secret. Yet, here was Marisol. We both liked her very much, but we suspected the idea of doing abortions would horrify her.

She stopped as she came into the room, quite aware that she had interrupted what we meant to be a confidential conversation.

"Lo siento, I am so sorry," she said, as she backed out of the room.

"Wait, Marisol. Are you aware of what we were talking about?"

"Of course," she said. "I see that you don't want me here, so I will never speak of it. But I am glad you are doing it."

"You are? Would you want to help us?" I asked.

"More than anything," Marisol replied. "My sister died of an abortion that was not done properly. She was nineteen. I was just eight years old when it happened. I only learned about it through what I overheard. I didn't understand it then, but I understand now. I would do this work in her honor and memory. I know that abortion is about love."

"Well, I am not sure about that. I think it is more about survival."

"You are young. You'll see. But if you let me do this work with you, I won't tell Felix about it." She smiled. "Remember? 'Ojos que no ven, corazon que no llora.' A woman doesn't have to tell her husband every little thing."

CHAPTER 29

GOODBYE PAPA

Connecticut, December 1943

In December, my mother called with impossible news. My father had died of a heart attack. The Navy gave me three days of compassionate leave. Not much compassion when it took a full day to get home and a full day to get back.

Over the phone Mother assured me that she was all right. She said Papa, true to form, had left a draft of an obituary, detailed plans for his funeral, and an account book. I was relieved to know that she wouldn't need to worry about money.

Levy picked me up at the airport in New York late Monday night. Even though I wore two sweaters and my warmest coat, I was freezing. It had snowed the day before and although the Merritt Parkway was plowed, the trees were covered in snow and looked like lacey valentines.

The grinding engine of a garbage truck woke me at 6 a.m. I was groggy, but I knew my mother would already be up, so I found an old plaid robe and fuzzy slippers in the closet, splashed cold water on my face, and joined her for coffee. We sat at the kitchen table leaning against each other. When the pale winter sun finally rose, the birds woke and chickadees and juncos came to her feeders. We didn't need to speak.

The service was all Dad. The pastor was his friend, and spoke of my father with real fondness. I read a passage of a book my father read to me when I was a child, *The Velveteen Rabbit*, by Margery Williams.

"'Real isn't how you are made,' said the Skin Horse. 'It's a thing that happens to you. When a child loves you for a long, long time, not just to play with, but *really* loves you, then you become Real.'

'Does it hurt?' asked the Rabbit.

'Sometimes,' said the Skin Horse, for he was always truthful. 'When you are Real you don't mind being hurt.'

'Does it happen all at once, like being wound up,' he asked, 'or bit by bit?'

'It doesn't happen all at once,' said the Skin Horse. 'You become. It takes a long time. That's why it doesn't happen often to
people who break easily, or have sharp edges, or who have to be
carefully kept. Generally, by the time you are Real, most of your
hair has been loved off, and your eyes drop out and you get loose in
the joints and very shabby. But these things don't matter at all, because once you are Real you can't be ugly, except to people who
don't understand.'"

My papa was real.

After the service, a line of people we didn't know formed to tell us how
my father touched their lives. Through countless small bank loans, he helped
them buy a house, pay for their grandmother's medical bills, and go to school.
He made a difference to our little town that I never realized. He was conse-
quential.

Then Levy, the Goldfarbs, and Lucie encircled me and mom with hugs
and kisses. Lucie was so tall! Eleven and a half. Hard to believe. Good friends
came back to the house to eat the tiny sandwiches that Mom and I had made.
We cut the crusts off and quartered them into triangles so they would look
fancy. I made a huge pitcher of fresh lemonade.

It was my only chance to visit with Lucie. Letters are no substitute. She
came into the kitchen to help me refill the tray of sandwiches. I just wanted
to hold her in my arms. But I didn't want to scare her.

"Mam'selle, I am so sad your papa died. I loved him. Did you know he
used to blow smoke from his pipe into my ears?"

"He used to do that to me, too." I closed my eyes and summoned the smell
of that pipe. Rose, jasmine, clove, balsam—smoke and leather. I remembered
his gruff outside and his tender insides. "Thank you, chérie."

"No one calls me that anymore."

I didn't know how to bridge the miles and the years. How to know her
and make sure she knew me. We shared a bit about the details of our lives. I
left out more than I included. When Lucie said goodbye at the end of the day,
it was almost worse to be so close and feel so far away.

CHAPTER 30

SO MUCH SHAME

Alameda, 1944

Back at work in California, my visit home seemed like a dream. I smiled at letters from Lucie. I still imagined my father at his desk, smoking his pipe. I worried about my mother, although I trusted Levy to look after her. As I had done so many times, and seen so many other people do during the war, I stashed my grief away under busyness—under my work—and hoped it would stay undercover.

After a long clinic day, Sally, Eddie, and I got back to our dorm to find Clarice curled up on the couch, weeping.

"What's going on?" I mouthed. Edna shrugged. Sally sat down next to Clarice and took her in her arms.

"Shh—shh—what is it, child?" she asked.

Clarice couldn't stop crying long enough to answer. I got some Kleenex and helped her blow her nose. She shook her head.

"I'm sorry. I had a hard day," she said.

Edna knelt down on the floor. "Clary, whatever it is, you can tell us."

Clarice took a deep breath, looked at each of us, and sighed.

"A girl I took care of came to the clinic today for her postpartum check. She was a mess." She was overwhelmed with tears again, and we sat quietly while Sally held her hand.

"Did something go wrong with her delivery?" I asked.

"No. Her parents forced her to give the baby up for adoption."

"Oh, I'm so sorry—poor lamb," Sally said. "I'm sure you helped her."

"I didn't help her at all!" Clarice cried. "As soon as I heard what happened to her, I ran out of the examining room. Lorna had to fill in for me, and I didn't even explain why I had to leave the clinic. I… I just couldn't stay in that room."

"Why not, honey?" Sally asked.

Clarice began again. "Because it reminded me of a secret—something I wanted to forget." She sat up straight and moved out of Sally's arms, then closed her eyes and put her head in her hands. "I can't even look at you. Can you just listen to this and not say anything?"

We murmured yes.

"When I was eighteen, I fell in love with a sweet boy. I didn't know thing one about my body. My monthlies were never regular, so I wasn't worried when they stopped. I had no idea what was happening to me—or maybe I knew but didn't want it to be true. It was summer, and Cody left to work on his cousin's ranch for a few weeks, so I had no one to talk to. My mother kept harping on me to go swimming with my friends like I usually did, but I made one excuse after another. One morning, she came into my room while I was getting dressed, and she saw... she saw what I could no longer deny. She threw a blue fit, yelling and screaming that no daughter of hers would disgrace the family with a bastard child."

"Oh Clary, how awful!" Edna said.

"Thank goodness Cody left town, because when my daddy learned about it, he got out his rifle. Before Cody even got back, they shipped me off to a home for unmarried girls. I had the baby on September the first. They wouldn't let me look at her or hold her, but they told me it was a girl. They said I was doing the right thing, giving her to a good Christian home."

"And you have never told anyone about it?" I asked. I knew how heavily secrets could weigh on you.

"How could I? My parents made sure I understood how much shame I had brought on our family. I never saw Cody again and got out of Texas as fast as I could. It was unbearable to think that I could be walking down the street one day and my daughter might be right next to me. I would never know if she was happy—or safe. What must y'all think of me? How could any woman do that—give her baby away?"

Edna hung her head. "*I'm* not judging you," she whispered. She sighed. "I guess I am even worse. I got pregnant at twenty-two—old enough to know better."

"Eddie, you don't need to..." Sally said.

"I want to. It's time I told someone. I was going to a Catholic college far away from home, and I was so lonely. I didn't even know the name of the man I slept with. It was obvious pretty quickly that I was pregnant, but I did not know what to do. If my school found out, they would have expelled me for bad morals. I was the first person in my family to go beyond high school, and I just couldn't humiliate them by coming home with a baby who had no father. I asked everyone for help. Of course, it wasn't legal, but I finally got the name of someone who was supposed to be a real doctor. The address was in a poor neighborhood. I was the only white person in his waiting room." She looked at Sally apologetically. "He was very nice and professional. He wore a white coat and all. His office smelled like Mercurochrome. He asked me about my period, did a quick exam, and said that I still had two weeks before I was too far gone for him to do it—and that it would be six hundred dollars.

"Six hundred dollars! He might as well have said six million. I had twenty bucks in my Christmas Club account, and an old beat-up car that got me to school. I sold that for one hundred and fifty dollars. And that was all I had—no friends or family who could lend me money. One day I was crying in the ladies' room, and a classmate persuaded me to tell her what was wrong. She said, 'Leave it to me, We'll have a rent party.'"

Edna looked at us. "You've heard of rent parties, right?"

"Sure. Friends pitch in when someone can't come up with the money they need to stay in their apartment," I said.

"Right. I had been to rent parties before, but my situation made me wonder if some of those parties had paid for the woman's life, not just her rent. My friend handled everything because I was pretty much in shock. We had the party at her apartment. Everyone brought something to eat, some booze, and a contribution. Over one hundred kids came in and out that night. We collected more than eight hundred dollars! She insisted I keep the extra to get another car so that I could finish school."

Edna continued. "The doctor had told me the rules of abortion. You had to go at night; you had to go alone; and you had to pay in cash. For the two days before the appointment, I sat in my apartment terrified—certain someone was going to break in and steal the envelope of money I had hidden under the ice cube tray in the freezer.

"The day finally came, and I followed all the directions. I don't remember any of it, except that when he had finished, the doctor said, 'Now you can go back to normal.' Normal? My life never really went back to normal. I did the best thing, and I thank God there was a doctor, but I never have felt quite… quite clean, maybe? Not quite good? I heard a man say one time, 'You play, you pay,' and that has stuck with me. I guess I am still paying."

She turned to Clarice. "I understand why you think we would judge you. I'm thinking you're judging me, too. At least you were in love. I didn't even know the guy. Doesn't that make it worse?"

Clarice shook her head.

I started to speak, but Sally stood up and gave a bitter laugh. She paced around the room as she talked. She said, "Girls, it appears that we are some birds of a feather here. I was only thirteen. I loved my Uncle Jack—Mama's brother. But they didn't get along. Mama wouldn't let him come over, but she would never say why. When my brothers and I stayed with my grandparents, Uncle Jack used to bring candy and play games with us. One time when my mother was at work, he came to our house. He wasn't supposed to be there, but he was a grown-up, so what could I do? That day, he wanted to play a new game.

"Mama blew a gasket when I got up the nerve to tell her. She said he had done that same thing to her. Daddy nearly beat him to death, and told everyone what he did to me. They drummed my uncle out of the neighborhood. But just that one time was all it took.

"Mama took me to a neighbor woman who gave me something sour to drink and put something up inside me. After a few days, I had terrible cramps and there was blood and a soft slimy thing came out of me that looked like a pippin—you know, a baby chick in the egg that didn't hatch? Mama never mentioned it again. Until now I haven't thought about it more than once or twice. It is almost like a story that happened to someone else."

"Oh, Sally," I said.

Clarice started crying again. "I don't know whether I am crying for myself or for all of us," she said, laughing through her tears. "You make me brave enough to tell the truth. There's another thing I never told anyone. *Anyone!* I think about that baby once in a while, but not every day. That is a lie I tell myself so that I seem like a better person. But I didn't want to be a mother. I never wanted any of it to happen. All those months, I prayed every day for a miscarriage. Then I prayed to the Blessed Virgin to forgive me for not wanting her. When they took the baby away, it broke my heart, *and* I felt relieved. Like I said, I regret the whole thing, but I don't regret that I wasn't a mother at eighteen."

Edna put her arm around Clarice. "That's just what I thought. I didn't want to have a baby. I thought that made me an unnatural woman."

Sally stood at the end of the sofa. "Are we a fallen group, or do you think there are other girls—other women—with stories like these?" She slumped down on the couch like a deflated balloon. After a moment of silence, they all looked at me.

"Jane, are you disgusted with us?" Sally asked.

My face was hot, and I was crying, too. Were the tears for these friends I loved so much? For Françoise and Mimi and all the other women whose stories I carried in my heart? For myself? Sally's story of rape at such a young age by someone she trusted almost made me sick. For all my talk about working through shame, I was silenced by my own. A part of me that had never grown up had learned to keep secrets. But I saw the fear on their faces, so I took a deep breath.

I pulled my friends into a tight circle and told as much as I could. "Girls, you are not alone. I'm not disgusted. I am amazed at your courage. There are many good women who have stories like yours," I began. "Let me tell you about Paris in 1939."

I told them about Levy, and Françoise, and some of the women we helped. I didn't tell them about Mimi. I'm not sure why, but I didn't tell them about wearing the habit or Our Lady. I wanted to tell them about those soldiers in Paris, but my shame wouldn't let me. I wanted to run away. And I didn't tell them... well, I didn't tell them everything. They had been so vulnerable and so courageous, but my grandmother's fierce warning still haunted me. Her words, "No one wants to hear about the dirty parts. There are some things you don't talk about," swirled around in my brain.

But I *did* talk with my friends about forgiveness. I told them they were being awfully hard on themselves for doing what they had to do to survive—for making the best choices they could. I was adept at giving advice I could not take myself. We spent the rest of the evening together, eating dinner and being kind to each other. Finally, I decided to tell them about doing abortions with Dr. Nick.

"That's great, Jane!" Sally said. If you ever need another hand, I would love to help."

Clarice was quiet.

"Do you disapprove, Clary?" I asked her.

"No, no, not at all. I am trying to imagine if I had known you then—if I had been able to do that."

Edna touched her shoulder. "Hey, don't get stuck in 'what ifs.' That won't get you anywhere. We all just get to live our lives the best we can every day."

I smiled. "You know, that's what my little students in Paris figured out. We decided the stories I told them should end with 'They had their good days and their bad days and they took care of their problems the best they knew how.'"

Edna laughed. "I'm going to remember that."

Sally sat back on the sofa. "These stories are so sad," she said. "So much shame."

"The world is sad," I added with a sigh. "And I hope giving women a way out of one of their problems makes it just a little bit less sad, and a bit less shameful."

"Jane, I agree it's great you and Dr. Nick are doing that," Edna said. "It's not the work I want to do—I just love Obstetrics—but I'm so glad there is a safe place for women who need help. And..."

Clarice butted in. "But aren't you scared? Couldn't Dr. Nick lose his license and you both get court-martialed and put in the brig?"

"I worried about that, too. But Nick says he has enough connections to protect us." I trusted Nick, and I didn't like to picture the consequences to us both if anyone found out. The ghost of the guillotined Marie-Danielle Giraud had joined the ghost of poor Mimi in my nightmares from time to time. But I shook my head and said, "So far, so good."

Sally nodded her head. "Well, God knows we need all the help we can get."

And with that, we gave each other hugs and went to bed.

August brought the wonderful news of the end of the occupation of France. I could almost hear the bells of Notre Dame ringing again. My beautiful city would come out of its wartime wrapping. Then Lucie sent word of her planned bat mitzvah. My gift to her was a silver Star of David necklace that Sadie bought on my behalf. Once again, I was an ersatz presence in Lucie's life.

August 14th, 1944

Dear Mam'selle,

I love, love, love my necklace, I wear it every day. Thank you. I wish you were there. I remembered all the Hebrew prayers and stood up with the Torah in front of everyone. It means that I am grown now. I am a daughter of the Commandment. That's what bat mitzvah means. I am in charge of myself. I think you would have been proud of me. Here are two pictures that Papa Hymie took.

XXXOOO,
Lucie

P.S. Should I call you Jane now that I am grown?

I laughed to myself. Ah, yes, my dear. Grown at twelve. I wrote her back that we'd continue with Mam'selle until she was at least sixteen. I slid the pictures out of the envelope. It wasn't even a year after I saw her at my father's funeral, and she was taller than I remembered. In the second photo, she was standing next to the beaming Goldfarbs, with my beaming mother and a beaming Dr. Levy on the other side. At least I had done something right—I had bequeathed Lucie a family.

Most of the abortions we did that fall went smoothly. We brought Sally onto the clinic staff right away, and she was great. It was a lot easier to work with Dr. Nick now that I didn't have to worry about sneaking around behind my roommates' backs. I still insisted upon talking with the women and explaining the procedure, as Levy had taught me. I explained, and Marisol translated. Because of our "special clinic" status, we helped our patients with no fee. By the time they lay on the examining table breathing nitrous oxide— also known as laughing gas—they felt calm.

The gas was one of Nick's brilliant ideas, inspired by an old roommate who trained as a dentist. The whole D&C only took ten or fifteen minutes. After their abortions, we gave them cookies and juice in our recovery room, and they chatted with each other. We tried to get them to return in a few weeks for a check-up, but since we realized that was impossible for most of them who had to work, we gave every woman a little packet of penicillin, and instructions in Spanish on what to do if she had cramps. Each woman we cared for also left with the admonition to keep our secret, except when they encountered a woman who needed us. It was dangerous, but they risked a lot to come to us. They trusted us. We trusted them.

Marisol and I got into the habit of eating our lunches together. She'd share her posole, I'd share my tuna salad. I told her how afraid I had been that she would be against abortion. Another lesson in not assuming anything.

"Marisol, can I tell you what I have noticed?"

"What chica?"

"At the core of every woman's story is the same thing. It's love, just like you told me. The love and loyalty a woman feels for the children she already has—the love that keeps a woman from bringing a new life into the world when she can't care for it—even the love a woman has for herself that pushes her to be honest with herself and to follow her own conscience and her own knowing. I am thinking of writing a training manual called *Abortion Counseling and Other Love Stories.*"

Marisol smiled that special Marisol smile. "I knew one day you would see it."

CHAPTER 31

I'M GLAD YOU DIDN'T

Alameda, January-April 1945

One afternoon, I filled a large tub with water, and found it too heavy to carry. Nick walked into the room and watched me use a siphon to empty some of the water into a pail.

"Janie, you are a genius!" he exclaimed. "A siphon. How simple." He twirled me around like a square dancer. I had no idea what he meant.

"Don't you see?" he exclaimed.

I didn't see.

"THAT is the way to do an abortion!"

The rest of that year, we experimented with his brainchild. We began in the laboratory, searching for ways to make a siphon safe enough and strong enough to empty a uterus. By May, he'd created a prototype. We planned to use nitrous oxide gas and the usual local anesthetic for comfort, even though the abortion procedure would be much quicker than with the traditional D&C. When we knew the device was safe, we needed to find the right patient.

On April 15th, 1945, we used what we named the Uterine Siphon Apparatus—nicknamed U.S.A.—for the first time. Our patient, Mary, was 22 years old and early in her pregnancy. She had an abortion with us once before so she trusted us. She felt embarrassed that she needed another abortion, but was also matter-of-fact that it was the only reasonable choice. We asked her permission to use the uterine aspirator, and explained the difference in the procedure. Her abortion went smoothly, and when I removed the nitrous oxide mask, she grinned up at me.

"Amazing!" she exclaimed. "It took longer for me to get pregnant than to get unpregnant!"

In an unanticipated consequence of our new method, Nick insisted I could do an abortion as well as he could. I wanted to believe him, but I was afraid. The memory of Mimi's terrible death hovered over me. But Nick persisted.

His confidence was so inspiring that I learned to do the simple and quick abortion procedure.

After I performed my first abortion, I sat in the staff room by myself and breathed. Hard to believe I had become the elusive clinician women needed. I cared for six women that day. Having another abortionist gave us a lot more flexibility, and I felt proud of my new skill. We traded off because I still wanted to counsel, and I had to keep up with my classwork.

I took deep breaths when the patients experienced cramping and wondered how the sensitive Dr. Levy handled the experience of hurting the women he was saving. I decided to write to him. I thanked him for being such a wonderful teacher in Paris and proceeded to tell him about the siphon procedure Nick invented and that I was doing abortions myself, but that I did not plan to share any of this with my mother. I didn't expect to hear back. He was not much of a correspondent, but I knew he would understand.

We were supported by a wonderful staff, but I was still glad to have Dr. Nick around in case of emergencies. As I got more experience, I thought I could handle almost anything. Almost.

It was a routine Wednesday afternoon in the clinic. We had seen six women for abortion procedures—three of them still sat chatting in our recovery room. Sally attended to them as I prepared to see the last patient of the day. Dr. Nick was in his office, catching up on paperwork.

Alicia was 38 years old. She didn't speak English, so Marisol translated. She was calm, and clear about her decision, about eleven weeks from her last period. Our limit was twelve weeks, which kept our cases simple and safe. She reported spotting, but that wasn't unusual. Sometimes it meant an imminent miscarriage, but not nearly as often as our patients hoped.

I did her pelvic examination twice, because I found her uterus smaller than I expected. The blood on my glove was a combination of very dark, almost black, and very, very bright red. Through Marisol, I instructed Alicia to change into a gown and left the room to pop my head into the office, though I hated to bother Dr. Nick with every little thing.

"Hey, Janie. Can it wait? I have to get these biopsy reports signed."

"Sorry. It's just... I'm seeing something unusual." I explained about the pelvic exam results and the dark and light blood, but before I finished, Nick sprang out of his chair and pushed past me.

"Move. She's going to the hospital now. What room? Get the wheelchair. What's her name?"

"Her name is Alicia. Room 2. She can walk fine." I ran after him. He threw open the door of the small procedure room and barked, "Alicia, you are going to the hospital." She was confused as I pushed the chair into the room.

He refused to let her get dressed. "Put a blanket over her. We are going NOW." He charged ahead, wheeling Alicia in the unfamiliar chair. As we slammed through the front door, I waved at Marisol and Sally and Sally said, "We'll take care of the patients."

He careened down the wheelchair ramp, Alicia crying, and I'm sure wondering what was wrong and where we were taking her. I tried to keep up with Nick and, at the same time, searched the Spanish-English dictionary to try to explain what I didn't understand myself. We rumbled across the parking lot and across the small lawn that separated the clinic from the hospital. I was out of breath by the time we sailed past the admissions desk. Nick hadn't said a word to me, but the dark cloud over his face spoke volumes. The receptionist tried to stop us, but Nick instructed her to call up to OB/GYN surgery to prepare for management of a miscarriage.

"Why are you getting her blood type?" I could hardly speak, panting for breath.

"To save her life."

Alicia and I looked at each other, but even though I understood the words, neither of us knew what was happening. Dr. Nick ran down the hall pushing the wheelchair in front of him, me jogging behind him, with several near-misses. But although Alicia must have been terrified of the ride, otherwise she seemed fine. I thought he had lost his mind taking an abortion patient with no documentation and no insurance into the hospital.

Nurses in surgical garb met him on the second floor and took the chair, running themselves. As he raced through the swinging door to the surgical suite, he looked over his shoulder and said, "Wish me luck." Nick didn't believe in luck.

I sat, dazed, in the antiseptic-smelling waiting room with families waiting to celebrate babies. I didn't dare ask anyone about my abortion patient who had suddenly become Dr. Nick's emergency. After half an hour, I returned to the clinic, the empty never-before-used wheelchair bumping in front of me like a baby carriage, over the gravel and grass and pavement. Sally sat on the front steps of the now-empty clinic. She handed me her partly drunk Dr. Pepper.

"You need this more than I do. You look like a mouse at a catfight." I hated Dr. Pepper, but I took a long slug and sat hard on the steps next to her.

"I have no idea what that means, but yes, that's exactly right." I described the inexplicable events until her expression changed.

"I saw a pregnancy like that in the hospital where I worked. The fetus had died. When that happens, it becomes foreign tissue that the body perceives as dangerous. Sometimes, that causes hyperfibrinolysis. The blood stops clotting."

"DIC?" I used the initials for Disseminated Intravascular Coagulopathy, since no one can say that.

"Yes. Our patient had two units of blood, but they couldn't save her. She was only thirty years old and had five other children."

"This woman is early in her pregnancy. Surely that will make a difference."

"I hope so," Sally said.

Later that night, I had a drink with Dr. Nick at the Officer's Club. Alicia survived. They gave her a transfusion which allowed them to manage her clotting. I was relieved when Nick told me a Spanish-speaking nurse had explained everything to Alicia once she was out of anesthesia. He had to do a fancy two-step to explain her presence in the Navy hospital, but Nick was always light on his feet.

"I'm sorry I was such a maniac. I have seen this before and it didn't end well."

"Nick, I almost did the abortion without checking with you. What if I had?"

"I'm glad you didn't."

CHAPTER 32

HAND THEM A KLEENEX

Alameda, May 1945

Though I had a knot in my stomach that didn't go away after Alicia, I continued to do abortions. As always, I talked with each patient and explained the process, whether I acted as the counselor or the clinician. Most of the women said they were sure of their decisions, and when we used the new siphon technique, the procedure was quicker and easier than ever. Almost all the time our patients left us with hugs and smiles, and I was happy to help them.

Once in a while they were struggling—not sure of what to do. Not sure if they were still a good person. Not sure if God, or the baby, would forgive them. Or, most important, if they would forgive themselves. I remembered what Edna had said about never feeling back to normal. I remembered what donning my black robes as Our Lady of Perpetual Grace meant for those patients. I wondered how to help the ones who were struggling. It might have been because I missed my father, but questions about life and death swirled around in my head.

One afternoon, our patient was a woman named Catalina. She was having a hard time deciding what she wanted to do about her pregnancy. Marisol translated that the woman's favorite uncle had died recently, and she feared that her pregnancy was his soul's way of coming back into the world. But she also had three children and not enough to money to feed them, so having another terrified her. Catalina was crying so hard that Marisol could hardly understand her. She translated the best she could.

She was Catholic like most of the migrant workers we saw, so it surprised me she believed the soul could re-enter the world. Marisol explained that Catalina also practiced a much older religion based on the cycles of Mother Earth, where all souls recycle in the same way that water does as it changes form from water, to rain, to mist, to snow. We worked with her for over an hour, but didn't get any closer to a resolution. She had come to the clinic from far away, so we couldn't send her home to think about it more. She begged us to do the abortion despite her misgivings.

Marisol told me, "She is afraid we are going to judge her." She turned to the distraught woman, saying, "Arrieros somos y en el camino andamos." That seemed to make Catalina feel a little better. Marisol later told me it translated roughly into "We are all imperfect humans doing our best, and we can't judge each other."

Catalina whispered to Marisol that she wanted to get it over with. She said she could not bear to see her children hungry. She started crying again. I was well aware that tears made Dr. Nick uncomfortable and cranky, which made the whole situation worse. I loved him, but he had a mean streak that came out when he couldn't admit he was scared. He was waiting for us in the procedure room.

"What's going on?" he asked. "Aren't you ready?"

"I'm not sure about this one," I said. "She is so sad."

"Yes or no, Jane. It's just a medical procedure," he said, pulling on his surgical gloves from the sterile package I held open. "Hell, it's not even surgery. Why do we even use that word? It's as simple as one-two-three—that's why even you can do it."

"I hope you didn't intend that to sound as insulting as it did," I said, scowling. "Besides, it's not always simple. Sometimes the women are upset."

"They are upset because they are poor and their lives are shitty. There is not one thing you or I can do about that except make sure they don't have to bring another screaming baby into their shitty world. If you ask me, that's doing quite a lot."

I winced at the brutality of his description of our work.

"Are we going to do this or not?"

I hated it when he was impatient. But maybe he was right.

"I guess we are, but what about when they are crying so hard that I can't put the nitrous mask on?" I asked.

"Do what I do. Hand them a Kleenex and tell them they can either stop crying or have a baby. It's as simple as that."

Nick and I rarely disagreed, and I had never seen him more disagreeable than that day. But his suggestion worked, even though I recognized it made Marisol as uncomfortable as it made me. When faced with an ultimatum, Catalina stopped crying so we could administer the anesthetic.

I couldn't let it go. "It's just horrible to make them stop crying by threatening not to do their abortion. They are damned if they do and damned if they don't. They want to do the right thing, and there is no right thing. How are they going to live with what they have done if they think it is wrong?"

"Jane, you are overthinking this," Nick said.

"That's just it," I insisted. "It's not about *thinking* at all! It is about feeling, Nick. *Feeling*."

Catalina's abortion went well, and she thanked us profusely for doing it. I knew I wouldn't be with her to see how she coped the next day. I'd have to hope she'd be all right. As I took her vital signs in the recovery room, it dawned on me what to do. I scurried to find Marisol, and the three of us found an empty room. Catalina had to catch a bus in forty minutes, so I didn't have time to explain what I was doing. I just depended on Marisol to keep up with me.

"Catalina, you have shared your sadness with us, and you have wondered if you have done the right thing," I began, with Marisol's lilting translation following closely. And then, in a brief but intimate talk, I asked her to summon her uncle so that she could ask whether his spirit was trying to come back into the world through her pregnancy, as she had feared. I told her to let him answer with her voice. Her uncle said that he was at peace. Then she asked God for forgiveness and God told her he knew there was nothing but love in her heart. The Virgin Mother thanked her for taking such good care of her children. We worked as long as we could without making her miss the bus. She blessed us as she hurried out the door.

After she was gone, Marisol said, "That last thing you did was a bit of magic. It even soothed *my* soul."

"Do you think she'll keep worrying about her dead uncle?"

"I don't think so. She was glad he was at peace. Having her ask for God's forgiveness was brilliant. And you know, the Virgin is like her patron saint. Jane, I think what you have done will change everything for her. What kind of wife or mother would she have been if she were carrying deep hatred for herself? What life would she have had? Thank you for helping her in that way. Besides, she will be busy. They will move camp in a couple of weeks. But I did tell her she had to stay away from her husband from now on if she doesn't want this to happen again. 'Ahogado el niño, tapando el pozo.'"

I only understood one word—niño—meaning child. "All right, smarty. What does that say about the child?" We had a running joke that I should try to decipher the meaning of her aphorisms, which I was never able to.

"Seal the well before the baby has been drowned."

"That's horrible! There is a much kinder version in English: 'A stitch in time saves nine.' But that other phrase you told her about not being perfect—that is so important. Let's put it on a sign and post it in the waiting room, so the women will be sure we are not judging them."

"Oh, Nurse Jane," Marisol said patiently, "no one has taught these women to read."

Once again, in my well-intentioned ignorance, I'd "hung the picture at eye level."

I posted the saying anyway, if only to remind myself. I also insisted that everyone on the staff learn it, including the recalcitrant Dr. Nick. I'd swear he said it with a British accent just to irk me! When Marisol and I worked together, I routinely said to patients, "Arrieros somos y en el camino andamos" in what I thought was a pretty good Spanish accent. It seemed to make all the patients laugh, so Marisol finally explained to me that the literal translation was something like, "All of us are just mule drivers, plowing the land." It made me laugh too. One more in a lifetime of lessons.

CHAPTER 33

NURSE SMITH, WILL
YOU STAY BEHIND?

Alameda, California, 1945

Most of our teachers were women, since the men were on bases at the front. Nurse Lawrence, who taught Obstetrics and Gynecology, had an ulcer, so we were expecting a substitute. I was sitting in the back of the room reading my notes when the instructor came in and introduced herself.

"Good afternoon. My name is Betty Marston."

I dropped my notebook on the floor. One of the girls sitting behind me whispered, "Isn't that the nurse on the recruiting poster?" Indeed, it was. The one and only. I picked up my binder, but didn't lift my head until Betty turned around to write something on the chalkboard. Even from the back of the room I smelled her perfume. I recognized her wavy dark red hair and the energetic way she wrote "disseminated intravascular coagulopathy" on the board. Her perfume was called *Joy*, but in me it inspired nothing but terror.

At first she didn't look my way, but Sally, sitting in the chair next to me, just *had* to ask a question. Betty's smile broadened when she recognized me. Although we had never spoken more than a few words to each other, I felt like we were the only two people in the room, exactly the way I had at the enlistment office.

I have no idea what happened in that class. I do know that I thought I was having a heart attack. I couldn't breathe and I was struck dumb. My classmates were used to Jane, the "know it all," whose hand was perpetually waving in the air to answer every question. Though I knew more than I wanted to about DIC, I didn't say a word the entire period.

Later, I laughed when I saw that I had covered my notebook page with doodles of flowers. When the bell finally rang, I had a bizarre combination of relief and grief—an experience I was to have many more times in my history with Betty Marston. I gathered my books and began to file out of the classroom with the other students when I realized she was talking to *me*!

"Nurse Smith, will you stay behind?" she said—more of an instruction than a request.

"Of course," I said, almost choking.

Sally gave me a questioning look, but I motioned her to go on, so she gathered her papers and left with everyone else.

Then it was just the two of us.

Betty leaned back against the desk with her arms crossed. She smiled that crazy smile of hers.

"Relax. Were you not going to say hello?" she asked.

"I, um, I didn't realize you remembered me," I said, feeling quintessentially stupid.

"Of course I do. I've followed your career since you enlisted. Very impressive. But you never called me."

I stammered something about being busy, or not wanting to intrude on her, or something.

"Nonsense. I'm never in one place for long, but it is nice to see a familiar face. Let's have a drink sometime."

"Are we allowed—I mean, is it all right?"

"Is it all right for you to have a cup of coffee with an instructor? I think so, Smith. What is your concern?"

I was again struck dumb. Did I have a concern? I knew there were rules against officers, which all of us nurses were, fraternizing with enlisted men. But surely there were no rules about women. Why would there be? And this wasn't fraternization, was it? What did you actually do when you were fraternizing? Of course I could have a cup of coffee with an instructor.

Really, this is so embarrassing to recount. I don't even know what I said next. I'm thinking I looked down at my wrist at the watch I wasn't wearing and said something about being late for my next class.

CHAPTER 34

HER FATHER IS AN ADMIRAL??

Alameda, California, October 1945

The next few weeks are a blur. I couldn't concentrate. I was acting like a dope, and phrases that had been unintelligible my whole life made sense: "Head over heels—a fool for love—lost my heart." I should have had an experience like that when I was thirteen, but I didn't. So here I was, thirty-two years old, and acting like a teenager.

I sneaked into the back of classrooms where Betty was teaching. I followed her around like a puppy when she did hospital rounds. I "coincidentally" took my lunch in the cafeteria when I knew she would be there. But I was too nervous to have the drink she had suggested. I was so lost that it didn't occur to me to wonder what anyone else thought of my strange behavior until one night Sally said she wanted to talk.

She patted the side of her bed and I sat down.

"Jane, I don't mean to get into your business, but you need to be careful about who you are associating with."

I blushed. "I don't know what you are talking about."

"Oh, honey," she said, "Falling in love is like inviting people to sightsee inside your heart. You might not mean to show it, but you can't help it."

"It can't be that obvious!" I protested.

"Only to anyone with eyes in their head," she said. "Now you be careful. You don't want to mess up what you have going with Dr. Nick. That would be bad for both of you."

Did she know everything? Did everyone know my secrets?

"I don't think I am breaking any rules…" I managed.

Sally replied, "You just keep telling yourself that. In the meantime, look in your Code of Conduct manual under 'moral turpitude.' I have heard stories about your Miss Marston—that she doesn't always treat people the way they ought to be treated. And she is not always discreet, which I guess doesn't matter if your father is an admiral. I am not judging what you do, but this is messing with your mind. Just be careful."

"Her father is an admiral?" I blurted.

"She didn't tell you? Now what does that say?" she asked.

"Thanks," I said, giving her a hug. The information Sally shared stunned me, and I resolved to be more careful, although I wasn't sure if I could.

CHAPTER 35

THEY ARE NOT MAKING
ANY GIRL ADMIRALS

Alameda, California October 1945

The next time I saw Betty, we were finally having that cup of coffee. I realized I had to screw up my courage to confront her.

"Is your father really an admiral?" I asked, feeling like a child.

"Oh, no. Not that question again. Yes, he is. How else do you think I ended up on that damned recruitment poster? He is like an albatross around my neck—and yes, I get the naval metaphor. How did you find out?"

"One of my roommates told me. I guess everyone knows. Everyone but me."

"So you're angry that I didn't tell you? You think I should confess my lineage with every measly cup of coffee?"

"Well, it is a pretty big deal," I said.

"Yes. It is a *big deal.* Okay, here goes. What do you imagine Betty is short for?" she asked.

"I don't know—Elizabeth?"

"No. It is short for Betton. *His* name. He wanted a son. He insisted on naming me after himself, even though I disappointed him by being a girl. Betty was my mother's idea of a compromise. So I began life a disappointment, and it went on from there."

"What do you mean?"

"When I was little, my mother got sick, so she couldn't have any more children. For years, I did everything I could to make him proud of me. I got all A's in school; was always voted class president; served the community through our church; even got the highest score ever recorded on the math portion of the Navy enlistment test. None of it was enough for him."

"But you are a successful Navy nurse. An instructor. An officer. What more does he want from you?"

She shook her head. "If only I knew. Whatever he wants, I can never give him because I am a woman. As you may have noticed, they are not making any girl admirals. Some of the enlisted men resent us. They treat us like KP staff. They don't salute half the time, even though we are officers. The Navy isn't even willing to assign nurses any rank."

"Can't your mother help?"

"She died when I was fourteen. That removed the little bit of a buffer between me and my father. He's like those men who don't salute, so I don't care anymore. I do whatever I want, and he has to catch the flack." She lit a cigarette and offered the pack to me. I shook my head no.

I was rattled by what she had said, and somehow even more rattled by what she did. I wasn't hopelessly old-fashioned. Levy smoked, of course, like every French man I'd ever met. I can't even picture his face without seeing what he called a "fag" hanging out of the side of his mouth in that insouciant Gallic way. My father smoked his pipe after dinner in his study, and I found that smell very reassuring. Betty's smoking was altogether a different matter, and anything but reassuring. Looking back, I recognize that I was an unwitting victim of the cigarette advertisers' campaign to make smoking seem sophisticated and alluring. Because it was!

I haven't really described Betty. She had lustrous auburn hair and pale skin… I think you'd call it porcelain. She had dark brown eyes. Her makeup was always perfectly applied—well, at least during the day. She looked like a Breck Shampoo girl, if you remember those magazine ads. And her voice was like warm corduroy. Some might tell you that Betty's husky voice came directly from a two-pack-a-day cigarette habit. But in those days, it was just— I sort of hate the word *sexy*, but that's just what it was—what she was.

Most of the time, Betty seemed in charge of everything. I guess she was used to people either keeping a wide berth (yes, I know, another nautical reference), or else toadying to her. Before I learned about her father, I thought it was just because she had a commanding personality. As I look back, I can see it came from insecurity. She both craved and hated being treated differently because of her father's rank.

Despite Sally's warning, I found myself spending more and more time with Betty. We developed a sort of banter during the Obstetrics and Gynecology class. It must have been uncomfortable for everyone else, because we acted as though there were just the two of us, making funny references to the stodgy textbook, and recounting stories of our favorite patients. I'm embarrassed that my crush must have been so painfully obvious.

As the end of term approached, I experienced that strange relief and grief phenomenon that I didn't know what to do with. I was crazy for Betty—there wasn't any other way to put it. But I hadn't even held her hand. *The Well of Loneliness* was no help at all in figuring out what to do. I imagined that Betty was experienced in these matters. She was seven years older and a world traveler. I figured she must have love conquests in every port, yet I was stuck hoping and fearing that she would make a move.

At the same time that Sally was warning me, Dr. Nick was teasing me. He didn't realize how naïve I was.

"Hey, it's the girl who has won the heart of the Admiral's daughter," he said, grinning one afternoon in the stock room as he was putting boxes of sanitary pads on the top shelf.

"Dr. Nick, don't be mean. I am so confused," I said.

"What is there to be confused about?" he asked. "Love is love. Enjoy it where you find it. But don't be too obvious. I need you to keep up our masquerade." Leaning back against the counter, he said, "Meanwhile, I don't mean to put any pressure on you, but I've had a letter from my mother. She wants to know when she can expect grandchildren. Greeks are relentless about grandchildren."

"Well, if you are looking at me, I am afraid she is going to have a long wait!"

"I know," he laughed. "She is going to have that same long wait with me. But it would mean a lot to her if I were engaged. Do you think...?"

"You're kidding. Nick, that is going too far."

"I know it is asking a lot, but it would satisfy all the questions we both get about when we are going to get serious. Please, Janie? Nothing would change. We're already putting on a performance. What is it they say, 'In for a penny, in for a pound'?"

"All right," I answered. "As long as we have a party, and I get a really enormous diamond!"

In my letters home, I shared new things I learned, books I enjoyed, interesting sailors I had met, the beauty of California. I never told any of them about my pretend engagement. I didn't write about Betty. Only Dr. Levy knew about my work in abortion. There are just some things...

CHAPTER 36

BUT SHE'S SO TALL

Alameda, California, November 1945

Nick bought me a beautiful art deco-style diamond ring for everyone to ooh and ahh over. He insisted on holding our engagement party at the French restaurant where we had our first dinner together, even though I worried it was too expensive.

"They have a private party room in the back," he said. "We'll just serve champagne and hors d'oeuvres." He invited the officers and their wives, and some of his father's friends. I was well aware they would all be looking me over to see if I was good enough for their Dr. Nick.

Once again, I relied on my roommates to make me presentable. I wore a fitted pink Shantung silk dress that belonged to Edna, pearls with matching earrings that belonged to Clarice, and a beaded belt that belonged to Sally. I emerged like a patchwork quilt pieced together from their closets. With Edna looking on, Sally and Clarice swept my hair up into a French twist, and applied the rouge, mascara, eye makeup, and lipstick that I never bothered with. They had me walk through a spritz of Rive Gauche perfume, so I smelled like a dream of Paris. Looking in the mirror, I had to admit I was, indeed, presentable.

The whole point was to put on a show, so I had to pretend with them as well as with everyone else and invite them to the party. When Nick picked me up in his convertible, the girls stood at the door to watch. They were triumphant when he gave a long, low wolf whistle. With a scarf protecting my updo and a pair of sunglasses, I felt like a movie star, even if we were in Alameda and not Hollywood.

The restaurant was as beautiful as I remembered, with soft lights twinkling on the walls. Nick took my wrap and scarf to the coat-check room. When he returned, a waiter carrying a tray offered us glasses of champagne. I was so nervous that I grabbed one right away and took a big sip. A voice from behind startled me.

"So you are the Janie who is stealing our Nick away?" The voice came from a short, heavily made-up blonde woman in her forties. She looked me up and down and said, "Nick, she's lovely."

I hope I never have to live through that kind of "compliment" again.

"Janie, this is Mrs. Arthur Kennedy, Dr. Kennedy's wife. You remember, he's the head of my department?"

The woman smiled and held out a limp hand for me to shake.

"Call me Loretta, dear," she said. "I have the honor of regularly beating your beau in tennis," she said, smiling as if she owned him. "He is our favorite bachelor. I was hoping to save him for my cousin."

I tried to smile. Nick put his hand on the small of my back and ushered me through the crowd until we were standing next to an older couple.

The white-haired woman said, "Hello, Nick dear. Such a pleasant party."

She wore one of those fox stoles where the poor animal's mouth is clipped to its own mid-section with its feet and tail hanging down. I always hated them. She leaned on her bald husband's arm and looked up at me.

"But she's so tall," she said, as if my height were akin to having a large piece of spinach on my front teeth.

Nick jumped in. "She's just perfect for me, Aunt Mandy." He turned to me.

"Janie, dearest, I'm delighted for you to meet Dr. James Kemp and Mrs. Amanda Kemp, friends of my parents. This is Officer Jane Smith, my intended."

"I am so pleased to meet you," I said, not sure whether I should shake hands or curtsy.

As we made our way through the crowd, being scrutinized was very uncomfortable. I couldn't tell if any of Nick's people thought I was a good enough specimen. I kept trying to sidle off to sit at the table with Sally and the girls, but Nick had me clamped to his side. Honestly, you would think he had birthed me himself, or that I was some kind of science experiment he had entered in a junior high school competition.

It seemed the evening would never end. I'm not very good with champagne, so by the time the party was over, after all the silly and suggestive toasts, I was smashed. I don't remember the goodbyes, but Nick put me in a cab with my roommates.

"I think she's had it," he said to Sally. "I've got to go for another drink with these department heads. Will you take her home and get her into bed?"

I guess they did. I don't remember much of it, except being sad that Nick had fabricated such a horrible version of himself for these people. Apart from the fiancé thing, in front of them he was a callow, supercilious, arrogant man—not the usually kind, smart, wry Nick I knew. I wondered if being homosexual meant you could never show your true self?

CHAPTER 37

YOU CAN'T FOOL A
FELLOW TRAVELER

Alameda, California, November 1945

I put off eating with Betty, though I'm not sure what scared me so much about having supper with her. I finally gave in to her repeated invitations. I discretely borrowed Edna's most sophisticated shirtwaist, but I didn't tell my roommates about my date, and didn't get their help with my hair and makeup. Somehow, this was different. This was a secret I couldn't share.

We met at the Officer's Club. After enjoying a fancy dinner, Betty asked me to come home for a nightcap. I was terrified, but I wanted to go. I said yes, hoping no one would see us going in together. Her apartment was set away from the regular nurses' quarters—another perk of being the Admiral's daughter. As I looked around her attractive suite, I didn't see anything of her in it. It looked more like a hotel room than a home. Betty lit a fire and then put on a record—the soundtrack from *Pal Joey*, a Broadway show I had heard of—and we sank together into the soft brown leather of the couch.

I smiled. "I like this music."

Betty reached over to the cut-glass decanter on the coffee table and re-filled my glass. I have never been a drinker, although I enjoyed wine with dinner in France. But this was scotch. Betty insisted on single malt, and I couldn't keep up with her.

"My father is a big fan of Broadway musicals," she said. "He took me to see this one when it opened—before I had disappointed him so irrevocably by growing up into a woman. A lovely show."

The fire warmed me and crackled in a friendly way, smelling of cedar. As she moved closer, Betty started to sing with the record.

"If they asked me, I could write a book... About the way you walk, and whisper, and look..."

Her voice was like warm honey and I couldn't help it—I melted into her arms, and in the words of Radclyffe Hall's *The Well of Loneliness*, "That night we were not divided."

I woke the next morning with a terrible headache and a terrible start when I realized I was in Betty's bed. I heard her humming in the kitchen and smelled coffee brewing. I was mortified to realize that I wasn't wearing a stitch. I pulled the coverlet off the bed, wrapped it around myself, and ran into the kitchen.

"Betty, I didn't check out of the dorm last night. They are going to wonder where I am—they'll be looking for me." We still had the old model of bed checks every night.

"Calm down. It's all right. I know your housemother, and I told her I needed you overnight for a special project. She didn't bat an eye."

"But... but when did you?... how did you...?"

"I did it last week when we made the date for dinner. And how did I get the idea you would stay over? Well—really, I didn't know. I just hoped you would."

"Betty, I can't... I can't do this."

"You said that last night... several times," she said, smiling and tending to the crackling bacon that sent delicious smells through the kitchen. "Relax. Have a cup of coffee." She gestured to the percolator on the counter. "You like cream and sugar, right? The cream is in the fridge. But before you do that, you might want to put something on," she laughed, pointing to the swath of bedclothes I had pulled around me. "There is a robe on the back of the bathroom door. And aspirin on the counter."

As I left the kitchen, I realized it surprised me that she had noticed how I took my coffee. That Betty. Full of surprises. But how did she know I'd need aspirin? When I came back into the kitchen, I wore a thin silky garment that barely reached my knees because Betty was a good bit shorter than me. But the robe was at least more presentable than sheets. I got my coffee, stirred in the cream and sugar, plopped down on one of the kitchen chairs, and took the welcomed aspirin. As it always seemed when I was with Betty, I felt exhilarated and defeated in the same moment. I did not know what to say.

"Betty... last night... I didn't mean to..."

"Oh yes you did, chicken." (Why did she call me that?) "You meant to and so did I. Why can't it just be a lovely memory that we'll have when we are thousands of miles apart?" she asked, smiling that crazy smile.

How could this be so easy for her? Making coffee and cooking bacon as if the world hadn't just shifted on its axis? I tried to smile. Betty lifted her fork from the frying pan and looked over at me.

"Oh, my, I am such a fool," she said, turning back to the bacon. "Honestly, chicken, I didn't know. Oh, my," she said again.

"I have no idea what you are talking about."

She was silent for a moment as she lifted the pieces of bacon out of the pan and placed them on a rack to drain. She came and sat across from me at the table.

"It was your first time, wasn't it? Not just with a woman—but really, your first."

I blushed deeply and lowered my head in assent.

"Oh, honey, I had no idea. Did you?… are you sorry?"

"Sorry… no. I wanted to. But I know it's wrong."

"Well, that's a crazy thing to say. Is that what you tell your best friend, Dr. Nick?"

"Dr. Nick is not my friend; he is my fiancé. We had our engagement party last week."

"Oh, come off it, Jane. He is as queer as a three-dollar bill. I saw that the moment I met him."

"How… how…?"

Betty lit a cigarette. She released a long exhale.

"For one thing, he is way too nice to women. And for another, I just didn't get a romance between the two of you, especially because of what I sensed about you right from the start. I've been around long enough to see a few "arrangements" like you two have. I say bully for both of you. But you can't fool a fellow traveler."

"Right from the start? I always wondered… was it my imagination or were you smiling at me that night at the recruitment center?" I asked.

"Not your imagination." She blew out a thin stream of smoke.

"But why—how did you pick *me*?" I asked.

"Oh, Jane, you are really green. You mean, how did I know that you were one of us? That you love women?"

"I'm not—I don't—I mean, I don't love women. I just love you," I said, blushing again.

"That's what we all say the first time. It's all right. There will be others."

"No—never! I don't want any others," I protested.

Betty put her arm around my shoulders and held me tight.

"I know," she said.

We ate breakfast making small talk, like how good her scrambled eggs were and how windy it was. She kept offering me more food.

"I need to use this stuff up or it will get thrown out," she said.

Abruptly she looked at her watch and stood up. It hadn't registered on me that she was in full uniform, while I was still pulling the too-small robe around me.

"Just leave the dishes," she said. "The maid is coming this afternoon. She'll clean out the refrigerator. If you want anything in there, help yourself. I have a meeting with the Dean of Nurses. You can stay as long as you want and let yourself out."

I began to get up, but she motioned me back into the chair. "Finish your orange juice," she said. "And you'd better put a happier look on your face or people will think I don't know how to cook breakfast!" And she winked. She actually winked at me.

"When you leave, turn off the percolator and push the button in on the door so it locks behind you."

"But when…?"

She kissed me and strode out of the apartment, picking up her briefcase on the way. I looked at the clock. I calculated that I would need to stay at least another half hour in order to avoid passing anyone going to classes. I found the switch on the percolator and turned it off. Then I unplugged it, for safety's sake, the way my mother always did.

I realized I had no clothes to put on other than the dress that I had worn the night before. Dinner at the Officer's Club was always a rather elegant affair, so, true to form, I had worn Edna's prettiest cream-colored shirtwaist and Clarice's pale green silk kimono.

The dress and kimono were draped over a chair, and my underwear, slip, and stockings were neatly folded underneath. *I* had not folded them, so that was humiliating. Seeing my white nylon underwear with the utilitarian name-tapes made me think of my first abortion patient, Françoise. I remembered her pretty silk underthings and rosary beads on the chair. I had no rosary beads, but I sort of wished I had.

I got dressed and hung Betty's robe on the back of the bathroom door, marveling again at how neat everything in her apartment was. It could have been a picture in a magazine. I sat down on the couch and waited for half an hour longer, attempting to calculate the time everyone would be in class. I finally screwed up my courage and left Betty's apartment, looking both ways as I walked out the door, with all the confidence of a six-year-old crossing the road. To my great relief, I didn't encounter anyone on my way back to my room. I changed out of the fancy clothes and lay on my bed, feeling utterly lost.

I skipped the rest of my classes that day and was noncommittal that evening when Sally asked if I was all right. I mumbled something about cramps when she asked if I was going to dinner. I turned off my bedside light and curled up with my back to her bed. When she came in from studying, she tiptoed in and slid under her covers without making a sound. I got up very early the next morning after a restless night. I took my clothes and dressed in the bathroom so I wouldn't wake anyone. If only I had listened to Sally's misgivings about Betty.

CHAPTER 38

MAKING NOISES LIKE A CHICKEN

Alameda, California, 1945

The following day I passed Betty talking with another instructor in the post office, and she didn't even make eye contact. The next morning she grabbed me by the hand as we passed each other in the hallway, pulled me into an empty classroom, and kissed me passionately. Then, without a word, she ran down the hallway in the opposite direction of where I was headed. I expected I'd get a phone call or at least a note from her, but there was nothing.

Within two days of our evening together, Betty was gone. Disappeared. She didn't say goodbye or tell me where I could reach her. Was I supposed to have realized she was leaving? I was so confused that I didn't even know if I had any kind of claim on her. I felt ashamed and humiliated.

When I was in college, I went to see a hypnotist's show. I still don't understand how he did it, but the man in the top hat put an entire stage full of people into a trance and made them do crazy and funny things. Each of them was clucking and barking until he snapped his fingers, and instantly they all went back to normal. That's what being with Betty always felt like to me. I made noises like a chicken, and waited for someone to snap their fingers and put me back to normal.

Sally was kind enough not to pry, although I finally said something about wondering where Betty could have gone. I was sure that I was making a fool of myself, but Sally reassured me.

"You are not the only one. Everyone here is a bit in love with Betty," she said as we filled our lunch trays one day. "Both the men and the women. I heard one of the doctors asking where she was, and the billet officer said that Nurse Lawrence was back, so Nurse Marston has gone on to her next assigned post. I'm sorry, hon."

"I feel like such an idiot," I said. "I can't believe she didn't tell me she was going—that she didn't even say goodbye."

"You know, relationships are harder for some people than others. You are such a nice girl, Jane. I hate to see you get hurt by someone who doesn't deserve you."

Of course, that's not what I thought. I was afraid I had done something to offend Betty and make her leave.

"Thanks, Sally," is all I said.

Amid the tumult of my personal life, that entire term was terrible and wonderful in equal measure. In mid-April, we mourned the loss of our beloved President Franklin Delano Roosevelt. I was just nineteen when FDR was elected, so it was as though he had been President my entire life. His dying was like losing my father all over again. As though the whole world was losing its father. The base just about shut down, with all of us crowded around the radio in the officers' mess. Even after all these years, I feel sad when I remember that day. The father of the country had left us in perilous times.

Just a couple of weeks later, Hitler killed himself, and Germany surrendered. I wish Roosevelt had lived to see that, but perhaps he trusted it was coming. As morbid as it sounds, we all celebrated Hitler's suicide as much as we celebrated the surrender. We didn't yet know the full extent of the evils of the Third Reich, but we knew enough to be glad that Hitler was gone from the face of the earth. The more we learned about the death camps and the horror committed by the Nazis, the more we feared for the future of the human race.

In August we were stunned to hear that the United States had dropped a new weapon—the atomic bomb—on a city in Japan. On Monday, August 6th, 1945 at 8:15 a.m., a B-29 called the Enola Gay, after the pilot's mother of all things, dropped a nine-thousand-pound bomb. Overnight, the word "Hiroshima" became an indelible part of our lexicon. Ninety percent of the city was wiped out. Eighty thousand people were killed instantly, including most of the city's medical personnel.

My roommates and I, and most of our classmates, wept that a weapon like this could have been created by humans—let alone unleashed on other humans. After all, we were nurses. Some argued that the bomb saved millions of lives of Americans and other Allied soldiers, but that didn't stem our tears, especially when we saw photographs of the devastation. The American media had turned the Japanese into monsters, so there were those who believed they deserved anything we did to them. I listened to the arguments, my thoughts going back and forth, ricocheting like a pinball. I felt a deep desolation with each of the positions.

Then we learned that another bomb had been dropped on a different Japanese city just three days later. I cannot convey the horror I felt, and the shame that it was my country that had done this. Yet most of the sailors around us were cheering, as if we had won some kind of sports competition. They had heard about and experienced the atrocities that the Japanese inflicted on our prisoners of war, and they were relieved that the fighting would be over soon.

I still can't imagine why the Japanese didn't surrender after that first bomb, but I know with all my heart that they would have given up soon. We were killing civilians! Did we drop that second bomb just because we had it? We nurses kept our tears to ourselves as much as we were able. After all, we were not the ones whose lives were on the line. But it left a sour, brittle place in my heart when I thought about my role in the military.

In September, we finally celebrated the end of the war. It was as though the bombings were the finale to a macabre concert—one that had to come before the curtain call. On a mundane level, we were getting close to graduation, and there were many questions about what we would each do now that the war was over. I still hadn't heard a word from Betty.

By fall, my entire class was abuzz with speculation about the future. A lot of the girls were going to leave the Navy. As the war was grinding to an end, the military seemed to want women to disappear as easily as we had appeared. At least a third of my class had decided they would use their newfound skills at local hospitals instead of continuing in uniform, and there were those who were excited to go back to being "ladies." In the hallway, I overheard a conversation that was repeated many times in different versions:

"I can't wait to get home. You know, Teddy won't hang around forever just because he put a ring on my finger. We are going to live in Levittown. They are building a fantastic new bunch of houses, and the GI bill is going to make them affordable. I am going to be just like a lady in *Home and Garden!*"

Having never been a "lady," I didn't see a home *or* a garden in my future. I had no desire to return to Connecticut, so I didn't care much about what was next. The truth is, after Betty disappeared, I didn't care much about anything.

One afternoon, Nick asked me to have a drink with him. After our shift we went to the Officer's Club, the scene of my ill-fated dinner with Betty. Dr. Nick was always flush with cash, and he preferred the club to the cafeteria or local coffee shops that the nurses frequented.

"So, how are you doing?" he asked after we had ordered our coffee. Nick was the only person besides Sally I'd confided in about my feelings for Betty. I thought he would understand, and I hoped he would be kind.

"I'm okay," I answered, although we both knew I was not. "I don't want to talk about it," I said, looking down. We were quiet for a moment.

"Hard to believe it's almost graduation," he said.

I knew that something was on his mind, so I said, "Nick, I know you. You are not one for small talk. What do you want?" I didn't mean to sound impatient.

"Well, they are sending me to Japan, to Kyoto, to head up one of the civilian medicine programs as part of our supervision of the country."

"Oh God. How awful! I didn't know. I am so sorry! Are you scared? Can't you request another assignment? I can't imagine how the Japanese are feeling about us. They hated us before, but now the defeat—and the bombs." I was getting myself all worked up.

"You don't understand. I requested this assignment. This is going to be one of the most important jobs I could ever do. I will be helping to rebuild a country—a people—that this war has decimated. I'll be in charge of an entire region. If we don't help the Japanese get control of their population, the entire country could face mass starvation so, believe it or not, the Top Brass has decided that we'll be doing abortions. Janie, would you... I would like you to go with me. We're such a great team. Won't you go with me?"

At first I was so shocked that I didn't say anything. The fact that I was "officially" Dr. Nick's fiancée meant nothing to the Navy, so I didn't know how he could proffer this invitation as if he were asking me to the prom. I had just read a harrowing story about American nurses who had been prisoners of war in Manila, the so-called "Angels of Bataan." They had spent nearly four years in horrible conditions and had only been liberated at the beginning of the year. There would be no love lost between me and the Japanese.

"Even if you could make that happen, I just don't think I could do it. I don't think I'd *want* to do it. After everything—after all the boys we've seen maimed and killed in this war. It would be like asking me to move to Berlin and be nice to Germans. I just can't, Nick," I said.

"I understand. But will you please read about the posting?" he asked. "We're talking about women and children here—people who had no part in making war. People who are suffering from malnutrition and whose children are dying. Just read the report they sent me." He handed me a sheaf of papers. "I can make it happen if you agree. There's an officer in charge of billeting who, shall I say, owes me a favor." He chuckled which I thought was in very poor taste in the middle of such a serious conversion. "I have to know in two days," he added, looking hopeful.

"Okay. I'll read it," I said, finishing my coffee. "But I make no promises. I might be better off with the luck of the draw."

He grinned. "But then you wouldn't have me."

I read the report and I was appalled. It wasn't enough that there was a total lack of health care, but they had included pictures of children who looked like skeletons. I had seen enough of the photographs from Europe to realize that it wasn't only the Allies who had paid a terrible price for this terrible war. I thought about how much I loved working with Dr. Nick, in spite of his occasional personality flaws, and finally decided to go. It seemed as good a future as any.

CHAPTER 39

GRADUATION DAY

Alameda, then Kyoto, Japan 1945

My mother got a terrible case of the flu just before graduation. Dr. Levy was looking after her, so they didn't come to watch me receive my hard-earned diploma. Although Lucie begged and begged, the Goldfarb's decided that, at thirteen, she was too young to travel to California alone.

Dear Mam'selle,

I simply cannot bear it that I am missing your graduation! And I won't see you before you go off to Japan. I tried so hard to think of a graduation present for you. Mama suggested you would like a poem, so I wrote this:

In Paris many years ago
You were my teacher dear
You saved me from the Nazis
And you brought me over here.

And now you're in the Navy
And your special day is near
When you'll earn your diploma
And get all your nursing gear.

I'm awfully proud of you, Mam'selle,
For overcoming fear
And though I miss you very much
I always feel you near.

I hope graduation is wonderful and you like the poem.

Love, Lucie XOXOXO

P.S. When are you ever coming home?
P.P.S. Absolutely nothing rhymes with Paris!"

On November 20th, 1945, I walked across the stage to the polite applause of my classmates and other people's parents. Just wishful thinking, but I could have sworn I saw Betty standing in the back of the room. When I looked again, she wasn't there. My overactive imagination.

My beloved roommates and I were sad to leave each other. Sally took a job at a hospital near her family. "I miss them so much. And truth be told, I'm looking forward to not being the odd one out all the time."

They deployed Edna to an island in the Pacific where some wounded sailors were still too sick to be transported home. "It's in the middle of nowhere—almost didn't find it on the map. I can't believe I'm leaving you gals," she said, giving each of us a huge Eddie hug.

Clarice didn't know what she was going to do. Returning to Texas was out of the question. "There is no home to go back to," she said. "I'll never forgive my parents for not listening to me. I'm going to move to San Francisco to make a new life."

We had all enlisted to help with the war, and it was perplexing how quickly nurses, who had once been deemed essential to the war effort, had become simply women—always expendable. We said tearful goodbyes, hoping we'd be together again one day.

Thank goodness my mother recovered from the flu. I'm sure she was surprised and hurt that I didn't come home before I went to Japan. But I couldn't face the questions about why I was so unhappy, and I just couldn't tell her about Betty. It was one thing to be a misfit, but entirely another to be unnatural. I wrote to her that my orders had come through unexpectedly and they wouldn't wait.

The trip to Kyoto was long, tiring, and uneventful. But what an extraordinarily beautiful city, filled with temples and gardens unlike anything I had ever seen. I was glad to learn the Allies spared Kyoto from bombings. After I arrived, I settled into my plain little apartment. It became obvious that Nick really did have pull. He ran civilian medicine for the entire base. As a result, we only served the local people at our clinic. Dr. Nick had warned me that we were going to be working with the poorest of the poor.

Over coffee in the cafeteria, we talked about our new practice.

"The living conditions here make our farmworkers' lives look plush. Japan has been at war for five years, and they spared no expense for their military, so the people are starving. They have had to sacrifice everything, and they feel a lot of shame because their country lost the war." Nick got up for more coffee, tilting his head to see if I wanted any.

I signaled that I had enough, and picked up the thread of the conversation. "I have been reading about the importance of saving face in Japan. I don't want to be rude, but it reminds me of teenage boys and their cars. Too much pride can be a terrible burden."

"I guess it *is* mostly male pride, but it is males who run the world," Nick said, "so better watch out when their pride gets hurt." He poured canned milk into his coffee. "These people are living in a feudal society, and that includes an inferior status for women."

"Given that, I guess it is not surprising that it's hard to find anything written about Japanese women, besides a few things about geishas."

"There are so many problems for the whole population. They don't have modern medical care or dentistry. They have no sanitation, which makes them susceptible to all sorts of diseases. They are largely illiterate, and they believe their illnesses are coming from various local gods that are punishing them. The rate of maternal death is terrible, and many children don't live past five years old. We're going to have our work cut out for us, Janie!"

The Navy built a brand new, beautifully equipped clinic for women and an adjoining one for children. We had an enormous waiting room—more than twice the size of the one in Alameda. When spring came, the air was redolent with the scent of cherry blossoms. I liked to eat my lunch outside, when there was time for lunch.

The people we cared for came to us with a wide variety of ailments, most of which I had only read about in textbooks. In some ways, it was like our migrant workers' clinic with the addition of rickets (didn't British sailors get that?) and devastating malnutrition. In addition, we saw cholera, dysentery, and a host of parasites we had to research. The war had reduced many of our patients to a sort of hopeless numbness. They had become walking ghosts.

Abortion wasn't yet legal in Japan, but as the Supervising Authority, the policies of the American military were the policies of the country. I found it refreshing that most of our abortion patients were clear about what they wanted. There was so little of everything to go around that they were adamant about not having more mouths to feed.

I missed the migrant children with their earnest English, and I missed the ever-sunny Marisol. But as the Frenchman said, *"Plus ça change, plus c'est la même chose"*—the more things change, the more they stay the same. The first time I sat with a pregnant woman who already had an infant she could not care for, all the differences disappeared.

For most of our Japanese patients, religion was more a private thing than a set of rules, unlike the migrants' Catholicism, which had so much dogma to obey. There was no need for anything like Our Lady of Perpetual Grace who was so comforting in her habit. Yet there are always exceptions.

Occasionally, I saw women in every bit as much turmoil as women I had seen in Alameda. I tried to talk with Dr. Nick about those patients. He was usually overwhelmed by his workload, which impaired his ability to be empathetic.

"I thought we would be past all of that once we left Catholic-land."

"Oh, Nick, don't be mean. It's not that their religion is against abortion—it's… well, for some of them, it is their heart. As loyal as they are to their children, and as much as they know they can't feed one more, some of them already love the baby they are carrying."

"That's ridiculous. There *is* no baby. All that's in there are automatically dividing cells. You're the one always showing them pictures of embryos. Don't they see that there is nothing there to love?"

"You don't understand. What they love is the idea of what that life *could* be. Maybe no man can fully understand what it means to have a life growing inside you."

"Well, you've never experienced it either, have you? What's making you such an expert?"

"I… I have sat with hundreds of women, and I have heard their stories and watched some of them struggle."

"Well, what do you want to do about it? Or, more precisely, what do you want *me* to do about it?" Nick asked.

"I don't know," I said. "I really don't know."

CHAPTER 40

I'M HERE!

Kyoto, Japan, December 15th, 1945

One evening a few weeks after I got to Kyoto, I arrived at my second-floor apartment exhausted from a long day at the clinic, only to see an apparition. Betty Marston was sitting in a folding chair smoking a cigarette on the second floor landing next to my apartment door. When she saw me, she jumped up, ground the cigarette butt under her shoe, and reached her arms out.

"Jane," she called out. "I'm here!"

To say I was stunned would be an understatement. I stopped at the bottom of the stairs and looked up at the woman whom I had loved and hated in equal measure, who had occupied too many of my waking and fretfully sleeping hours, who had broken my heart and left me without a glance in my direction, and I simply stood, gripping the banister. At last, Betty started down the stairs, talking very softly, as if I were a bird who might fly away at the least provocation.

"I didn't want to say anything until I figured out whether I could swing it with my father. I had to meet with him in person, which was not a lot of fun. I actually convinced him that Dr. Nick had won me over with his vision of Americans helping the vanquished Japanese people, if you can believe it. Father agreed to station me here in Kyoto on the condition that I continue my usual schedule traveling to bases in the U.S. I agreed, so here I am! Surprised?" she asked. Then she saw my expression and added, "You're not mad, are you?"

About a hundred sarcastic answers ran through my head, but the scent of her perfume addled my brain and I ended up shaking my head no. That was always me. When it came to Betty, I always forgave her, except that last time. But I had to say something.

"You left without saying a word. I didn't know *what* to think."

"I'm sorry. I thought everyone knew I was leaving the base. I didn't talk about the future because I didn't want to get your hopes up if I couldn't make it work," she said, slower this time, coming down the stairs and reaching for me. "It scared me that I was falling in love with you. I went to the billet officer, who is an old friend, and got him to tell me where you were posted. I don't do this, you know. I have never done anything like this before. I try to keep my relationships casual, but I fell for you. I didn't mean to, but I did. And I brought a Christmas present for you. Are you going to let me come in?" She smiled that damned Betty smile.

"Of course." She followed me back up the stairs and I fumbled to find my key. As we entered the small, sparsely furnished apartment, I was suddenly ashamed, as if the apartment represented my shabby self.

"Would you like something? Scotch?" I asked.

"Sure," she said, sitting down on my rickety sofa and taking off her camel-hair coat. She was out of uniform, wearing an expensive beige cashmere sweater set and a brown tweed straight skirt with crocodile pumps. She looked even more beautiful and put together than usual. In my pitiful room, she was a gem on a junk heap.

I poured two glasses of Glenlivet and put them on the table, then joined her on the couch. "Betty, I ... Were you at my graduation?"

She took a sip and turned to me. "I wouldn't have missed it. But I didn't talk to you because my plan wasn't in place. Please forgive me. I was so excited that I didn't even think how you would feel. Please, please forgive me." She took my hands in hers, and the horrible month of anger and shame disappeared. "You have to open my Christmas present right away. I hope you will love it." She reached into her coat pocket and pulled out a small jewelry box tied with a ribbon. I took it in my hands and warily removed the bow.

Inside the box was a key.

"I found the most perfect apartment," she said. "It is just a short walk from your clinic. It has a bedroom for each of us, and two rooms that can be offices. There is a fireplace and one of those amazing Japanese soaking bathtubs. It is just swell. I want you to live there with me. It will be our home— our first home together. I'm going to be traveling so much that you'll have it all to yourself half the time, anyway. Please say yes?"

It was a fateful yes.

CHAPTER 41

FIRST CHILD

Kyoto, Japan, December 1945-January 1946

The apartment was everything Betty had promised. I moved my meager belongings in the next day and informed my landlord. The high demand for housing for military personnel guaranteed that she happily accepted my key, especially since I had already paid for the month. I wondered what Dr. Nick would think, but decided that he might want me to be happy. And I was. We were. We had a lovely Christmas, with a fake tree made from bristle brushes dyed green that Betty had shipped from England. We decorated the apartment and invited Dr. Nick to Christmas dinner. Steamed dumplings stood in for the usual roasted potatoes and Betty snagged a juicy roast beef that we somehow cooked to perfection. When we had eaten and drunk our fill, and Nick had bid us a warm goodnight, we cuddled on the sofa enjoying the scent of cedar in the fire, and talked about our future together.

Betty was traveling two weeks out of the month, so I made a cozy nest for myself in my bedroom. Photographs of my parents, Lucie, my Paris girls in front of the Eiffel Tower, and Levy looking important in his New York office, crowded my bedside table. In my office I had a fancy desk where I wrote letters. When Betty was home, we had a wonderful time. She'd quiz me on Japanese words for basic things like pain, menstrual period, and medicine. That really helped me in the clinic. We'd cuddle up together on the sofa with our books, stopping to read interesting things aloud. She'd dance me into the bedroom after dinner. We laughed more than I can remember laughing in a long time. Maybe ever. I felt safe with her, and I knew that I was well and truly loved. That almost made up for not being able to tell anyone except Dr. Nick about our relationship. Thank goodness for him. In my letters home, Betty just was a nice roommate.

Having love in my life made me care even more about the women who came to us for help. There are as many reasons for an abortion as there are women. Most of our patients were certain about their decision, and they handled the experience with the same resolve as they handled other challenges in their lives. It was truly extraordinary to have the freedom to provide abortion care without being afraid of the intrusion of men's laws. But there were still some women who struggled. I found it deeply rewarding to work with the women who were more troubled than they were confident. It challenged me to think about the deeper parts of their lives—their hearts and their spirits. And my own. I remembered Dr. Levy telling me how similarly rudimentary his tools were when he first started doing abortions. I was beginning to hone my counseling skills. It was just luck—or grace—that allowed me to come up with the prayer that promised women grace and forgiveness, and honored their goodness, love, and courage. I had come a long way as a guide for women through the crucible that a decision about pregnancy can be. I didn't tell the woman what I thought she should do. That was only and always her choice. I was like a midwife, birthing a marriage of her head and her heart.

Sometimes conflicts arose when women had religious, moral, or spiritual reservations about taking life. Does it surprise you that I am phrasing it that way? Of course I know abortion is an ending of life—a kind of killing—and so do our patients. That's what they want and need. But for me, and for most of those women, the nature of the life that they are ending differs from the lives of their husbands, or their friends, or their already-born children. I have searched for ways to express the inexpressible nature of an embryo or fetus. Perhaps it is just as simple and as complicated as the difference between a pregnancy that is wanted and one that is not. In choosing abortion, a woman sometimes takes on pain to prevent a child from being born into suffering. One woman who had a hard time after her abortion told me, "The abortion was for the baby, the grief is for me." Grief was what she had left to hold on to. Abortion and birth. Both choices are sacred. We can honor life when we say yes. And we can equally honor life when we say no.

Some women believe that the spirit comes from heaven and returns to heaven when it is not accepted on earth. In Alameda, a lovely woman named Deborah told me that her abortion was like "flinging a star back into the sky." Still, the choice of abortion often represents an inherent contradiction. How can it be that a life—a potential child—can be valued and loved and still not chosen? I can't explain it. A baby can be a blessing or it can be a terror. Motherhood is a complicated proposition, especially for the very young. That's why I had compassion for a patient who came to us that fall.

Betty could be a good listener. She knew that my work meant everything to me, even though she didn't always understand what I was trying to do. Over a glass of wine, comfortable on our living room sofa in front of the fire, without saying the patient's name, I told her about Ami.

"Her chart said she was 17—hardly a woman. The moment she came into the clinic, I could see that she was going to have a hard time. I am used to crying, even from women who are confident about what they want, but she was sobbing and literally could not stand up."

"Poor dear. But that's extreme, isn't it?"

"Yes. And it got worse. When the receptionist called her name, she dissolved into loud wailing. We sat in a counseling room, and she finally calmed down enough to talk. Through the translator, she told me that she desperately wanted to have the baby, but her husband's mother was demanding she have an abortion. The mother-in-law was angry that she got pregnant because the family isn't able to feed another mouth. Her husband works miles away in the mines, and her entire family was killed in Nagasaki."

"How terrible," Betty replied. "Just a teenager, and she lost everyone. How did you figure out what to say?"

"I've worked with young women before, so I had an idea. I told her that I understood her situation, and of course, we would not do an abortion. She stopped crying as if I had shut off a faucet. The translator turned to me and said, 'She wants to understand what you mean, that you will not do it?' I explained that, regardless of the wishes of others, the woman *herself* must choose about her pregnancy."

"A bit of reverse psychology?"

"In a way. When I said we needed to make a plan so she could keep her baby, she looked stunned. Then she told me that she had never taken care of a baby, but she was so lonely, she just wanted something of her own."

"So, what did you do?"

"When I understood what she really wanted, I explained that new babies are completely dependent, and that it is the role of the mother to give to the baby, not the other way around. When I shared what it would take from her to care for an infant, she gave me a very serious look and said, 'I have just realized that the baby would be born under the sign of the rat. I am under the sign of the dragon. I will be angry and critical like my mother-in-law and never accept a rat child. I will choose an abortion.'"

"So she really wanted an abortion?"

"Well, after talking more about it, I felt confident that she saw abortion as the best choice. We did her procedure, then I called Sue Blake, who raises Shiba Inu dogs. I paid for a lifetime of food and care for one of them and gave the patient a darling puppy. She named it Hatsuko, which means first child."

"I don't understand. Did she want a baby or an abortion?"

"She wanted love."

"Ah. I see. You are so smart. Have I ever told you how much I love you?" Betty wrapped her arms around me.

"Yes, but don't ever stop," I said, laughing.

She went back to her magazine, then looked at me again. "Why do you care about this so much? Why not let the girls with husbands sort this out for themselves?"

"I like women," I answered.

"That's obvious," she pushed my shoulder playfully.

"I don't mean just that way. I actually like and care about women. Maybe you can't see it, but we live in a world that hates us. Fears us. Doesn't trust us. Notice they have pinned the 'sins of man' on the figure of Eve."

"Isn't that a bit of an exaggeration?"

"I wish it were. Look at how your father treats you. How the Navy treats us nurses. Women were property until nearly 1900. Now that the war is over, we are expendable again, and they are sending us home to be good little wives and mothers—under *their* terms." I sighed. "I'm in the same boat as the women I help."

At the end of the year, something troubling appeared in the form of a letter from my mother, followed the next day by letters from Sadie Goldfarb and Lucie.

December 30th, 1945

Darling Jane,

I miss you as always. I hate to write with bad news, but our precocious Lucie seems to have gotten in over her head. It's about a bit of anti-Semitism at the school. I love Miss May's, but it has always been very Christian and straight-laced. Remember all the hymns you had to learn in glee-club? But I think what she is encountering will stand her in good stead for being Jewish in a Christian nation. This surely won't be the last time she hears things she doesn't like. Lucie is very resilient, and I'm certain she will weather this storm. I just wanted to warn you that you will probably hear about it. I hope you can stay calm and trust that the Goldfarbs are dealing with the school. This isn't a time for you to interfere. I don't mean to sound unkind, but you are a Mama Bear when it comes to Lucie. Somehow, she shares your fierce passion for fairness.

That's all for now. I'm good. Spending a lot of time helping to set up a literacy program to teach immigrants how to read and write English. Without those skills, they just don't have a chance.

All best,
Your loving mother

January 1st, 1946

Dear Jane,

I hope this letter finds you well. I'm afraid we have run afoul of the school. There have been some distressing incidents with a student taunting Lucie by saying the Jews killed Jesus. She came home very upset. Hymie and I sat down with her and talked about prejudice, but I don't think she understood. She kept asking, isn't that what the war was all about, to end religious prejudice toward Jewish people? Last week we took Lucie to see Gentleman's Agreement *with Gregory Peck as a reporter who pretends he is Jewish for a newspaper story. Of course, he experiences terrible anti-Semitism which ruins his life. Perhaps at nearly fifteen, Lucie is old enough to understand that people are imperfect, but it breaks my heart not to be able to tell her when this hatred will ever be over.*

She wrote a school paper about the book the movie was based on. The teacher said it was inappropriate to base an assignment on a popular book, as if Gentleman's Agreement *were some kind of pulp fiction. This went all the way up to the headmistress, who, I am happy to say, ruled in favor of the importance of learning about prejudice in order to combat it. There is still a bad feeling between Lucie and the student who has been told that* our people *killed her Lord and Savior. Perhaps they neglected to mention the fact that Jesus was himself Jewish. She is still upset. She sent a letter to you today, so I hope you can help.*

All my best,
Sadie Goldfarb

January 1st, 1946

Dear Mam'selle,

I got in trouble at school, but it wasn't fair. Last year there was another Jewish girl in my class, Wendy Fink, but they moved to New York. Now there is just me, and I don't fit in. I wasn't born in Connecticut (which my classmates seem to think is where the Mayflower landed); I have a funny accent; and I'm the wrong religion! I tried to tell them about living in Paris when the Nazis occupied, but they weren't interested. I told them that the whole point of the war was to stop religious *hatred, and they said no, the war was to save Europe, and that Jewish people aren't really European and don't belong anywhere. They said there is going to be a country just for Jewish people and I'll have to go live there. That's not true, is it? Anyway, I read a book about a man who pretended to be Jewish so that he could write about living in a mostly Christian country. He told everyone that hating Jewish people has been going on for a long time. They made a movie about it. My teacher didn't like my paper. But Hymie and Sadie talked to the headmistress, so they made everything all right. You probably don't have time to see many movies, but "Gentleman's Agreement" is a really good one.*

Hymie and Sadie told me that people like me will have to keep working all of our lives to make things different. So that's really hard. I don't like to get in trouble, but I like to tell the truth.

I hope you are still my friend.

Love, Lucie

P.S. Do you think the Jews killed Jesus?"

I adored that child. I was challenged to be as honest as Lucie deserved.

January 7ᵗʰ, 1946

Dear Lucie,

Of course I am still your friend. I'm sorry you got in trouble. I think of Jesus as a great teacher who had a message of love that scared almost everyone. Neither the Jews nor the Romans could figure out what to do with him. When human beings don't understand something, they often try to destroy it.

According to Christianity, God arranged for his son to die to save humans from their sins. So obviously God killed Jesus, and the Jews just went along with the plan. I'm not sure your classmates would be very happy with that answer, but it is the only one that makes sense.

The country they are talking about is called Israel. They are proposing it be established in an area where Jewish people have lived for centuries. Jews will be able to live there if they want to, but you will not have to move.

Remember all those years ago in Paris when I was not able to explain why some people hate the Jews? I still can't. I wish the

Second World War made religious prejudice go away, just as I wish the Civil War made racial prejudice go away. But wars never seem to solve anything. I'm afraid people have a long way to go before we are actually fully human. I wish I had a happier message. The good thing is that there is no one *better than you to continue the fight for justice.*

I love you and I am very proud of you.

Jane

Betty was impatient with my "tales of Lucie," as she called anything I told her about my home life. I wished I could confide in her, but it was just something I had to accept. Little could I imagine that kerfuffle at Lucie's school was going to be the *easy* one.

CHAPTER 42

SANDI SENDS A POSTCARD

Kyoto, Japan, May 1948

If you are like me, your journals are filled with stories of strife. When life is good, my journals are empty. A year and a half went by, filled by the mundane aspects of life, and a mostly blank journal. Betty and I had been together for two-and-a-half years, but as far as my family knew, she was just a roommate who was conveniently away half of every month, leaving me the run of the apartment. I wanted to tell them—wanted to share my happiness—but I had never known another woman like me, except Betty, and I had no idea how to bring the subject up. So I stayed silent. Another secret.

I enjoyed my work at the clinic and relished the challenges of bringing healthcare to an unserved population. As painful as it was to see the effect of war and poverty on the women and children who came to us, I could also see that, little by little, we were making a difference.

At first it was hard being by myself half the month when Betty was working at other bases, but I came to enjoy my time alone. I wrote letters, kept up with my mystery novels, and occasionally wrote in my journal about an interesting or challenging patient—and about missing my mother and Lucie. Being alone for half of every month seemed a small price to pay for having someone, even if it was just the two of us. Even if loving Betty meant I could never be honest with my family. Even if it meant I had to get used to living without Lucie.

Each time Betty returned from a trip, she brought me a trinket from wherever she had been, though I told her she didn't have to.

"I'm not a child," I said. But I really loved it. I put all the little tchotchkes around the apartment so that she would know how much they meant to me. She traveled all over the United States, and she always sent postcards from the cities she visited—Boston, Pittsburgh, San Francisco. Now that there was no push to enlist new nurses, she substituted for nursing faculty who were ill or on leave, and sometimes filled slots of nurses who had withdrawn from the service to get married. I was always excited to get the mail. I'd curl up on the sofa with a scotch and look through it, hoping for something from Lucie or my mother, a postcard, or one of Betty's rare letters.

Spring brought some surprises. One day my pile of mail had two letters from home, one from Sadie Goldfarb, and the other from my mother. I didn't get many letters from Sadie, but they were always long. I opened hers first.

May 3ʳᵈ, 1948

Dear Jane,

I hope this letter finds you in good health. We have had an encounter with Lucie's school that I thought you should hear about from me, since I know you'll hear about it from Lucie. Where to begin? You know that Lucie is a voracious reader. I'm glad I am a librarian, because she is constantly in search of books on new subjects. She is fascinated by everything from classical poetry to rocket science. I'm afraid school is sometimes a little bit dull. Between the two of us, Hymie and I have to work hard to keep her engaged.

This year she started reading plays. She went through Euripides and Homer, on to Shakespeare, and finally came to the contemporary section. Recently she read Lillian Hellman's The Children's Hour, *which caused a stir on Broadway in the 1930s. In the play an unhappy student falsely accuses two women teachers of being in a homosexual relationship. The accusation ruins their lives. At the end, the one who really does have those tendencies kills herself. You can only imagine how upset Lucie was about that terrible ending.*

This was the first time Lucie heard anything about sexual aberration. As you know, Hymie and I are open-minded. We prefer to discuss complex issues rather than to avoid them. But Lucie didn't talk to us before she wrote a school paper about the history of homosexuality, starting with the Greeks, including citations from Twelfth Night, *ending by asking who benefits from laws making homosexuality illegal? It was as if Oscar Wilde himself was whispering in her ear.*

Perhaps it wouldn't have been such a problem if the teacher, Mrs. Brooks, hadn't invited students to read their papers aloud before she looked at them. According to her, there were girls in the class whose innocence was fractured by Lucie's paper. Mrs. Brooks stopped Lucie from reading as soon as the nature of the discourse became clear, but apparently the damage was done. Now parents are complaining. It is ironic because Lucie is a model student. She has always been class president, tutored younger students, volunteered at the rehabilitation center, and coordinated clothing drives for the poor. Still, Mrs. Brooks went directly to the headmistress with concerns that the topic Lucie chose was "age-inappropriate." Lucie will be sixteen this summer and she has been through a war. She is not a child. Mrs. Brooks said it was "beyond the pale," not that I think she had any true understanding of the 13th century Irish idiom she was citing.

The headmistress called us in. She insisted on punishing Lucie with a week's suspension. Hymie's and my subsequent conversations with Lucie centered around censorship and justice, and an exploration of the varieties of human sexuality. Then we played cards and baked cookies. It was an altogether enjoyable punishment.

I hope you don't think we are leading our dear Lucie down the road to depravity!

Best,
Sadie

My mouth was dry as I folded the letter and put it back in the envelope. I wanted to throw it away, but I laid it on the sofa next to me and slit open the one from my mother. It cheered me to see her familiar handwriting in the blue fountain pen she always used.

May 2nd, 1948

Oh, love. I'm afraid we are in quite a brouhaha. Lucie has apparently written a paper about sex. I'm not sure why she thought that was appropriate, but she did. It's not just that it was about sex, but about sexual perversion. I didn't know about such things when I was her age. We are lucky she was just suspended and not expelled. I'm going to suggest that she limit herself to subjects she finds in the school library. Sadie is too lenient, allowing her free rein of the stacks of books in the reference center. Those were never meant for teenagers. I'm afraid, as you always say, that Lucie is fifteen going on thirty.

I don't mean to interfere, but I think the school administrators are worried that Lucie could have unnatural urges, and might attack an unsuspecting girl. We'll have to straighten that out.

I'm sure we will.

Your loving Mother

Between the two letters a few things stood out.

- _ depravity
- – ruins their lives
- – sexual aberration
- – those tendencies
- – kills herself
- – innocence was fractured
- – the road to depravity
- – unnatural urges
- – sexual perversion
- – suspended from school
- – attack an unsuspecting girl

I was so hot that I opened the front door and stood in the breeze. I wish I had thrown Sadie's letter away unopened. And my mother's too. My eyes were jerking around, and I couldn't catch my breath. I wished it was something I could have talked about with Betty. I ate leftovers for dinner and had a stiff drink that knocked me out for the night.

The next morning I ran down to my mailbox even before I had coffee. As I suspected, Lucie's letter was there. I opened it right away.

May 3rd, 1948

Dear Jane, (At fifteen, Lucie had convinced me to let her call me Jane.)

I got in trouble again. This time they made me stay home from school, and they won't even let me do my volunteer tutoring. Anyway, you won't believe why I am in trouble. Because I read a play! Aren't I supposed to be learning about new things? This new thing was that a woman might love another woman. Do you know about that? I still don't understand why it made the teacher and the headmistress so crazy. They said I am not allowed to talk to my classmates about it. If they only knew what those girls are already talking about! Boys. How to kiss boys. If you should let a boy touch you when you are dancing. If you can get pregnant from kissing. It is ridiculous. I told them what Sadie explained to me about periods and eggs and everything, but they didn't believe me. Their mothers don't talk about any of this. They aren't even allowed to use Tampax because they think it means they aren't a virgin. I am SO LUCKY to have Mama Sadie who tells me the truth.

Anyway, I know this was your school too. Did you ever get in trouble for knowing too much?

Love you forever (don't worry, not that way!),

Lucie

Not *that* way? Oh, Lucie! If there was ever a time I imagined I could tell anyone about my relationship with Betty, I could see I was so wrong.

I started a reply.

Dear Lucie,

Then I finished doing the dishes, paid bills, watered the plants, and cleaned my hairbrush and comb by soaking them in hot water and ammonia. When I had nothing else to do I sat down again.

Dear Lucie,

I'm sorry you got in trouble. Of course you should be able to write about anything that interests you. People are scared of things they don't understand. I'm glad you're not scared.

Love,
Jane

I wrote identical letters to my mother and Sadie:

I'm sorry Lucie got in trouble. She has always had a lot of curiosity. People are afraid of things they don't understand. I hope it will be forgotten soon.

Best,
Jane

I knew Betty would be impatient if I brought this up when she got home. She would just tell me to forget it, and I assure you that is what I did my best to do.

A couple of days before Betty was scheduled to get home, the mail contained a second surprise. I was curious to see a postcard with a picture of a city I didn't recognize. When I turned it over, I saw that it was written to Betty, addressed to an FPO I didn't recognize. FPO is the mailing system for the Navy, Coast Guard and Merchant Marine, like the APO for the Army. The address was crossed out, and our correct FPO scrawled in.

The postcard read, "Miss you, darlin.' Wish I could come see you there. You know what I'd like to say, Sandi." The card was postmarked from Savannah, Georgia.

I read it about a dozen times, trying to figure out an explanation. I couldn't find one. So I did what I had so often done in my life. I tucked the problem away. I stacked Betty's personal mail on her desk the way I always did, pulled out the bills and paid them, and went on with life.

But life didn't just go on in spite of my best efforts. My mother's words haunted me. "Sexual perversion." No matter what my future with Betty was, I would never be able to share it with my mother. Maybe I could never see any of the people I loved most again—wouldn't they recognize I am an unnatural woman? But with all the fears raging, I held them inside, locked in a steel box. I didn't cry. I couldn't cry because I might never stop. Until one afternoon.

The patient had been dropped at our doorstep—dumped, I should say. She had a sign around her neck that read: "Su-mi. Liberated in Berma. Born in Busan, Koria. Age twenty-five?" written in large letters. Nick told me it seemed to be the only identifying information she had. She looked more like fifty than twenty-five—not much more than bones, with graying hair and patches of naked scalp—and she hadn't said a word to anyone.

"Berma, Koria?" I asked.

"Well, clearly, the soldier who left her behind didn't know how to spell."

"Oh, Nick. How can we help her?"

"She has a rash on her hands, so I'm guessing she has syphilis, but it will take a blood draw and a Wassermann test to be sure."

"She looks broken."

"She's certainly suffering from malnutrition, and who knows what else? But she is so fragile. I don't even want to touch her—I don't want any man to touch her. You have heard about this, right? These comfort stations?"

"Yes, but I had a hard time fathoming it. The soldiers raped them?"

"The Japanese kidnapped thousands of girls and women and held them hostage wherever there was a Japanese military presence. Soldiers raped them repeatedly, day after day, for years."

"How did she survive it?"

Nick shook his head solemnly. "If someone liberated her in Burma, maybe they thought she was dying."

"*Is* she dying?"

"We won't know how serious her condition is until we run some tests. She doesn't seem to understand Japanese. Perhaps she is mute or else in shock. And of course, syphilis can cause neurological damage. If the sign around her neck is accurate, then some poorly educated American soldier is telling us that she is from Korea, and I don't have a Korean translator here. This needs your most delicate touch. I don't think it matters that she can't understand your words. Will you see what you can do?"

I was a bit scared of Su-mi. I had cared for many women with difficult or troubled lives, but this was beyond anything I could comprehend. I nodded yes to Dr. Nick and motioned for her to come with me. She followed obediently into a treatment room. Her face was blank, like some soldiers I had seen. I motioned for her to sit on the exam table, and she did. I carefully took the sign from around her neck. Her body was rigid. I pulled my chair closer to her, but not too close. Sensing her energy, I remembered a feral kitten who lived under the porch one summer when I was a child. It took a couple of weeks and a lot of patience to get the frightened animal to eat from my hand. I hoped I could get the kitty comfortable enough with me so that we could find it a home, but that never happened. Every day it came out from under the porch and I fed it, until one day it didn't come.

As I looked at Su-mi, I despaired. There wasn't even enough light in her eyes for me to tell whether she was frightened. As I had with the kitten, I spoke to her in my most gentle voice. She probably didn't understand anything I said, but that didn't matter. It was how I was speaking to her that mattered.

I turned my hand palm up and put it on my knee, near her but not touching her, in an invitation. And then I just sat in silence. She was trembling. I didn't look her in the face. I didn't want her to feel like a specimen.

As we sat, the weight of all the horrors—the bombs, the camps, the murders, the tortures, the lives lost, the soldiers and sailors on both sides who would come home but never be right again, the kamikaze, the brutality, the hatred—and my fears for myself and my own tiny family finally broke something inside me.

With this woman whose life I could not imagine—with this stranger—I closed my eyes and cried, really cried for the first time in so long. I cried for myself and my losses—Lucie, my father, German soldiers in an alley, the innocence of thinking I had the power to make things better, my mother's judgment, Betty's mysteries. And I cried in despair for the human race. Then I let out an enormous and overdue sigh. Nothing was solved, but my tears dissolved a great lump that had been weighing on my heart.

After a moment, she slid her small hand in mine. With a few sniffles, my breathing returned to normal and I opened my eyes. Her expression was still flat, but tears welled up in her eyes. We sat, hand-in-hand, until I heard her breathing change, and she sighed. I realized the irony that I could only let my feelings out with someone who could not judge me.

I hoped I could make her feel safe enough for me to do an examination. I found a gown and mimed that she should go behind the screen and take off her rough cotton kimono. She moved as if in slow motion and emerged wearing the gown.

I led her to the examining table and helped her get up. I dreaded what I might see, so I started out by drawing blood. She sat on the table like a rag doll, and I gently moved her arm in order to apply the tourniquet. After I had the blood samples I needed, I motioned her to open her mouth. The few teeth she had left had been worn down and chipped. I noted several lesions. Her clavicle had been broken and not properly set. She had an elevated temperature, and as I palpated under her jaw, I felt swelling in her lymph glands. Then I lay the table flat and had her lie back, putting a small pillow under her head. I touched her shoulder, and said, "I apologize, my friend, that this examination may remind you of the Hell you have been in." I motioned her to move down on the table, and she did. Before I put her knees in the stirrups, I clasped her hand for a moment.

As I released her hand and sat on a stool between her legs, I wanted to weep again. Her right leg had been badly burned—the scar still raw and angry-looking. Her left leg had been broken, and there were traces of old bruises on her thighs. The syphilis rash appeared on her palms and the soles of her feet. Her pubis was nearly hairless. As I separated her vaginal lips, I found abscesses and tearing. She winced as I applied ointment to relieve some of the discomfort, but never uttered a sound.

My brain could not find the language to describe what they had done to her. Penicillin would cure the syphilis, but we had no medicine that could heal this woman's spirit. I removed her legs from the stirrups, helped her move back onto the table, and covered her with a blanket.

Then I said, "You have taken such good care of yourself, Su-mi. When it was too brutal, you survived by leaving your body. My prayer is that someday there will be a place safe enough and people kind enough that you can come back into your body, and into this terrible and wonderful world." I'm sure she didn't understand me, but I thought I saw the slightest sign of life in her eyes.

I don't know what became of Su-mi after we transferred her to a refugee camp, but in the dark times when humans reveal their enormous capacity for evil, I think of her. Our dilemma is that human beings are not quite *human*. As for what became of me, well, you shall see.

CHAPTER 43

WHAT DO YOU WANT FOR DINNER?

Kyoto, Japan, May 1948

Months later, when I was missing Betty, I found myself humming a tune I had heard a thousand times in Paris. *"J'attendrai"—I am waiting for you, day and night I wait for your return.* There were so many people who waited in vain during that terrible war. I smiled to myself, feeling a little self-satisfied because I knew that *my* love was going to be back home soon.

I was happy that there was a postcard from Betty at the bottom of the stack of mail I had just picked up. It was from Boston with a picture of Faneuil Hall, and said, "Miss you, see you soon, Betty." I think it was just because I was lonely that I read the card over and over as if I could somehow discern some secret, deeper message in it. I had never really examined the cards she sent, but I noticed it was postmarked from Boston just two days before.

That was impossible. There was no way mail could get from Boston, Massachusetts to Kyoto, Japan in two days. I had pinned all of Betty's postcards to a bulletin board in my office. I pulled them down and took the cards in a stack to the living room to look at them. I wasn't an expert on the postal service, but it surprised me that the postmarks were identical except for the name of the city. I rifled through my drawers to find letters from my mother, Lucie, and Levy. The postmarks looked different on those letters—different colored ink and different designs. That left me with a mystery.

I am not, by nature, a suspicious person, but my heart felt cold, and I was trembling as I tried to empty my mind of that nagging postcard I'd seen last spring. I refilled my glass of scotch to find, what did they call it? "Dutch courage?" This was a mystery. Where was Nancy Drew when I needed her?

It might seem strange, but Betty locked her door when she was traveling. She told me it was a habit from the days she had shared quarters with untrustworthy roommates. But I knew where the extra key was. I downed the rest of my scotch and pulled the kitchen drawer all the way out until I could feel the key at the very back under a swath of cellophane tape. My hand shook as I took it out. As if in a trance, I walked to her door and unlocked it.

Betty's room looked the way it always did. It was painted pale blue with a pretty damask bedspread that had been her mother's. I tried to think like

Betty. Where would she hide something? I opened the top drawer of the dresser where she kept her accessories. At first I didn't find anything, but then I could feel papers wrapped in fabric.

I drew the packet out of the drawer and laid it on the bed. Tucked in a green scarf made of kimono silk was a pile of brand-new postcards from all the cities where she worked. They were addressed to me and filled out with a variety of innocuous messages—all the kinds of messages I had received—"Miss you, see you soon"—generic enough not to be connected with any specific date. At first I was perplexed, but then I imagined that what had, at first, been enjoyable, might have become a burden. I could understand if she bought the postcards ahead of time so she didn't have to interrupt her busy schedule to buy one in every city.

But just as I was being understanding, I found a new mystery. Under the postcards was a pile of envelopes, all addressed to the same person—Lt. Ted Sanders–FPO Master #400, Tokyo, Japan. Who the heck was Lieutenant Ted Sanders, and what did he have to do with my postcards? I took one postcard and one of the Ted Sanders envelopes from the large stack. Then I wrapped everything else in the scarf and put it back in the drawer in what I hoped was the same place. I closed the drawer, backed out of the room, and locked the door, as if I had been on reconnaissance. I replaced the key in its hiding place, went into my office, and sat down to devise a plan. I wrote a brief letter:

Dear Lieutenant Sanders,

>*I seem to have received a mailing intended for you. I opened it without noticing it wasn't addressed to me, and then I was perplexed because it contained a postcard from Boston addressed to someone in Kyoto. I am returning it to you, but I wonder if you can clear up this mystery for me."*

>*All best,*
>*Dr. Nicos Ariti*
>*FPO # 233*
>*Kyoto, Japan*

I signed Nick's name just as I did dozens of times each week in the clinic, added his return address to the envelope, put on my jacket, walked briskly to the base post office, and mailed it before I could change my mind. I knew I was going to have to explain to Dr. Nick that I had used his name in a letter, but I didn't want to tell him everything. I felt ashamed, as if I had done something wrong.

We had the same schedule, so I thought I'd find him at home.

"Hey Dr. Nick," I said, coming up behind him in the little park outside his quarters.

"Hey, Janie, what's cookin'? Is that beautiful gal friend of yours coming home any time soon? Bai and I would love to have you over for dinner. He is experimenting with some new dishes that he wants to try out." Bai was Dr. Nick's new Japanese boyfriend who was a chef at the Officer's Club. They had moved in together, and the four of us often socialized when Betty was in town. Two couples going out was much less conspicuous than just two men, though no one seemed to notice when it was two women because women are invisible.

"She'll be home next week. I don't know the exact day. She likes to surprise me." I was struck by the thought that she was surprising me in a new way. "I have a favor to ask you," I said.

"Anything," Nick answered, smiling.

"I'm planning something for Betty," I said, haltingly. "But I don't want her to find out. I needed to ask something from a friend of hers in Tokyo, but I don't want it to slip that it came from me, so I signed the letter with your name and put your return address. So if you get a letter from a guy named Sanders in Tokyo addressed to Dr. Nicos Ariti, it is for me, okay?"

Nick was not stupid, and he knew me better than almost anyone.

"Janie, what is going on?" he asked. He pulled me over to sit on a bench in front of a gurgling fountain. "Talk to me. What is this about?"

"Nothing," I said. "It is just a surprise," I insisted. But to my consternation, I started to cry. Then I blurted out the whole sordid story.

"Oh honey, I am so sorry. But let me get this straight. You found a bunch of brand-new postcards with messages to you already written on them?"

"Right."

"And then you found envelopes addressed to some guy in Tokyo?"

"Yes. It looks as if he is the FPO Master—you know, the person in charge of the post office."

"But why would Betty do that? I don't get it. Of course I'll give you the letter if it comes—if you are sure you want it. Sometimes mysteries are best left mysteries. Do you want to come stay with us?" He had a lovely guest room I had stayed in once when our apartment was being painted.

"No. I'm good to stay at home. But thanks."

Then I put the whole thing out of my mind, as I know how to do so well. I realized I would never confront Betty because–

- I knew something was wrong.
- I didn't want it to be true.
- She would invent an excuse to slip out of it.
- I loved her and didn't want to lose her.

It wasn't until much later I could see that by trying to keep her, I was losing myself.

After a week, Nick stopped me in the middle of a busy clinic day and pulled a letter out of his pocket.

"I got it this morning. Janie, are you sure you want to read this? You might want to let sleeping dogs lie," he said.

I reached for the letter, but he wouldn't let go of it.

"No dogs are sleeping, Nick. I need to find out what is going on."

He released the letter. "Do you want me to stay with you while you read it?"

"No. I need to do this alone." I smiled at him wanly. "Thanks, though." I took the letter into a janitor's closet and with trepidation, slid open the envelope. It was a short letter—short and not sweet. And it turned my life upside down.

Dear Dr. Ariti,

Sorry the mail got mixed up. There is not much to the mystery. I am the FPO master here in Tokyo. I have a friend who sends me postcards that she wants to appear to have been mailed from various cities in the U.S. I stamp them with the postmarks of those cities and send them on. Just a favor for a friend, but I'd appreciate it if you didn't mention this to anyone. It's not strictly by the book. Thanks for sending this one to me.

All best,
Lt. Ted Sanders, FPO Master

I forgot to breathe.

Insistent knocking snapped me back to consciousness; then Nick barged in and closed the door behind him. There was hardly space for both of us. I was dizzy from the smell of ammonia in the mop bucket behind me. I handed him the letter, and he squinted at it in the low light and swore under his breath. He handed it back to me as if it were something dirty. He pulled me out of the closet, and we sat down in a small deserted waiting area.

"I don't get it," he said. "All these years you have been getting postcards from Betty—from these different cities—and this guy is saying he actually mailed them from Tokyo?"

"Yup."

"But if Betty wasn't in these cities, then where was she?"

"That is the question. Well, one of the questions. And why did she want me to think she had been mailing them from those other places? Is it possible... Nick, do you think there is any chance that she could be—I don't know—that she could be doing something for the government that she has had to keep secret?"

"She has been keeping a secret, all right," he said ruefully. "But I'm afraid I don't think it was for the government."

I hung my head.

"What are you going to do?" he asked.

"I have no earthly idea," I replied, and I began to cry again.

Nick gave me his handkerchief so that I could blow my nose, and insisted I take the rest of the day off. I felt an overwhelming sense of sadness. When I opened the door to my apartment it was as if I was attending the funeral of my tiny family. I sat down on the couch with my jacket still on. Mixed with the sorrow was a horrible feeling of shame.

One part of my mind was asking what I had done wrong that would cause Betty to trick me. Another part was saying, *Now Jane—you don't really even know what this is about. There may be a perfectly innocent explanation for all of it*, although most of me knew that couldn't be true. And simmering under all of it was the kind of anger I hadn't felt since watching the Nazi soldier march our old bookseller friend away in Paris all those years ago. Anger and betrayal braided together. I sat still, not crying, my mind a raging torrent, until I decided what to do.

I decided to do nothing.

I tucked the letter from Lt. Sanders away in my desk drawer and put on my nightgown and bathrobe. I lit a fire, curled up on the couch with a mystery novel and a bottle of scotch, and fell asleep. I woke in the morning with a stiff neck and a terrible headache, but ignored it and set about getting ready for work.

I went through the day seeing patients, giving information, doing pregnancy tests, and taking care of problems the best I knew how. With a glance, I admonished Nick not to try to talk to me about it. As I had done with the letter, as I knew how to do very well, I put the entire thing into an emotional drawer and locked it.

But fate, or whatever it is, has a funny way of having the last word. As I was rummaging in my purse for a roll of Butter Rum Lifesavers, I found a little wadded-up piece of paper. I prepared to toss it into the trash, thinking it was a gum wrapper, when I noticed that there was writing on it. I smoothed it out on the kitchen table. It was from a fortune cookie Nick brought me all those years ago in California. *Never forget that half a truth is a whole lie.* I found a thumbtack and added it to my bulletin board.

I had a patient the next day who was as emotionally armored I was. She stayed in the back of our waiting room and didn't approach the desk until everyone else was gone. Nick was out of town, and it wasn't a day we usually scheduled abortion patients, but I had come in to finish up some paperwork. I stood behind the front desk. She barely bent at the waist and whispered to the receptionist that she wanted to see the doctor. The receptionist glanced up at me, and I nodded that I would take over.

I had never met a geisha and only learned about them from books. She stood ramrod straight and looked just like a porcelain statue. She had chalk-white skin, her eyes were blackened with kohl, and she wore a silk kimono of brilliant orange with gold chrysanthemums. Her hair was pure black and looped around her head in a complicated way, with a silver headdress with little dangling ornaments that, to my untrained eye, looked as though it belonged more in a Mardi Gras parade than in a doctor's office.

I smiled at her. "Do you speak English?" She nodded. "My name is Nurse Smith. Will you come with me?"

She nodded again and followed me down the hall with the tiny steps necessitated by the kimono. I gestured to a chair in the small room we used for consultations, not sure if she would be able to sit in the elaborate costume, but sit she did.

"How can we help you?" I asked.

She looked uncomfortable. "I must speak with the doctor."

"Your English is excellent. How did you learn to speak it so well?"

She lowered her head. Not once had she made eye contact with me. "My danna—the gentleman I.... my patron... is British," she said. "He prefers me to speak to him in his own language."

From the woman's reticence, I thought it would be wise to proceed carefully. I did not know what she needed.

"I am so sorry Miss..."

"I am called Kikuyo." She shyly told me that her name meant "Chrysanthemum Evening."

"The doctor is not here today. He is in Tokyo. I expect him to return in two or three days. Is there something I can help you with?"

She looked at the floor, then shook her head slightly.

"I must have help today. I understand you help many women here. It is not the usual way for me to come to you. My mother should arrange this, but she has been very ill. I need..." she said, and stopped.

I had talked with enough unwillingly pregnant women to recognize that exact silence. Although most in the counseling profession may prefer difficult conversations to be broached by the patient, I had the feeling that the two of us would still be sitting in silence at midnight if I didn't ask directly.

"We see women for many problems here," I began. "Some women are pregnant at a difficult time, and they come to us to end their pregnancies. I wonder if that is how we can help you?"

She nodded, almost imperceptibly. "Yes, please," she said, looking at me for the first time. She was younger than I had thought.

"I must do it today... now," she said, almost pleading. "Mother will be expecting me back soon."

"We need to start with some questions. Then, if you are sure about what you want, I'll explain everything to you. The abortion will just take a few minutes. It shouldn't hurt—maybe some cramping like your monthly period. You will also probably bleed like a period afterward, depending on how long your pregnancy has lasted, so we'll give you a pad. Can you estimate how far you are in this pregnancy?"

"I know exactly. Eight weeks ago. The date of my mizuage." It shocked me when Kikuyo explained that her mizuage, the term for her first sexual experience, her "deflowering," had been sold to the highest bidder.

"Normally my mother would have been very careful to schedule it at a time I was not fertile. This is information only she knows. She tells the patron she is being guided by ancient Shinto teachings. But Mother has been very confused in her mind, and she allowed the gentleman to schedule the ceremony when he wanted. I cannot go back to my okiya, the House of the Flower, where I live, until this is taken care of. Mother would send me to the old woman who uses herbs and pessaries to treat this difficulty. I am afraid of that. I have heard that you have a superior method."

That launched me into my usual explanation of the siphon method of abortion. Kikuyo's eyes widened.

"You are sure this is safe?" she asked.

"It is very safe."

"And no one will know?"

"You will bleed like having your period, so you can explain it that way."

"That is good," she said.

"Kikuyo, is this what you want in your heart? Or do you wish to have a baby?" I asked.

She looked at me as if I had lost my mind.

"I do not wish a baby," she answered. I didn't hear any ambivalence.

"And are you at peace with this choice?" I asked, determined not to skip my usual questions just because this was an unusual person.

"I pray on this," she said. "I am at peace."

When I was assured that she understood everything, I gave her a gown and an opportunity to remove her complex wardrobe in private. She had cleverly found a large glass jar filled with cotton balls to serve as a wig stand. How stupid that it hadn't occurred to me that the coiffure wasn't her real hair!

It was startling to see the normal skin color of her neck and chest, in contrast to the pure white makeup that covered her face and continued down the nape of her neck.

A net cap covered her cropped hair, like the ones nuns wear. She had folded her beautiful kimono on the back of the chair and put her wooden sandals on the floor. I couldn't help but think how completely we women are defined by our costumes. Even without her elegant raiment, she was lovely, although she appeared vulnerable, like a newly hatched chick.

Kikuyo seemed astonished that I would do the procedure myself, but resolutely declined my offer to bring someone else into the room to be a support to her.

"Only you," she said.

The abortion was quick and, from what I could tell, not uncomfortable. Yet I already had a clear sense that a geisha, like other women warriors, would be adept at hiding pain. When she got off the table I led her to the recovery room and gave her a blanket, a heating pad, and some refreshments. We sat and talked.

As she sipped her tea, Kikuyo explained that the mother she had spoken of wasn't related to her. She was the head of her okiya—her geisha house.

"My parents live in a tiny village. I have two younger brothers and a baby sister. We were starving. I came to learn geisha to save them."

"I don't understand," I said. "How does it help them for you to be here?"

She looked down again. "I was sold as a geisha—three years ago when I was fifteen," she said. She didn't need to say anymore.

Kikuyo also told me about the tradition of Jizo, a small stone god found at Japanese cemeteries. She said she would knit a red hat for the Jizo statue at the Yasaka Shrine. Again, I looked at her in confusion. There was so much I didn't know about the people I was trying to help.

"This tradition is many centuries old," she said. "A baby that dies before its mother goes to *Sai no Kawara* on the banks of the Sanzu River and cannot pass into the afterlife. Jizo Bosatu smuggles their souls across, so we give clothing and gifts to Jizo so he will help the soul of the one that is lost.

"In many cemeteries, you will find hundreds of these, with red hats, bibs, fruits and toys. It is not just for geishas, although many of us care for several Jizos. This is for all women who have lost children. It helps us be sure we are doing right by the souls of the water babies."

"Water babies" was her translation of the Japanese term that so eloquently described the "almost but not quite" status of an embryo or fetus. I couldn't think of a term in English that conveyed the delicate meaning. When she explained the Jizo, I saw the healing power in having something external and concrete to represent an internal process. Loneliness and shame can be overwhelming when you are mourning a secret. I knew that myself.

Then I helped Kikuyo dress, and she took her wig into the bathroom to adjust it properly. With her kimono on and obi tied, she looked, again, like a doll—just as she was supposed to. She bowed to me. I bowed back. I resisted the urge to hug her.

I watched her leave, taking tiny, graceful steps. I was struck by the delicate intersection between feminine beauty and objectification; between choice and survival.

It wasn't until I was home that I could see myself in her. She was perfectly balanced—nothing released from her inner life, nothing touching her from the outside. Kikuyo's armor was made of silk. Mine was invisible, fabricated of fear and shame. Yet we were the same. If we did our job well, always serving, no one would think to wonder what was beyond the wall. We were both invented and defined by our work. I had let Betty slip past my defenses—for all these years, I trusted her in a way I had never trusted anyone.

Just a few days later, Betty came home with the usual little gift—this one from Boston, of course, home of the most recent postcard. I put the stuffed Boston Baked Bean pillow on the bed and thanked her, as usual. If she could tell that anything was wrong, she didn't say so.

"It's great to be home," is what she did say.

"I've missed you," I said. And that was true. I was already mourning her as if she were gone.

"Missed you too, chicken," she said. Her use of that endearment rankled me even more than usual, but I said nothing. Perfectly balanced, nothing in, nothing out.

I asked, "What do you want for dinner?"

CHAPTER 44

I'M HERE!

Kyoto, Japan, December 18th, 1949

I'd like to tell you about the following year and a half, but my journals are silent. I thought that if I didn't write anything down, I could make believe nothing was wrong. What I can remember of that time is working hard and doing my best to pretend that everything was fine between me and Betty. I got the usual postcards from her when she was gone, but I stopped tacking them up on the bulletin board and just threw them away. The holidays were coming again, our fourth anniversary, but I was going through the motions. I didn't even haul out the box of ornaments and decorations from our storage closet. Everything seemed so different to me. I was miserably worried, but Betty didn't even notice. She was in San Francisco on a special assignment and promised to be home just before Christmas. I had a week off for the holidays, but the time I usually spent decorating I spent drinking and listening to old records. That damned *Pal Joey* album always turned up at the top of the pile. Listening to "*If they asked me, I could write a book,*" wrenched my heart apart.

On the afternoon of December 18th, I was sitting on the sofa reading a magazine when the doorbell rang. A loud voice with a Southern drawl called, "I'm here! I'm here, darlin'! Surprise! I did it. I didn't think I could, but I did. And now I am here as the best Christmas present ever! And you can unwrap me! Let me in, let me in!!"

Perplexed, I put down my drink and answered the door. A petite, heavily made-up young blonde woman was standing on our landing beaming at me insanely.

I smiled back at her and said, "I'm sorry. You must have the wrong apartment."

"It can't be—isn't this Tokaido Road number 2 B?" We pronounced it Tok-eye-doe. She pronounced it like Tokeeyahdeeo.

"Yes, that's right. Who are you looking for?"

"The 'who' I am looking for is the lovely Betty Marston. Doesn't she live here?"

I stood there for a moment before answering.

"Why, yes. She does live here. Won't you come in?"

The woman hopped into the apartment, clutching a purse and a small suitcase. She was wearing a pink wool suit with pearls, a matching hat, and white gloves. She was shivering a bit when she came in and marched over to the fireplace.

"They said it would be colder here, but this is crazy. It was 65° when I left Savannah. Of course, that seems like weeks ago," she said, with a shrill laugh.

"Can I get you something hot to drink?" I asked. "Some tea?"

"Oh Lord, no, I would never drink hot tea! What would my mother say?" she said, laughing again. "I'm okay. It's better in front of the fire. I'm sorry. Where are my manners? I haven't introduced myself. My name is Sandra Babbitt—of the Savannah Babbitts? Actually, I prefer Sandi with an "i"—it just seems more—*modern*, don't you think? Of course Betty calls me 'chicken'—isn't that darlin'?"

I wondered why she ended all her sentences with a question mark. Truly, I did not know what to think, though the name Sandi with an "i" rang an old alarm bell. And when she said "chicken," I wanted to throw up.

"I'm Jane Smith," I said.

"Oh, you are Jane! Of course. Betty has told me all about you." She gazed up at me. "You are the girl who waters her plants when Betty is at home in Savannah? That is so nice of you. I have a black thumb, so I don't even try to grow anything indoors, but our garden is beautiful. Of course, Betty has a lovely African gentleman who takes care of everything for us. But you are so tall!"

Sandi looked around the room and took off her white gloves, pulling them from each finger, as I had seen my mother do. Then she took off her jacket and draped it over the back of the sofa like she owned the place. She looked around the apartment as if doing some kind of inspection.

"Well, I'll be darned." She picked up a shell that Betty had brought me back from a trip to Florida. "That darling must have gotten two of all the little gifts she has brought me so she wouldn't miss home as much. Isn't that sweet?"

So sweet. I'm not sure if Sandi with an "i" was nervous, or if she was just naturally voluble, but she didn't stop talking for twenty minutes, so I was free to enter a coma. She told me about her career as an office manager for the Daughters of the Confederacy, about how she and Betty had fallen in love, about their beautiful home in Savannah, about how she never telephoned Betty in Japan because she understood the work here was top secret, and about her concern that no one found out about their relationship.

"Betty said she told you all about us?"

Of course, I thought. Why not?

I nodded lamely.

"It's really very dangerous, so I don't just tell every old person who comes along. Did you know they can kick you out of the Navy for being... you know?"

"Yes, I did know that."

"Betty has been completely honest with me about her past. She hasn't always been a faithful girlfriend. In fact, she told me she has stepped out on every girl before me. And she had one girlfriend who was actually two-timing her with another girl? And when that other girl found out, she sent an anonymous letter to the Navy Brass? And they kicked her out."

Besides losing track of who was Betty's girlfriend, and which girl was two-timing whom, and who was kicked out, I got the idea.

"That's terrible," I said. "The woman did it for retribution?"

"I don't know about that," Sandi said, scrunching up her face in concentration. "I think she just wanted to get back at her. And she wanted to get the other girl out of the way. And it worked," she said, with a wry smile.

"How awful. Um, how long have you two been together?" I asked casually.

She scrunched up her face again. Thinking seemed to take quite a toll on Sandi with an "i."

"Almost four years," she finally said. "We met just after they stationed Betty in Japan. Since then she's been able to work at the base in Savannah, so we have hardly been apart for a minute—except when she had to travel and when she had to be here, you know?

"This is a really fabulous surprise for Betty—me being here and all? We have missed being together every single Christmas, and she was really broke up about missing another one. But she just had to be here in Japan—for something top secret, you know? She told me she wished I could come because she was going to have some R and R time—that's what they call it when they can have some fun? But I am so afraid of flying that I knew I'd never be able to get here. But guess what? My doctor gave me a sedative, so I just slept the whole way and only threw up the two times. Won't she be surprised?"

"I think she will be very surprised," I said. The words "four years" were ricocheting around in my brain like a metal ball in a pinball machine.

"Where is Betty, anyway?" she asked. *Good question. Where the hell is Betty?*

"She is working in San Francisco. I expect her back tomorrow."

"Okay. I guess I can just make myself at home?" she said, motioning to her suitcase. I wondered if she thought I also provided maid service.

"Sure," I said, dully.

"Gee, I am starving," she said next, with her hand on her stomach. "Is there any place nearby where I could get a sandwich and a coke or something? I don't want anything too foreign."

I am really not a vindictive person, but I just couldn't help myself. "There's a place right across the street. It serves Japanese food, but the Navy runs it. They don't speak English, so just point to the #2 special and they will fix you up. When I'm finished with the plants, I'll leave the door unlocked for you and a key on the kitchen counter."

"Thanks, you're a peach," she said. She put her suit jacket back on and waved to me as she left, putting on her white gloves as she went down the steps. I didn't have a lot of time before her first bite of the #2 special, "octopus in extra spicy sauce," would set her hair on fire.

I hurried into my bedroom, packed a bag and the little travel alarm clock that my mother gave me when I first went to Paris. The inscription, *I Love You to the Moon and Back*, was really painful to see. As I was gathering the photos from the bedside table, I smiled at my favorite picture—of Lucie, the girls, and me standing in front of the Eiffel Tower on a sunny day in June.

Then, believe it or not, I actually watered the plants. They were all mine, anyway; Betty never cared a whit for plants. I glanced at the photographs of me and Betty scattered around the apartment that Sandi missed when she was doing her "gifts from Betty" inventory. I picked up the framed picture of us caught in a passionate kiss under the mistletoe, and sighed. I almost smiled as I imagined how Betty was going to explain that one to little miss Sandi.

I took one last look around the apartment, knowing I'd have to come back one day to get the rest of my belongings. My emotions threatened to jump out of the metaphorical drawer where I had stuffed them, so with a grunt I pushed them back in. I put on my jacket, and with a stony expression on my face, I lugged my suitcase the twenty-minute walk to Nick's apartment, hoping, hoping he would be home. His boyfriend, Bai, answered the door, and Nick was standing behind him.

"CanIstaywithyouIamsorrypleasedon'taskmeanyquestions."

Bai let me in and they both said, "Of course." Nick grabbed my suitcase and followed me down the hall to their little guest room. He started to say something, but my look stopped him.

I barked, "I would love a scotch. I can't talk about it right now," and I plopped down on the bed. In the background, I heard Bai in the kitchen and the clank of bottles. He came back and passed the glass of scotch to Nick, who had stopped in the doorway. Nick gave it to me, and I drank it down like medicine.

"Janie," he began. I glared again, looking, I am sure, like a lunatic. "Okay. I get it. You'll talk when you want to talk. We'll leave you alone." Bai called to me over Nick's shoulder, "Let us know if you need anything." And then they were gone, with the door closed behind them.

I had to decide whether it was the right time to let my feelings go. I decided against it. I took a long soak in the guest bathroom tub that was identical to ours. Then I went back into the bedroom wearing a beautiful crimson silk kimono that was hanging on the bathroom door. I curled up on the bed like a puppy and fell into a deep and mercifully dreamless sleep. After some time—maybe minutes, hours, or even days—I heard a tapping on the door. Bai opened it a crack and poked his head in.

"Jane, dear," he said, "I've got dinner ready. You really need to eat something. Pardon me, but you look like hell."

"Thanks, Bai." I knew Nick had sent him because it was so hard to say no to Bai. He was a lovely young man who had studied to be a chef and hotelier at UCLA before the war.

"I don't want to eat right now, but maybe I will have another drink."

"Nick said no more drinks for right now. Come on and eat—I made your favorite. Don't even bother to get dressed. We'll have drinks later."

I'm not sure if it was his kind tone or the promise of alcohol in my future that got me to go to dinner. I couldn't imagine I would be hungry, but Bai had indeed made my favorite—steamed dumplings and chicken with snow peas and cashews. He really was a marvelous cook. Dinner proceeded with Nick and Bai making small talk, gently inviting me to participate, which I did not. Finally, we were done. Nick made a fire while Bai cleared the table. I moved to the edge of the sofa and pulled a blanket over my lap, savoring the warmth from the cozy flames. Bai had the sake that he always enjoyed after a meal, and Nick poured scotch for himself and me. As he finished pouring mine, I motioned for him to put in more, but he shook his head.

"Janie, you've already had a lot. Getting plastered will not change whatever is wrong," he said firmly.

"Maybe not, but it can help me not think about it."

He couldn't argue with that, so he added a splash to my glass. I drank my scotch the way Betty did—neat. No melting ice cubes to water down the taste of dirty socks that I had come to appreciate.

We sat in silence for a while. Nick and Bai exchanged worried glances. Finally, I said, "Betty has been leading a double life. She has another girlfriend named Sandi, spelled with an "i," who is in our apartment right now. Sandi came to visit Betty as a surprise Christmas present. She knows no more about me than I knew about her. She thinks I'm the girl who waters the plants. I didn't tell her who I really am. Frankly, I wouldn't even know *what* to tell her. That will be the 'lovely Betty's' job when she gets home. That's all, and I don't want to talk about it."

After a few minutes of fending off their concerns, I got up, said goodnight, and went back to the guest room. Nick refused to let me take the bottle with me. I put on my nightgown, climbed under the covers, and prayed for sleep to come.

Nick had a rare private telephone in his apartment because he was on-call for emergencies. Starting the afternoon of the next day, Nick and Bai fended off multiple phone calls and even a visit from Betty.

"No, she doesn't want to talk to you. No, she doesn't want to see you," were the phrases they repeated. Over the next few days, I stayed in their apartment as if it were a hideout. I played gin rummy with Nick; completed a huge jigsaw puzzle of the Eiffel Tower that had two pieces missing; and made a list of things that they could do to help me, which included getting a new FBO box so that I would still get my mail. I washed my hair with Bai's fragrant jasmine shampoo; did my nails; and wrote chatty letters to my mother, Lucie, and Levy, as usual, leaving out everything important that was happening in my life.

I made a list of things I still needed to remove from the apartment, including my extra suitcase which would have been easy to forget because it was tucked behind the Christmas ornaments in the storage closet. I took walks behind their house in the private gated area and read a bit of *Crime and Punishment*. I had somehow avoided that book in all my years of formal education, but it was in Nick's collection of leather-bound classics. I didn't really get into it—I had no ability to focus. But the title seemed appropriate. After a few days, I ventured out with Bai to the outdoor market and bumped into one of my neighbors, Miss Wright, who worked at the base library.

She pulled me aside and whispered, "Oh, Jane, are you all right?" She looked very concerned. "I don't mean to meddle, but I couldn't help but overhear the arguments you and Betty have been having. I've never heard either of you raise your voices before, so I know there must be something terribly wrong, or I would not mention it. Is there anything I can do to help?"

Very interesting.

"Thanks so much for your concern, Miss Wright. That actually wasn't me. I've been away from home. Betty has an old friend visiting, and I guess they must have had some disagreements." I couldn't help but smile just a little at the thought of the formidable Betty, and Sandi of the Savannah Babbitts, duking it out.

"Oh. Well, I'm glad it wasn't you. I'll just be going," she said as she grabbed her string bag full of vegetables and hurried off.

"What was that?" Bai asked.

"Oh, nothing," I answered. "My reality," I said grimly.

Even though we were both off for the holiday, Nick went to the clinic several times—once when an officer's wife had a ruptured ovarian cyst (he was the best surgeon on the base), and once to oversee a drug inventory. Each time, he assured me there was no gossip about me and Betty.

"No one is going to know anything. It's none of their business unless you want to tell them."

"I don't," I said, pleadingly.

"Then it will be our secret."

Great. Another secret.

Secrets can kill you.

CHAPTER 45

SANDI SENDS A LETTER

Kyoto, Japan, December 23rd, 1949

Then, the shit hit the fan, as they say. After my encounter with Miss Wright, I refused to go out again. Bai brought the mail from my new FBO, which included some letters forwarded from the box I shared with Betty. There was a Christmas card addressed to both of us. I crossed out the address and scrawled "Return to Sender" in big black letters. I wondered if the postmaster was going to divide the mail addressed to both of us the way you deal cards—one to me and one to Betty. There was a copy of the lease for the cheap furnished apartment Nick had found for me in a nice enough building. At the bottom of the stack, there was an envelope from the Navy. It looked very official. The hair on the back of my neck stood up as I opened it.

Office of Naval Discipline
FBO Box 759
Kyoto, Japan

December 22nd, 1949

Dear Officer Smith,

We are in receipt of an allegation that you are in violation of Section AR 635-200 of the Navy Code. Specifically, it alleges that you have engaged in homosexual conduct. As you are aware, this behavior involves moral turpitude outlawed in the United States Navy and is grounds for dismissal.

If you dispute these charges, you will be scheduled for a Court Martial to hear testimony. If found guilty, you will receive a Dishonorable Discharge.

If you wish to submit the name of others involved in this prohibited behavior, we will offer you a General Discharge.

If you accept the charges lodged against you and wish to take no further action, you will receive an Undesirable Discharge.

Please indicate your choice, sign at the bottom of this form, and return it to our office.

> *Sincerely,*
> *Matt Haven*
> *Vice Admiral*
> *United States Navy*

I must have cried out because Nick ran in from the kitchen.

"What is it? What's wrong?" I handed him the letter.

"This is Sandi's doing," I said. "She wanted to get me out of the picture and she has succeeded."

"How do you know?" Nick asked, rereading the official document.

"She told me a story about someone else who got kicked out of the Navy in exactly this way. All it took was an anonymous letter."

"They can't do this to you. We'll find a lawyer—you've got to fight this," he exclaimed, shaking his fist.

"What good would a lawyer do when it's true? What I am is bad enough, I'm certainly not going to lie about it. And don't even suggest that I might implicate Betty. I won't."

Nick took me in his arms, and I sobbed. Tears I had held back for days came cascading out. "I just can't have a dishonorable discharge! I just can't, I just can't."

For a long time, we stood that way, me clinging to Nick and weeping, him holding me, not knowing what to say. Finally, I stopped crying. He found a handkerchief in his pocket and I wiped my eyes and blew my nose. I was clear about what I had to do.

"Thanks, Nick," I said. "You are swell." It meant more than I could tell him to have a friend I could count on. I took the letter over to the desk and signed it, accepting an Undesirable Discharge. I folded the document and licked the flap on the pre-posted envelope. Funny how glue tastes the same, whether you are sending a love letter or an admission of guilt.

"I'll be back in a minute," I said.

"Janie, I can take that to the FBO for you. It will go right into the officer's box," Nick said, reaching out for the letter.

"Thanks. I need to do this myself." I put on my hat and coat, slipped off the Japanese house shoes that they always wore inside, put my shoes on and, head held high, I trudged off to the Base FBO office. On the way, I passed a few people who said hello and Merry Christmas, but I didn't answer. In the post office, as I stood in line to hand my letter over, I was sure everyone was looking at me. My face burned as I imagined the judgments and pity they were surely sending my way. I wondered if I would ever feel respectable again.

I walked to my old apartment, my heart pounding. I hammered on the door as if it were a police raid. No one answered, so I used my spare key to let myself in. I was shocked to see that the apartment looked exactly as it had when I left. I don't know what I expected. I dug the extra suitcase out from under the boxes of Christmas decorations and hoped it would be big enough for everything. I pulled the list from my pocket. Bathroom, bedroom, study. I had things in every room. I went into my bedroom and pulled things out of drawers and off shelves. I piled everything on the bed. I didn't go into Betty's room. Anything I had in there would be sacrificed to the god of failed relationships.

I noticed that all the photographs of Betty and me were gone. For a moment, I considered looking for them—in one of the drawers? In the trash? Then I remembered what she had done and was furious. I was glad never to see those pictures again. My toothbrush, soap, and face cream had been put in a dish in my bathroom drawer. Why was I ashamed to see them there? Why was *I* ashamed about any of this?

A week after I mailed the signed form, I received another official envelope with my discharge papers, instructions about what to do with my uniforms and identification badges, and an admonition that my discharge would result in the loss of all benefits, including health care and educational stipends. The official document read, "Undesirable. AR 635-200." According to the Code of Conduct, my discharge was for "Homosexuality; Qualified Resignation, unfitness; Disloyal and subversive; Security violation." I have never felt so wretched.

Despite Nick and Bai's insistence that I stay with them, I spent that Christmas alone in my new empty apartment. It matched my new empty life.

CHAPTER 46

SHUT UP

Kyoto, Japan, December 25th, 1949

Thank goodness Dr. Nick had found a small, sparsely furnished apartment for me in the civilian section right behind the clinic. He promised to use his contract labor fund to keep me on staff. He was a good friend. I didn't mean to be ungrateful, but I couldn't bear to be around him or anyone. I skipped Christmas altogether and threw out the presents from my mother and Lucie without even opening the packages.

On Christmas night, as I folded my clothes into the cheap dresser, I kept thinking how much a drink would help. I had a bottle of wine in the tiny kitchen, but it was the scotch I turned to. Before long, I was splayed out on the bed. I slept through dinnertime and woke, my clothes rumpled, in what I assumed were the wee hours of the night. The clock on the bedstand said 11:30. The room was stuffy, so I put on a sweater and coat and went outside into the crisp winter air. In a little park next to the building, I sat on a bench and looked at the crescent moon. Even in the face of disaster, nature had a way of making me smile. I dozed off for a moment and I awoke with a start to see Betty sitting next to me. At first, I wasn't sure if she was real or my imagination.

"How did you find me?" I asked, when I smelled her perfume and decided she was real.

"I wormed the address out of Dr. Nick. He didn't want to tell me. He is very protective of you."

"I appreciate that about him. What do you want from me?" I asked bitterly.

"Sandi has made quite a fuss. I'm leaving Japan. My father is having me reassigned. I don't know where yet. I wanted to say goodbye—and I am sorry."

"Well, *chicken*," I answered, "it is a bit late for that. You tricked me into thinking you loved me—that there was a place in this world where I belonged."

"Jane, I'm—I can't explain it. It's just that I have always needed to have two people—in case one left me. If it means anything, I really *do* love you. You were my favorite."

"SHUT UP, Betty!" I said through clenched teeth. "JUST SHUT UP! I don't want to hear anything you have to say!" To my chagrin, I noticed that I had started crying.

"No, I don't suppose you do," she said.

"I can't forgive you for this," I said. "I can't ever forgive you."

"Well, we're even. I'll never forgive myself either." She stood up, brushed off her skirt, and walked away into the night.

CHAPTER 47

SCOTCH NEAT

Kyoto, Japan, February, 1950

I hated telling you that story. You must think me as much a fool as I felt. But it explains the dark time that followed. I had a place to live, but what a step down. No fireplace—no soaking tub—the shared bathroom down the hall. But it was all I needed. A book and a bottle kept me company. I arrived at work mostly on time and did the bare minimum. Then I went back to my apartment and collapsed on my single bed, a fifth of scotch and glass within easy reach on the night table. Sometimes I had nightmares. Sometimes I didn't sleep at all.

Nick and Bai did everything they could think of to rescue me. They cajoled and threatened and entreated me to come eat with them. Occasionally I did, but it hurt to remember how wonderful it had been with the four of us, and I was certainly no fun. Eventually, they gave up.

"Jane, patients are actually complaining about you—you—the best nurse I know! When you go home for Lucie's graduation I am ordering you to take at least a month to get yourself together. This is not a suggestion or an offer —it is an order—do you hear me? Jane, you must get over this. And you *must* stop drinking. Betty is not worth it! I wouldn't treat my worst enemy the way she treated you."

That high school graduation was the only thing I had to look forward to. June seemed like a long way off, but I was determined to be there. Surely I would be able to pull myself together with a whole month at home?

Nick stopped by my apartment one evening. I had already had a scotch or two, so I didn't want to answer the door. But he continued to knock until I let him in.

"I'm so sorry, Nick. I'm lost right now. I promise I'll stop drinking when I go home. I'll be with my mother, Lucie, and Levy—all the people who really love me."

He raised his eyebrow.

"I'm sorry. I mean, besides you. I can never thank you and Bai for your love and support. It's just that being here is so hard. I am reminded of Betty everywhere I look. Drinking makes it easier."

"Have you told any of them about what happened?"

"You know I can't tell them! I said Betty was just my roommate to avoid their judgments about 'unnatural' women. And I didn't tell anyone about my discharge, let alone the reason. I would die if they knew. I am already so humiliated. How could I ever tell them?"

He sat down next to me on the sofa and put his arm around me. I put my head on his shoulder.

"Shh," he whispered. "Of course, you don't have to tell them anything you don't want to. A month back at home will make all the difference. I promise, everything will be better soon."

Even though I was in a fog, I remember that sweet moment so clearly. And I can recall the tears that I shed on the shoulder of that dear, dear man.

CHAPTER 48

GOING HOME

Kyoto, Japan, May, 1950

I don't like surprises. I don't enjoy being the one surprised or being the surprise. For me, there is always an unpleasant smell of deceit. But my mother and Levy persuaded me that Lucie would love my surprise arrival at her graduation, so I agreed. Lucie's letters brimmed with excitement about preparations for graduation. Mine were full of my busy workload, my supposed excuse for not coming home for her big day. I really *was* working double shifts and then collapsing into bed with a bottle. The exhaustion was almost enough to keep me from obsessing about Betty.

A month in Connecticut! Unheard of! I splurged on tickets for the best flights so I could sleep on the way and arrive refreshed. I was depleted from weeks of extra work and too much booze. I looked achingly forward to being pampered by my mother, and to seeing my friends and family.

I couldn't figure out what to get Lucie for a graduation gift. I abandoned the old standbys—a pen, a wristwatch, a suitcase—too boring. Besides, there were no shops near the base to purchase anything like that. I lingered over some colorful kimonos in the local market, but they seemed too much like a costume. In bed, just before falling into a coma-like slumber, I mused over memories of the seven-year-old Lucie: adventurous, funny, smart, brave, impulsive, fierce, kind. In those ways, she hadn't changed over the years.

Although they loved her dearly, I inferred from my mother's letters that the Goldfarbs sometimes found Lucie a handful. I looked at a photograph that was on every one of my bedside tables since Paris. In it, ten little girls and an impossibly tall, impossibly young, woman in a nun's habit are standing in front of the Eiffel Tower on an impossibly beautiful Paris day. June 8th, 1939, is inscribed in blue ink on the front of the photograph. As I ran my finger over the picture, I remembered each of the girls. In the picture, Lucie was front and center, making a funny face. It was the perfect gift.

My planned itinerary took me from Kyoto to New York City spanning three days. Mother would pick me up at the airport, and tuck me into my childhood bedroom for a day to rest, then we would all attend Lucie's graduation. Lucie was graduating from Miss May's Academy, an all-girls' college preparatory school. You might remember it because of the difficulties Lucie had dealing with anti-Semitism, and that other problem. But I don't want you to think badly of Miss May's. I graduated from the same high school and I loved it. It seemed impossible that I walked across the stage with my bouquet of red roses nearly twenty years before. Commencement at Miss May's was a lovely ceremony—out on the school's lawn if weather permitted.

I packed way ahead of time, as if I could will myself there. I wrapped the photo of the girls at the Eiffel Tower in a beautiful piece of silk and tucked it in the suitcase next to my meager travel wardrobe.

A week before my flight, after another grueling double shift, an ensign knocked on my door with a message. It said, *Urgent. Call Dr. Levy at your home.*

Panic. My mother? Mom hadn't been the same since Dad's death. It was nine in the morning yesterday in Connecticut. I rushed to the central office staffed 24 hours a day. I showed the duty officer the message, and he kindly set me up with the phone in a back room. My hands trembled as I dialed my parents' number. Levy answered on the first ring.

"Allo. Levy here."

"It's Jane. Is it Mother?"

"Non, Jane. Your mother is fine. I can hardly bear to tell you this. It is Lucie. She is gravely ill."

I was too stunned to speak. I sat down hard behind the desk. It made no sense. She was just a teenager. Lucie was safe—we did everything to get her out of France so that she would be. She had parents who loved her, a community that loved her. There was some mistake.

"Jane? Jane? Are you there?"

"Oh, Bernard."

"Can you come home?" he asked. "Now? We need you."

"Of course I will come home. But how? What happened?"

"She is in a coma. Jane, she had an illegal abortion. Please come as soon as you can."

I don't recall anything about the rest of the conversation—or the rest of the night, for that matter. Dr. Nick pulled every string possible to get me on a military transport plane designed more for cargo than people. Thirty of us were going stateside. They strapped us into uncomfortable seats in what sounded like the belly of a monster. I imagined they would at least give us ear covers like the pilots wear, but they did not. The din on the thirty-plus-hour, nearly seven-thousand-mile trip to Mitchel Air Force Base on Long Island was almost unbearable. I was a zombie as they herded us off and on the plane for every refueling. I tried to sleep—to stop my thoughts.

But I hadn't told Lucie how to protect herself. She was almost eighteen, but in my mind she stayed that lost little seven-year-old. I blamed myself that she didn't confide in me, but she didn't have a clue I knew anything about abortion. I had kept that secret from her, afraid she would think badly of me.

Lucie was a faithful correspondent. She told me about her best friends, and her favorite classes and teachers. She wrote about her excitement at being accepted into Barnard, her first choice of colleges, and her dream to work in medicine as Dr. Levy and I did. But nothing about a boy.

I had attributed the recent lack of mail to the stress of final exams and getting ready for graduation. My imagination exploded, picturing her terror at realizing she was pregnant. Every time I started to doze off, we hit turbulence, or there was another engine noise even louder than before. I gave up trying to sleep. I desperately wanted a drink, but we had been told in no uncertain terms that alcohol was forbidden on the flight.

When we landed, I found my duffle inside the terminal. My mother stood behind the wire fence waving at me. I had been holding on until I saw her. I burst into tears, ran, and grasped her hand through the chain link.

"Is she…?"

"She's the same, darling. The doctors are giving her antibiotics. They are hoping we'll see a change soon. But she is very, very ill." Unwelcome images of Mimi crowded my mind.

Mom looked at me, a furrow in her brow. "Jane, darling, are you all right? You look terrible. I am worried about you. When did you sleep last?"

"I'll be all right. I'll sleep when I know Lucie is all right. Let's just get to the hospital."

On the hour-long drive to the hospital, I didn't speak, although my mother made a few attempts at conversation. I found myself dozing, dreaming about the first time I met Lucie.

I recall so many details of that time. Lucie and I met in the spring of 1939, before the invasion of Poland destroyed our naïve belief that another world war would never happen. This small-town New England girl found France both beautiful and a bit frightening.

After my ship docked, I took a taxicab from Mantes-la-Jolie, the closest train stop from Cherbourg where the ocean liner anchored. The driver, a small wiry man, complained as he struggled to load my steamer trunk into the back of his small vehicle. He tied the lid of his luggage compartment with a long piece of twine, complaining furiously in rapid French that I was happy I could not decipher.

When I gave him my aunt's address, he abruptly smiled broadly and switched his tone to equally rapid, but now happy French that I still could not understand. I asked him to please speak more slowly.

He had smiled again and spoke as if in slow motion, so I got most of it. "Ah, I love Madame Mathilde," he said. "My daughter was determined to fail learning English. Madame Mathilde worked a miracle. Now Gigi speaks as well as the Queen of England!"

"Mathilde is my aunt," I said. "I will be very happy to give her your regards." I was proud to construct such a complicated sentence in French, but I must have said something funny because he laughed as he drove. The driver, suddenly my best friend, gestured to the points of interest and the different neighborhoods as we drove by.

"You are coming for a visit with your aunt?" He glanced behind at the trunk sticking out of the back of his car.

"Yes, well, sort of. I am going to be a teacher," I answered.

He harrumphed—to show his skepticism, I suppose. As he pulled up to the old mansion I had only seen in photographs, Mathilde Smith, a formidable woman if there ever was one, came out to greet me. When I stepped out of the cab, she kissed me on both cheeks.

"Welcome chérie! So tall!" she said. "I didn't realize. I'll instruct the seamstress to adjust your uniform." She turned to the cab driver, and it was as if I had disappeared.

"Hallo Jean-Guy. How is Gigi?"

The driver beamed. "Très bien, Madame Smith. Now where shall I put this?"

Mathilde swooped into the house, followed by Jean-Guy and my luggage, leaving me standing alone in the driveway. I was startled to feel a tug on my coat. A tiny little girl with long red hair. She took my hand and drew me down so my face was at her level.

"Bonjour Mademoiselle. Je m'appelle Lucie. Êtes-vous perdue? Je peux vous sauver."

That was Lucie. "Good afternoon, miss. My name is Lucie. Are you lost?" and not "Can I direct you?" or "Can I help you?" but "I can save you!"

"Non, ma chérie. Je ne suis pas perdue. Je suis la nouvelle institutrice! Je m'appelle Mademoiselle Jane."

"D'accord!" With that exclamation, she pulled me into the old house and down a hall into a small room filled with little girls napping on pallets covered with pink blankets.

"J'ai découvert la nouvelle institutrice! Elle s'appelle Mademoiselle! I discovered the new teacher!" Ah, yes, Lucie. You did. And from that time on I was known as Mademoiselle, shortened to Mam'selle.

In my reverie, I didn't realize my mother had pulled into the hospital parking lot. Before we got out of the car, she put her arms around me, which opened the fist I had held tight around my tears. I sobbed on her shoulder. Levy came out to the car. He didn't want to look at me because he didn't want to cry, but we all suspected that there were many, many tears to come. I wanted—needed—to hear more about what had happened, but first I needed to see Lucie.

She was in a private room with a breathing tube and an IV in her arm. The Goldfarbs were sitting beside the bed, looking haggard. I had seen some young wounded sailors in my time at the Navy Hospital, but nothing could have prepared me for the shock of seeing Lucie like this. I felt so helpless. And this terrible thing had happened to her somehow without my knowing. Should I have realized that something bad was happening to her? Shouldn't I have sensed that something was not right? I was as attached to Lucie as if I had given birth to her. Yet here I was, with no way to help.

"Who did this? What monster…?" I reached out to take the medical chart hanging at the end of the bed, but Levy caught my arm.

"Jane, come with me. I will tell you everything we know."

We walked down the corridor to the tiny chapel where Levy told me a story that broke my heart.

"It seems that Lucie had an illegal abortion two or three days ago. She developed septicemia despite the antibiotics and the D&C they did to remove retained tissue. She lapsed into a coma before any of us realized she was here." He looked down at his hands.

"I do not believe what you are saying. Lucie is just a child! That cannot be true… and an illegal abortion? With you right here? How was it possible?"

"Lucie has grown up a lot since you have been away. As always, she is fiercely independent. She told Sadie she was staying with a friend. She didn't have identification, but luckily the hospital found a library card in her coat pocket and called the Goldfarbs. As for me, I never told her anything about what I did… what you and I did together in Paris. She would never have thought of seeking my help. And for that, I shall never forgive myself."

I laughed a hollow laugh. "And what about me? I have been doing safe abortions for women thousands of miles away when my darling Lucie needed me here. I never told her either, Bernard. I couldn't bear it if she thought I was bad." I closed my eyes and wrapped my arms around myself. "Is she going to live? I am familiar with sepsis. Mimi, of course. And I have often seen its deadly march in the bodies of wounded soldiers."

"It appears she was brought to the hospital quickly after she started having symptoms. Thank God one of the staff, Dr. Hoffman, recognized the signs and got her on antibiotics immediately. They say the coma isn't unusual, and it doesn't mean she can't pull through. But there are no promises."

"Who did this?"

"Do you mean who did the abortion, or who was her lover?"

"Both, I guess. Either."

"The Goldfarbs don't seem to have any idea. They are gracious people, but Lucie has always been a bit of a mystery to them," Levy said, putting his hand on mine.

"How could there be a boy that no one knew about? Lucie wrote to me nearly every week. I never heard a word about a boy. After everything she went through, I just wanted her to have a normal life. Should I have tried to keep her myself?"

"It won't help to think of all the things we should have done differently. She knows you love her, and she always has. What more could you do than to surround her with people who care for her?"

"But then I left."

"Jane, don't. Let's just focus on Lucie and getting her through this."

Arm in arm, we went back into the room.

"The hospital staff is trying to limit how many people are in here at once," my mother said, looking at Levy and the Goldfarbs. "I'm bushed. I know we all are. Since Jane is here, what do you say we all go home and get a shower and some sleep? We can come back in the morning."

"Thanks, Mom."

Sadie Goldfarb was reluctant to leave, but she hugged me. Hymie looked at me mournfully. Everyone gave me a kiss on the cheek, and they filed out of the room.

Sitting by the bed, I studied the face I had known so well and now hardly knew at all. Lucie's red hair, darkened into auburn, was shoulder length, and splayed out on the pillow like a halo. Her face was longer, but still elegant, and as pale as it was the day she fell from the Linden tree. She had grown into a lovely young woman.

I reached over and took her pulse, even though she had a breathing tube. I placed the photograph of me, Lucie, and her seven-year-old classmates standing in front of the Eiffel Tower, on the table beside the bed. Even if she never saw it was there, I wanted those angels watching over her as they had always watched over me.

A few minutes later, her doctor came in. Whatever professional demeanor I might ever have had dissolved.

"Thank you so much for helping her. Is there any change? Is she better? Save her..." I grabbed his arm and held on. "You have to save her!"

He spoke quietly and firmly. "I'm not seeing any improvement, but she hasn't gotten worse, so that's a positive sign. It's a waiting game. We'll do everything we can, but I can't tell you whether she is going to make it. I am so sorry," he said. "The best you can do is to be here with her." He led me to the chair next to the bed and left me there alone.

As I sat by her, I began to speak in a low whisper. Words I had so often thought, but never said aloud. Never said to her. Never said to anyone.

"Lucie, chérie, I should never have left you. You needed me and I chose the coward's way. I couldn't see how to be in your life without disappointing you. Without failing you. There are things I have never told you about myself. I have loved a woman. Is that unforgivable? I honor all women, though they are so hated and feared in our world. I love them so much that I have risked everything to help them believe in their own goodness. I have helped them have abortions. Can you understand? I'm sorry. Please, please don't die. I promise I won't go away again. I promise I'll be here to see you grow into a woman. No more secrets."

Holding her hand and watching the IV drip, my eyes closed. Anyone walking by might have imagined that I was praying.

CHAPTER 49

A NIGHTMARE OF A FUNERAL

Connecticut, May 1950

None of us could stop crying. My mother, who never raised her voice, yelled, "It isn't right to cremate a teenager!" I yelled back, "Who said anything about cremation?"

Dr. Levy said, "The funeral has to be within 24 hours according to Jewish custom."

"But the Goldfarbs don't practice, do they?" I whined.

"Of course. They go to Temple Beth El. Shouldn't they be the ones to decide what to do? They are her parents, after all," my mother said.

"No. They are not really her parents. She is mine. I'm the one—I'm the one who always loved her," I cried out.

My father said, "She always liked my Episcopal church. They'll have bagpipes."

Mother countered, "They don't have bagpipes at a Jewish funeral."

We argued about how to make these hideous arrangements. Where do you hold a funeral for a teenager? How can any of us go on with our lives when half our hearts have been torn away?

I paced back and forth in my childhood bedroom, trying to decide what to say at the service. My father gave his advice—to speak from the heart. Levy said he trusted me to decide. Betty advised me not to let her father come to the funeral. My mother appeared in the doorway and asked if I needed help.

"I can't decide whether to tell the truth about what happened," I said.

"Dear, I recognize how much you value honesty, but are you thinking of Lucie—her reputation?"

"What good is a reputation if you are dead? Besides, some of her friends have already heard about it. *They* won't be keeping it a secret. It will just be like a poison that trickles out of an infection a little at a time. And her death will be for nothing. Nothing!" I pounded my fist on the desk.

"My darling, I understand. No matter what you decide, we'll support you." With that, she kissed my cheek and left me to my thoughts.

I was grateful that Lucie's friends filled the temple. Her schoolmates were packed into the back rows. Aunt Mathilde (how did she even get here?) had placed an enormous crucifix on the closed casket. The scent of lilies was intoxicating. It was a small building, small enough that I didn't need a microphone. If I was able to find my voice at all.

I cleared my throat and began. "Good morning, I am Jane Smith. Thank you for being here to share this goodbye to our beloved Lucie. This is a memorial that never should have happened. Most of you knew Lucie very well—and I can say that everyone who knew her loved her, even when she was a challenge."

Gentle laughter followed, as I expected.

"I met Lucie when she was a seven-year-old in Paris. A year after the Nazis occupied the city, I brought Lucie to this country with the support of my Aunt Mathilde." I gestured toward her in the front pew and she bowed her head. Mathilde was conspicuous in her black habit. She sat next to two sweet little seven-year-old girls in pinafores—Socorro and Paulette, Lucie's best friends. Of course they would come.

"And with the help of our beloved Dr. Bernard Levy," Levy wept, but he nodded as well.

"Here she had a new life with the wonderful Goldfarbs." They sat in the front row, next to my mother and father. They leaned against each other and didn't even acknowledge my words. Rosie, the cocker spaniel, was curled up in Sadie Goldfarb's lap, crying.

"We all loved Lucie's brightness, creativity, infectious spirit, caring, and mischievous nature. If Lucie saw a sign that said, 'Danger, Do Not Enter,' she read, 'Glorious Adventures This Way!' She charmed us all, and we loved her fierce loyalty." Heads nodded. I was still debating with myself, but seeing the kids made me bold.

"Lucie was honest, as they say, to a fault. And it is her honesty and her love—especially her love for her friends—that has made me decide to tell you the truth."

I stopped and took a deep breath.

"Lucie didn't have an accident, as you have been told. She had an illegal abortion that went wrong. That is how she died."

I heard a collective gasp. I didn't realize that saying it out loud would be so hard. My face felt numb.

"I failed her. We all failed her. Don't look around to speculate about the boy. He lives in another town. But it could have been here. In Lucie's memory and in her honor, I want to tell you what I have learned about abortion after nearly a decade of providing abortion care."

I heard the gasp that I had anticipated, but continued, though I couldn't look at my parents.

"Abortion is a sacred choice—just as sacred as the choice to give birth. It is not only a woman's right; it is her *responsibility* to decide when to bring a new life into the world through her body. Laws that make abortion and birth control illegal are crimes against women. In a different world, at a different time, Lucie would still have her whole life in front of her."

I could hear the people murmuring.

"I'm sorry if I have disturbed you, but the death of a young woman should be disturbing. This is a memorial that never should have happened."

With that, I left the podium, back to the front pew. The room had become awfully quiet, and I couldn't look at anyone. Then there was a noise behind me. Some of Lucie's friends had stood and begun clapping.

And it spread.

In a moment, half the people in the room were clapping and crying. And soon all the people who had known Lucie as their friend, their student, their babysitter, the girl who walked their dog, their daughter, and their beloved, stood and clapped. And finally, I joined them. It was noise like church bells.

The rattle of a medical cart startled me. The woman pushing it was short and plump, with white hair. In my daze, I thought she was Mrs. Santa Claus.

"Sorry to wake you, love." She bent over and took Lucie's temperature. "Her fever has broken. I shouldn't say this, but I think God has his eye on this little sparrow," she said, smiling at me. "I bet she's awake before you know it."

I shook my head and caught my breath. Lucie was alive? Still here in the bed, right next to me! She was breathing and her fever had broken! My nightmare had broken. I whispered to the nurse, "Thank you, thank you. Thank you!"

"It's not me you need to be thanking. This one is a fighter. We are all rooting for her." She finished her work and smiled at me as she left. "My name is Bridie. You call me if you need anything, dearie, anything at all."

I stood by the bed, watching Lucie's face as if waiting for the sun to rise. In another half hour, her eyes fluttered open. I leaned over her, tempted to remove the breathing tube myself, but I shook off that idea and pushed the call button. I put my hand on her arm and said, "Don't worry, my darling. They'll get that tube out in just a minute." Bridie came in. I smelled the starch in her white hat as she swooped past me to Lucie's side.

"Now dearie, I want you to cough and this will come right out."

Lucie looked at me, and I nodded. She coughed, and the nurse slid the tube out. That led to more coughing.

"Your throat is going to be a bit sore. That's normal. I'm just going to moisten your lips with this glycerin. You can have some ice if you want." She turned to me. "She may be a bit confused for a while. Just help her stay calm. She'll likely be in and out of sleep."

I nodded as if I were a child. She took Lucie's vital signs and smiled. "All good," she said. "There are ice chips in the Kelvinator next to the nurses' station. Call if you need me." I felt scared as she left the room. Then I remembered that I was a nurse.

I turned back to Lucie who burst into tears. In a hoarse voice, she whispered, "I am so sorry, Mam'selle. I wanted to wait for you, but he said we had to do it right away. Are you mad at me?"

"I'm not mad, but we have all been scared to death. You have been very sick." I wiped her face with a tissue. My nightmare was still hovering around my heart. She didn't die, but she could have died. Because abortion, the simplest of procedures, was illegal. So many have died. So many more will.

Lucie hung her head. I held her face in my hands and kissed her on the forehead. *My pulse.* "You know, you must tell me who did this."

Her eyes widened. Then a familiar Lucie furrow appeared between her brows. "I can't tell you. You will put him in jail for doing an illegal abortion." She seemed to have overwhelmed herself, and her eyes closed as quickly as they had opened and she fell back to sleep.

I thought about Mimi and all the other girls who died because they couldn't find someone safe to help them. I thought about how close Lucie had come to dying. With each thought, my resolve strengthened. I couldn't let the man who hurt Lucie harm other women. I *wouldn't*. More to myself than to the sleeping Lucie, I said, "I don't want to put him in jail, I want to teach him how to perform safe abortions."

-fin-

EPILOGUE

Albuquerque, New Mexico, Present Day

I shoved my way through the hostile crowd, walking backward, making a space for the young woman to follow. I stayed as close as I could, kept my eyes on hers, and spoke directly to her. I hoped she could make out my words above the din of the angry voices surrounding us.

In a commanding voice, I said, "You don't have to listen to them. They don't even know you. You are the only one who can make this choice. We will support you no matter what you decide."

The woman moved her head abruptly back and forth from one yelling protester to another, as if watching the tennis game from hell. I touched her gently on the arm to bring her attention back to me. As much as I tried to keep her focus on me, the ugly voices seeped in.

"You are a slut."

"The blood from your crotch will rise up against you, you whore."

"God will not forgive you."

"What kind of woman murders her own baby?"

"Mommy, mommy, don't kill me. Mommy, I love you. Mommy, I need you. Mommy, mommy, don't kill me. Mommy, I love you. Mommy, I need you,"—this a recording that repeated over and over in a loop, played at top volume with a background of a baby crying.

I estimated a hundred protesters. Some old women with rosaries. Mostly men carrying colorful signs of dismembered fetuses. On Saturdays they bussed teenagers in from local Catholic schools to harass women for course credit.

The woman I escorted was maybe twenty years old. She was pale and looked like she hadn't slept in a week. She had driven more than ten hours from Texas where abortion was all but illegal. We got to the break between the sidewalk and the front of the clinic. The security guard nodded at me and opened the door. I gave her hand a squeeze and whispered, "They will take good care of you." She didn't want to let go of me, her eyes wide and glassy, but the guard helped her inside.

I steeled myself to move back through the mob to the parking lot to help the next woman. Some of the protesters had learned my name, so I heard shouts of "Abbie, Abbie, you're so flabby." Really? That was the best they had? A tall man in a red cap screwed his face up and spit at me. I nearly fell back from the surprise, but I kept going and used my sleeve to wipe the tobacco-scented slime off my face.

June 24th, 2022. The overturn of Roe v. Wade. We recognized the day was coming, just not when. Part of me still can't believe it. When Senate bully Mitch McConnell refused to hold hearings on Obama's court nominee, Merrick Garland, we saw it as dirty politics. We didn't like it, but we thought Hillary would appoint someone younger and more aggressive. We knew having a woman president would turn the years of whittling away at abortion rights around. We knew.

Then came Trump.

With the perspicacity of hindsight, we traced back from Dobbs, to the hasty swearing-in of Amy Coney Barrett, to the tragic death of Ruth Bader Ginsburg, to the circus of adding another sexual predator, Brett Kavanaugh, to the "we got away with it" club of Clarence Thomas, to the happy-to-steal-the-seat appointment of Neil Gorsuch, to the presidential election. By the time the Dobbs decision was announced, a twice-impeached president had appointed one-third of the members of the Supreme Court. How they ruled was no surprise. They did what they had been hired to do. In a raw exercise of political power that ignored precedent, public opinion, and human decency, they used citations from the 1700s to cancel what had been guaranteed as a constitutional right for nearly fifty years.

I adjusted the purple vest I wore to identify me as an escort—someone who helped patients get through the mass of angry people whose only goal in life was to make women cry. I wasn't supposed to interact with them, but sometimes I couldn't help it. Roe was overturned—why did they have to be so ugly?

"Sore winners," I hissed, only partly under my breath. The old man we called "Friendly Freddie" laughed.

"Winners is right, Abbie. Before too long, you and your witch friends won't have anywhere to volunteer. Wah, wah. You'll have to eat magic mushrooms to make you feel better that you were not able to defend your sluts and whores."

He was right. After Roe was overturned, states with Republican legislatures fell over themselves to outlaw abortion, without exceptions when they could get away with it. A Republican Congress and another Republic president could ban abortion at a federal level. No. Choice. For. Anyone. Anywhere.

I understood the crowd. I was raised like that. For most of my life, I believed abortion was wrong. Evil. Unforgivable. Until I met Jane and listened to her stories.

I am Lucie's granddaughter. Jane and I began chronicling the stories of her amazing life. I promised her I would finish the book and get it published when she was gone. She died at 102 on October 23rd, 2016. I have done my best to keep my promise. There was too much life to fit into a single book, so you'll hear Jane's voice telling her stories in two more volumes. I had to cancel the airline and hotel reservations we'd made to attend Hillary Clinton's inauguration. Thank the goddess she died still planning to welcome our first woman president. I am glad Jane didn't have to live through the nightmare that was Trump. Or see Roe overturned. But I wish she were here to help us figure out a way to get what we need without begging men. Jane used to quote feminist theorist Sonia Johnson: "It's only when we have nothing else to hold on to that we're willing to try something audacious and scary."

Well, I'd have to say that time is now.

Sonia also said, "Although most women apparently did not hear the words spoken, every woman born gets the message subliminally, repeatedly and strongly from her earliest days that she does not belong to herself... Every time we lobbied them for the right to choose whether or not we will have children, we acknowledged that men owned us."

As we work to cast off that ownership and to regain women's rights state by state, we must also keep alive Jane's vision of what abortion can be—care tailored to the emotional and spiritual needs of each person, without the interference of men's laws. Jane provided the sacred service of abortion throughout her life. She did it with love and passion, and without permission, authority, or apology. We need her courage now more than ever.

Abbie Wilder

AUTHOR'S NOTE

Like Jane and Abbie, I started to write this book in 2016, anticipating the inauguration of the first woman president, Hillary Clinton. Republican state legislators passed insane rules and regulations designed to make it impossible for clinics to provide abortions. I wanted to write a story about providing abortion care as I hoped it would be—the way it *should* be done—without politically motivated restrictions, and with care for the emotional and spiritual wholeness of the patient.

By the time I was ready to publish, the Supreme Court had overturned Roe v. Wade. There has never been a more important time to share our stories about abortion.

Without Permission is a work of fiction based on real events in real life. However, some of the story comes from my imagination.

- Dr. Nick's invention of a suction device for abortion comes many years earlier than Lorraine Rothman's 1970s invention of the Del-Em, a DYI mechanism for menstrual extraction made with a glass jar, tubing and a stopper. During the 1970s, the vacuum aspiration machine developed by Dr. Harvey Karman and Dr. P.G. Sathe became the tool used by clinicians all over the world.

- A lecture by Carl Djerrassi in Dallas in the 1980s gave me the idea that the United States Navy had an obligation to provide abortions in Japan after the war as part of its guardianship of that country, as I depicted. I can't find any evidence that it actually happened.

- I loosely modeled the Fords in my book after Martha and Waitstill Sharp, who helped hundreds escape the Nazis.

- As far as I am aware, the concept of helping a woman *connect her head and her heart* to find resolution about her pregnancy choice began in the 1980s at the clinic I ran in Dallas. I have brought that work into the present with my website, beforeandafterabortion.com.

A word about language. In our modern world, people may identify themselves as male or female, non-binary, trans, gender neutral, or whatever works for them. People who do not identify themselves as women may need abortions. Jane's world is binary, so I use the word woman. But if you stay on this journey, in Book Three, you will see Jane assist a trans-man in having an abortion.

In the 1940s, the use of the words Negro and colored was common. Jane's dear friend Sally was ahead of her time. It wasn't until March 1945 that Phyllis Mae Dailey became the first Black woman sworn into the Navy.

Where are we now?

Where are we now, in February 2024 as this book was completed? For years prior to the 2020 election, abortion was being increasingly restricted with laws passed by Republicans who had Super-Majorities in state legislatures. The intention was to make it impossible to provide care. The width of hallways was policed, waiting periods introduced, strictures on the number of sinks, and impossible requirements for doctors to obtain hospital privileges were all part of a brilliant and destructive strategy to make sure that no woman of any age has the authority to decide for herself whether to continue or end a pregnancy.

As Americans, we don't like to see ourselves as extremists, but these policies are extreme. They echo practices of fundamentalists through history. Every fundamentalist faith and regime is dominated by men and controls women—how they dress, how they are educated (or not), when and whether they have children, and whether they are permitted or prohibited from being an equal part of society. We live in a society that talks about caring for women and children, yet accepts a shameful legacy of high rates of maternal and infant mortality, especially for Blacks, immigrant women and people of color.

The United States falls behind almost every industrialized nation in providing a social safety net. Legislators who oppose abortion recognize that some women are not able to care for a child financially. They pass bills to restrict abortion, yet fail to pass laws that guarantee all children safety, education, food and health care. Anti-abortion activists illustrate time and time again that they care much more about power than the lives of children and women. The overturn of Roe v. Wade in June 2022 was a task for which one-third of the Supreme Court justices were hired by a twice-impeached president. Since then, not only abortion care, but essential obstetric and gynecological care has been withheld from women whose most elemental rights have been stolen for political power.

How can you help?

At this writing, abortion is practically unavailable in half the states in this country. If you or someone you love needs an abortion, IneedanA.com is an excellent resource. If you want to donate, volunteer, or stay up to date, Google *abortion advocacy and activism* to find a list of groups that need your time and money. Make sure you are registered and vote, especially in the states where an abortion referendum is on the ballot. It can be hard to raise a controversial subject, but you can talk with your friends by saying, "I don't know where you are with the issue of abortion, but I believe strongly that parenthood should be a personal and not a government decision." You will find that most people agree with that. If we don't find the courage to risk and fight for our rights, we can't be surprised when someone more committed than we are erases them.

Over the past decades, I have specialized in working with women who were having a difficult time deciding what to do, or were troubled by their choice of abortion. I have written these books for you, too. If you are one of those people, please go to my website, beforeandafterabortion.com.

I have written this trilogy to share some of the stories I experienced in my work, and to leave the legacy of the importance of emotional and spiritual resolution in everything we do. If *Without Permission* meant something to you, please write a review on Amazon or Goodreads and tell your friends and post about it on social media. Most independently published books only reach about 200 people—roughly the friends and family in the universe of the author. Since Roe, more than 70,000,000 abortions have been provided. I know there are many people who would like to know Jane and the stories of her life. Please help me reach them.

DISCUSSION QUESTIONS

For Book Clubs, Women's Groups, or Personal Journaling

1) Can you imagine yourself in Jane's shoes—wanting so much to be good, but coming up against rules she feels she must break? Discuss challenges you have or had that create similar conflicts.

2) How does Jane navigate the societal norms and religious beliefs of the various settings related to abortion during the times and places depicted in the novel?

3) Discuss the differences and commonalities of the women's experience in wartime France, California and post-war Japan as Jane sees them.

4) Discuss the character development throughout the novel, focusing on how individuals grappled with societal expectations, religious pressures, and the need for spiritual resolution regarding abortion. Which character's journey resonated with you the most?

5) Explore the role of spirituality in shaping the characters' perspectives on women's reproductive rights. How do different characters interpret and reconcile their beliefs with the need for autonomy?

6) Jane breaks many taboos, including talking about abortion as a kind of killing, bringing Jesus and God into her counseling sessions, and saying goodbye to the spirit of the pregnancy. What was your response to these examples?

7) How does Jane's philosophy about abortion counseling evolve through-out the story?

8) Consider the friendships and alliances formed by the women in the novel. How did their unity contribute to their ability to navigate the difficulties of the time?

9) Consider the relevance of the book's themes to present-day conversations around women's rights and reproductive justice. How do the historical challenges faced by the characters resonate with contemporary struggles?

10) Dr. Levy asks Jane, "Are you willing to take a risk for something you believe in?" What risks would *you* take to defend something you believe in?

ACKNOWLEDGMENTS

I'd like to begin by thanking Hillary Clinton for inspiring this trilogy. I wrote hoping that during her presidency, abortion care could, once again, be provided with the patient, not politics, at the center.

Much gratitude goes to my partner Shelley Oram, herself a writer to envy, who read, re-read and skillfully edited the manuscript. She gave me good advice that I usually took and has been my champion.

Milles baisers to my trusty writing group, Annie Lewis and Phyllis Leavitt, who provided constant and unwavering support and saved me from my initial impulse to have Lucie die from her abortion.

The extraordinary Nancy McNary Smith was my 9th grade Ethics teacher. She opened our eyes to music and poetry. All my life, I said that if I ever published a book, I would dedicate it to her, so I have.

In 1959, my mother, Sylvia Weaver, self-induced an abortion with a knitting needle. Thank goodness she didn't die. She told me about it when I was eighteen. I share this because she told her story as part of a national speakout. She died in 2020, a lifelong contributor to organizations that support access to abortion. I'm sure her experience informed my choice to work in abortion.

My love to all the staff of the Routh Street Women's Clinic in Dallas, where I did my best, made so many mistakes, learned so much, and invested my heart.

Thanks to November Gang members, who taught me so much and helped me hone my skills in our constant pursuit of ideas to improve abortion care, and to my friend, Elizabeth Velez, who introduced me to the work that changed my life.

And thanks to my beta readers! There has never been a more wonderful group of humans! In alphabetical order, Annie Baker, Ray Harrison, Corlean Harvey, Arlena Ryan, Karen Thurston, and Alfreda Wright. They helped me remove 10,000 commas, researched and corrected myriad details, and told me the book *must* be published immediately! I hope the finished product will live up to their enthusiastic and loving support.

My long-time writing teacher, Anya Achtenberg, was the person who broke it to me that my original book was too long to publish, so, bingo, I had a trilogy! Her encouragement and insightful feedback are central to my writing journey. Stacey Pryor gave me great feedback and helped me with my French. The errors are all mine! My Anya classmates over the years from all your various locales and time zones have helped me make *Without Permission, Without Authority* and *Without Apology* books I am proud of.

My developmental editor, Diane Zinna, author of *The All-Night Sun*, gave me the feedback that spurred me on. "I don't think you know how good your book is." Every writer deserves to be read as closely and generously as Diane has read my work.

Jennifer Leigh Selig, who owns Empress Publications, was a skillful midwife to the birth of this book into the world. I am grateful for her experience and guidance.

Ashley Mansour's coaching program, LA Writer, helped me whittle my manuscript down to a workable length.

Thanks to Lee Avison, whose beautiful cover shares the sensibilities of my books even before you begin to read.

Edgard Rivera at the Step-Bridge studio in Santa Fe helped me create the audiobook I wanted to offer right from the start.

I am indebted to Wikipedia, and to the thoughtful writing of David Drake, *Paris at War,* and Ronald C. Rosbottom, *When Paris Went Dark.* I am forever grateful for the many sources of encouragement to publish independently.

My heart holds memories of the thousands of women who have trusted me with their most personal and intimate stories over the past half-century. I hope our work to meet your emotional and spiritual needs made a difference in your lives. I carry so many of your stories in my heart. I have recounted some of them in these books.

ABOUT THE AUTHOR

Charlotte Taft has worked in abortion care for more than half a century. Though most women do well with the experience of abortion, there are some who struggle. Charlotte developed tools to identify and assist the women who need deeper emotional exploration to find peace and confidence with whatever decision they make.

After earning a bachelor's degree from Brown University and a master's degree in feminist studies from Goddard College, Charlotte served as the director of an abortion clinic in Dallas, Texas, for seventeen years. During this time, she worked with her staff to pioneer a unique style of abortion counseling tailored to meet the emotional and spiritual needs of each patient, sometimes called Head and Heart Counseling.

In Dallas, Charlotte served as the media's go-to person on the topic of abortion. Charlotte was interviewed by national publications such as *The New York Times*, as well as appearing on dozens of local and national television programs including *The Today Show*. Her non-fiction publications are available at Rewire.com.

Charlotte is featured on the 2020 FX documentary *AKA Jane Roe*.

With her partner Shelley Oram, Charlotte created *Imagine* to provide experiential workshops and retreats to deepen abortion providers' understandings of themselves and their work. Charlotte served as the director of the national non-profit organization Abortion Care Network for six years, where she was at the helm of supporting independent abortion providers and fostering open conversations around abortion.

Today, Charlotte lives in rural New Mexico with Shelley, her partner of thirty-five years. She continues to work with women who need help looking deeper in order to make a decision and resolve difficult feelings after an abortion. Her website beforeandafterabortion.com offers insightful videos designed to further assist women in finding peace before and after an abortion. Visit her author website, charlottetaft.com, to learn more about *Without Permission*, *Without Authority* and *Without Apology*.

Made in the USA
Middletown, DE
21 May 2024

54437388R00145